HIS LORDSHIP'S MASTER

Book Two of

His Lordship's Mysteries

Samantha SoRelle

Balcarres Books LLC

ISBN-13: 978-1-952789-03-8
ISBN-10: 1-952789-03-6

Cover design by: Samantha SoRelle
Printed in the United States of America

BY SAMANTHA SORELLE

His Lordship's Mysteries:

His Lordship's Secret
His Lordship's Master
His Lordship's Return
Lord Alfie of the Mud (Short Story)
His Lordship's Gift (Short Story)

Other Works:

Cairo Malachi and the Adventure of the Silver Whistle
Suspiciously Sweet

CAIRO MALACHI AND THE ADVENTURE OF THE SILVER WHISTLE

"The first time I met the love of my life, he died in my arms."

Cairo Malachi, Conduit to the Spirits, is a liar, a thief, and a fraud. He may be building a reputation as one of the most fashionable mediums in London, but he doesn't even believe in ghosts and has certainly never conjured one. Which is why, after he witnesses the brutal slaying of a handsome young constable, he's shocked when the man's spirit appears in his home, begging for his help.

Constable Noah Bell is everything Mal can never be—honest, funny, and kind. But it's ridiculous to be attracted to a man he can't even touch, especially when every step they take towards solving Noah's murder is one step closer to bringing him the justice he needs to move on—and out of Mal's life forever.

As their investigation brings unexpected enemies to light, the secrets they're keeping from each other may prove even more dangerous. Mal and Noah will have to work together... or risk a fate worse than death.

To my 11th grade English teacher,
Mrs. Meer, who will not be surprised
by the contents of this book.

CONTENTS

CHAPTER 1

County Fife, Scotland
November 4, 1818

"When shall we three meet again," Alfie muttered to himself as the carriage trundled down a rough dirt road that had long since turned to mud. "In thunder, lightning, or in rain?"

He pressed his face to the window, trying desperately to see anything beyond the raindrops racing each other down the glass. The rain, which had begun as only a gentle patter against the roof of the carriage, now drove down in sheets, the wind lashing it ferociously against the glass. He thought they'd passed through an ornate gate moments ago, but try as he might, he could see no further than the lead horse.

He spared a thought for the poor driver with only the protection of his oilskins against the weather, and made a note to ensure the man was compensated generously when they reached the manor, as well as provided a hot meal and a place to spend the night. As it was, they would barely reach Balcarres House before nightfall, the charcoal skies already darkening at the edges to the true black of a Scottish night.

The carriage lurched as a wheel caught in a rut. Alfie's head knocked painfully against the glass and he pulled back, swearing colourfully.

"Mrm?" mumbled his fellow passenger.

"Yes, I'm fine," Alfie replied with a scowl, rubbing his head. He knocked one Hessian-clad foot lightly against the ankle of the man opposite him. "You'd best wake up though; we'll be there in a few minutes."

On the other bench, Dominick sighed, then stretched his arms as far as the tight confines of the carriage and his fashionably tailored jacket would allow. His fingertips brushed the carriage doors on both sides.

Alfie's mouth went dry. All these months later, he was still just as overwhelmed by Dominick as he had been the night of that illicit boxing match, and his feelings did not seem to be dulling with exposure. If anything, he fell more in love with him every day.

Dominick opened his eyes, his enormous yawn collapsing into a wicked smile as if he could read Alfie's thoughts. He probably could, curse him. Alfie kicked his ankle again, harder this time.

"None of that. I need to make a good impression on the staff and I can't do that with you leering at me like an ape."

"Leering? You're the one's been watching me sleep for the last hour, and don't deny it."

Dominick kicked back, careful to only make contact with Alfie's undamaged leg, a gesture for which Alfie refused to feel fond. He felt a blush rising on his cheeks and attempted to will it down. It wouldn't do to meet his new servants while looking like an infatuated schoolboy.

His hands shook faintly with both fear and excitement. He pressed them between his knees. In a few minutes, he wouldn't be able to just be Alfie, London orphan and street rat, but would have to be The Right Honorable Lord Pennington the Earl of Crawford. He'd been able to keep up the pretense while living in the townhouse in London, but every bump in the road now drew him that much closer to the family seat, where he would be expected to take up the role of country lord as one born to it. Which he very much was not.

In the five years since he'd inherited the title, Alfie hadn't had the courage to visit. It was one thing to pass as just another overly titled and entitled member of the aristocratic set in London, where any slip-ups could be put down to eccentricity, but the idea of taking up residence in the family seat seemed too much like being an *actual* lord.

But London held too many ghosts for him now, although in the gloom it was hard to believe that Balcarres would be any better.

The carriage swayed as Dominick switched from the bench opposite to sit next to him. His muscular bulk caused the cushion to dip and Alfie to slide into his side.

"You can do this," Dominick said, putting an arm over Alfie's tense shoulders.

Alfie leaned into him, enjoying a faint whiff of his cologne. Spanish Leather.

"And if you don't like it," Dominick continued, "We'll go to one of your other properties. Or to one of the ones so nobly gifted me by a handsome and generous benefactor."

Alfie sighed, "I told you, you don't owe me anything—"

"Of course not," Dominick sniffed, arranging Alfie more securely against his side. "I was the one who took the blame that time you put the matron's petticoat on that stray dog and let it loose in the girls' dormitory. As far as

I'm concerned, you still haven't paid that off."

Alfie couldn't help the laugh that escaped him. "And who dared me to do it in the first place?"

"Some scoundrel, I'm sure. An absolutely wicked beast."

"Unrepentant too."

"Naturally."

Silence descended on the carriage for a few more minutes. Dominick was warm against him, and Alfie relaxed as he drew both heat and strength from his lover. It might be a while before they had the opportunity to sit like this again, so he was resolved to enjoy it while it lasted.

The moment he had the thought, Dominick jerked away with a curse and cupped his hands against the window on Alfie's other side, peering out into the storm.

"Christ, is that it?"

Alfie struggled to see over him, but even through the darkness and rain, the house was unmistakable. Built halfway up a long sloping hill, the roofline was clearly outlined against the sky, its pointed turrets and countless chimneys silhouetted in the last breath of twilight. The dark grey of the stone walls and slate roof separated themselves only slowly out of the dark, seeming solid one minute, the next as ethereal as the mist rising up along the drive and spilling over the horses' hooves.

A shudder ran down Alfie's spine as a sense of foreboding washed over him. The windows in the house were all brightly lit, but their promised warmth felt like a trap, like the lights of a will o'wisp luring unsuspecting travellers to their doom.

Squinting further into the dark, he realised he'd been mistaken. Only the nearest half of the house was illuminated. The rest hunched in the darkness behind it, lost in the falling night.

Dominick, still leaning across Alfie's lap, looked up at him. "I suppose it's too late to turn back."

"I'm sure it's much more welcoming by day?"

Dominick looked doubtful.

"Regardless," Alfie pressed on. "We're here now and we've come all this way. We might as well give the whole country living a fair go. And if we don't like it…"

"If we don't like it, we can go back to dirty, smelly, rotten old London like other civilised folk." Dominick smiled and sat up, smoothing down his jacket lapels. "Either way, I'm with you."

Alfie took his hand and gave it a quick squeeze, one last show of affection as they pulled up in front of the house.

"Unless the ghosts are particularly ghastly," Dominick muttered. "Then you're on your own."

Before Alfie had a chance to respond, the carriage door was yanked open. A young man with a narrow nose and high cheekbones thrust his head into the carriage. The hood of his cloak covered his hair, but even the brief exposure to the elements had turned his skin fish-belly pale.

"Beggin' your pardon, milord. S-sir." He stuttered when he saw Dominick. Alfie felt a moment of dismay. He *had* written to the property overseer of his upcoming arrival and to make the house ready for himself and his guest. Surely the staff had been informed?

He bit back a sigh. It had been a long journey. Between the damp and the long periods of enforced stillness, the bullet wound in his leg had begun to ache. All he wanted was a hot bath and to go to bed, but if a second bedroom hadn't been made ready, propriety would keep him from even those simple pleasures until Dominick's quarters could be properly laid out. Of course he'd much rather share both his bath and his bed with Dominick, but it wasn't as if he could tell the staff that.

The young man regrouped his wits and continued. "Should I fetch coats and the like? Or you could run for it. It's only a few feet."

Alfie was shocked at the young man's informal manner. It was one thing for Mrs. Hirkins to speak to him that way, quite another for some gawking footman. Apparently things really were done differently in the country! He looked over at Dominick to share his amazement, but either he hadn't noticed, or he completely misunderstood Alfie's look, because he only grinned. "I think we can make it. After you, *milord*."

Alfie huffed and surveyed the distance as the young man stepped aside. It *was* only a few feet, but those feet comprised of either the thick mud of the drive or the slick wet stone of the entry steps. Either would be difficult enough to manage were he in perfect health.

He gripped his sword cane tightly. Before being shot by the mad Doctor Barlowe, the cane had been merely an accessory, at most a precaution against thugs and pickpockets, but now it was a necessity. He could usually go short distances on his own, but his leg had yet to regain its previous strength and after being folded for so long into the cramped confines of the carriage, he wasn't sure it would fully bear his weight, especially over such treacherous ground. It would hardly do for his first act as lord of the manor to be falling face-first into the mud, or cracking his skull open on a paver.

Out of sight of the footman, Dominick touched his back lightly. "I'll be right behind you," he whispered.

Alfie took a deep breath and propelled himself out of the carriage. The wind immediately tried to tear his jacket from his shoulders while the rain assaulted him in tiny droplets like frozen nails, seeping through his outer layers and down his collar. He stumbled, but caught himself with a lurch, biting back curses through the last uncertain steps. His first act as lord of the manor would be to have a damned porte-cochère built!

Finally through the door, he stepped aside to clear the way for Dominick and did his best to tug his jacket and waistcoat into some semblance of decorum. At a slight cough he looked up.

Good Lord.

The foyer opened onto a massive hall that stretched deep within the house, lit with chandeliers, candelabras, and two roaring fireplaces. On the walls hung faded tapestries and collections of weaponry from across the centuries—modern rifles crossed above heavy maces and fanned by swords in arrays as forbidding as they were decorative. There were even full suits of armor in every corner, each set of gauntleted hands resting on a shield painted with a different crest. With only his cane to hand, Alfie felt like a woefully underprepared attacker about to be overwhelmed by the castle forces.

Between him and the fires' warmth stood a line of patiently waiting servants.

Overwhelming forces indeed. He heard Dominick

stumble in behind him, a welcome, if insufficient, reinforcement for the battle ahead.

A man on the left end of the line stepped forward with a subtle clearing of his throat. He had the look of a bottle stood on its end. The formal black stockings and knee breeches he wore made his legs appear too weak to support his stout torso and square shoulders. Despite the unbalanced nature of his appearance, his bearing was that of a man not yet past his prime, though his saturnine features gave him a much older air.

"My lord, allow me to be the first to welcome you to Balcarres House. I am your butler, Mr. Gibson. Would you prefer to inspect the staff now or shall I show you and your guest to your rooms?"

Alfie would much prefer to curl up under a warm, dry quilt and sleep for a week, but as the servants were already assembled, it was churlish to make them all go through this again later. Besides, it was only right that he get to know those who would be living with and working for him as soon as possible.

He stood straighter and tried to project as much nobility as possible, even as water dripped off his hair. Another reason to get the introductions done now, before his hair oil washed away completely and his drenched locks resumed their natural shape. The staff would already be wary of an earl as young as himself; a headful of wayward curls would hardly inspire their confidence.

"A pleasure, Mr. Gibson. I would be much obliged if you would introduce me to the staff now. I'm sure an inspection won't be required. If they have your approval then doubtless they will have mine."

The exaggerated formality of Mr. Gibson's speech seemed to have brought out the same in him, and for a moment Alfie worried he might have laid it on a bit thick, but Mr. Gibson visibly preened. There was a rustle further down the line of servants, but by the time Alfie noticed, Mr. Gibson had already begun the roll.

"That was Jarrett the footman who greeted your carriage, sir. Most of the staff here have been with the house for years, but he is our most recent addition, hired in preparation of your arrival. He'll be leading the driver around to the stables and bringing your luggage in shortly. May I enquire as to whether your driver will be staying with us?"

"No, he and the carriage will be returning to Edinburgh tomorrow. If you would-"

"I'll see that Graham—that's the stablemaster, sir—finds him adequate accommodation for the evening. Graham is assisted by young Davey, the stable lad. I felt it better that they remain at their posts at present, but will of course arrange for them to be formally presented at a later time. Undoubtedly you will wish to return the Crawford stables to their former glory, and will seek to hire additional hands."

"Undoubtedly," muttered Dominick. Alfie resisted the impulse to elbow him in the side. He desperately wanted to mention that he'd spent the last several years with only a single housekeeper-cook, just to see Mr. Gibson's reaction. But Mrs. Hirkins would leave her cozy retirement and travel all the way to Scotland to take him by the ear if he intentionally shocked or mistreated his servants. Although in fairness, she would probably want to take the haughty Mr. Gibson down a peg or two herself.

Mr. Gibson gestured to the man on his left. "This is Mr. Howe. He will be your valet, sir. I'm afraid we do not have a full complement of staff at present, so Mr. Howe will have to assist both you and your guest. If he requires additional assistance, Jarrett will be able to assist in the more rudimentary tasks."

"I'm sure you're more than up to the challenge, Mr. Howe," said Alfie before Dominick could tell Mr. Gibson exactly how capable he was of handling his own rudimentary tasks, thank you very much. "I do apologise in advance for the current state of our apparel. I fear that long travel is just as hard on the wear as it is on the wearer!"

Mr. Howe bowed and a slight smile crooked the corner of his mouth. He was roughly of an age with Mr. Gibson, although his hair had already begun to thin at the top. He wore his servant's uniform in some indefinable way that seemed much neater; although looking between the two men Alfie wouldn't be able to point out any actual differences in their dress. He was a full head taller than Mr. Gibson as well, and skinny as a reed. If this were one of the tales of horror Dominick had told him as a child, he suspected Mr. Howe would have sunken eyes and a voice like the creaking of a castle gate, but instead his eyes sparkled with mirth at Alfie's jest, and when he spoke his voice was a pleasing tenor.

"No need to apologise for a bit of Scottish soil, my lord. We are rather proud of it after all."

Mr. Gibson continued, "The housekeeper, Mrs. Finley."

The woman in question gave a small curtsey and bobbed her head. In her early sixties if she was a day, and with a face as plump and cheerful as a Christmas goose. Dominick would have her thoroughly charmed in no time, and would undoubtedly be the one with the plumpest of pillows and warmest of hot bricks on cold nights. For these reasons alone, Alfie would have to ensure that he made his way into Dominick's bed.

Beside Mrs. Finley was the cook, Mrs. Buie—a hatchet-faced woman with eyes to match. Her curtsey was respectful enough, but Alfie couldn't shake the feeling she had already taken his measure and found him wanting.

On Mrs. Buie's other side stood a rather excitable but pretty young woman, a maid by the name of Janie. Her bright red curls put even Alfie's wayward locks to shame. They seemed ready to burst forth from her cap in the excitement of meeting an actual member of the nobility, if her stammered greeting was anything to go by.

"And finally we have the second maid, Mrs. Buie's daughter, Moira."

Moira, a mousy little thing, barely came up to Alfie's lapels. The young woman had light brown hair and a rather plain complexion. Although she kept her eyes firmly on her shoes, he could still see the similar features shared by her and the fierce cook. Perhaps a touch of flattery could reassure the former and soften the latter. Dominick wasn't the only charming one after all.

"Mother and daughter?" he exclaimed. "Mr. Gibson, I beg to differ, these ladies are sisters surely!"

Someone gasped and a silence fell over the hall, as dark and oppressive as the night outside.

"My sister is gone, sir."

Moira spoke the words softly, but they seemed to echo

throughout the cavernous space.

Mr. Gibson cleared his throat. "Aye, I'm afraid the other Miss Buie left rather suddenly not long before we received word of your impending arrival, sir, leaving us even more shorthanded. As such, I'm afraid we've not had time to thoroughly prepare the entire house for your use, but I assure you that we have quite comfortable rooms made up. I could show you to them now, unless there is anything else you wished to say while we are all gathered."

The man seemed to be awaiting some sort of speech, an addressing of the troops, but Alfie was still flustered from his unintentional blunder regarding the missing Miss Buie. Dominick gently nudged him.

"Oh, yes, of course. This is Mr. Dominick Trent, my cousin. He shall also be residing at Balcarres for the duration of my stay. I'm afraid neither Mr. Trent nor myself have spent much time in the country, but I'm sure we'll all be able to muddle along. I am already quite impressed by what I've seen. Mr. Gibson, Mrs. Finley, I commend you both in particular for getting the house in such fine shape on such short notice."

It was an embellished truth, but truth nonetheless. For all the house resembled the abode of the villain in a gothic novel, he recognised the amount of hard work that must have gone into making the manor ready for his arrival. Especially after his father's decades of neglect.

"Thank you, sir," said Mr. Gibson, chest puffed out like a black and white songbird. "If you will both follow me, I can lead you to your rooms. Would you care for a brandy or port before you turn in?"

Alfie shuddered. He doubted he would ever be able

to drink port again after Doctor Barlowe's poison. If Dominick hadn't been there…

"Tea for me," said Dominick. "Or a cup of chocolate if it's not too much trouble. Something to warm the inside as well as the out."

"Tea, only," grit out Mrs. Buie. Whether this was true or whether the cook just wanted to avoid the hassle of making chocolate so late in the evening, Alfie could only speculate.

Beside her, Mrs. Finley beamed. "The lasses and I will bring that and some hot water for the wash basins along in just a wink, Mr. Trent."

The women all bobbed a final curtsey and headed off, presumably towards the kitchen. Alfie pretended not to notice the final long look Mrs. Buie gave him.

Mr. Gibson picked up an ornate gas lamp and gestured along the hall. "The stairwell is just this way, please."

Alfie shared a quick look with Dominick and gripped his cane more firmly. Into the villain's lair they went.

CHAPTER 2

Alfie was thoroughly lost in his own home.

Mr. Gibson led them up one hallway and down another, across the landing for a third stairwell, or was it a fourth? The lamp he carried was unnecessary, their path having been well lit before their arrival, but the corridors on either side were dark. Each time Mr. Gibson passed one, it would be briefly illuminated for a few seconds before plunging back into darkness. The shadows slid and shifted as the light moved. At first Alfie tried to peer down each as they passed, hoping to orient himself. But the idea of seeing a ghostly face lit for just a moment or catching a door being closed by unseen hands came into his head entirely without permission and could not be dispelled. Perhaps it was best to just watch where they were going, and ignore anything he thought he saw out of the corner of his eye.

"As I mentioned, my lord," said Mr. Gibson, "We unfortunately have not been able to prepare the entire manor in time for your arrival. As such, I felt it prudent to focus on the main areas of the home, so that you may be comfortable while we finish."

Good Lord, if they had only walked through the "main areas" so far, Alfie had no idea how he would ever find his way around the whole thing!

"Unfortunately," Mr. Gibson continued, "The suite in

which the Earl of Crawford normally resides is somewhat secluded from the rest of the house, and there was not enough time to make that particular wing up to Your Lordship's standards. I therefore took it upon myself to have one of the larger family rooms made ready. It is in the same corridor as the room in which I had thought Mr. Trent might be most comfortable. I hope this is acceptable?"

Alfie looked over his shoulder and caught Dominick's eye. Well, that would certainly make visiting each other's quarters easier once they had figured out the servants' schedules. Not only that, but Dominick would be close by for companionship.

And protection, in case this place is as haunted as it feels.

He tried to ignore the thought, but the idea of being in an isolated wing of the house all on his own sent chills down his spine. He shuddered.

Dominick, clearly misinterpreting the motion, raised an eyebrow at him unsubtly and grinned.

Alfie ignored him, "I'm sure the rooms will prove most adequate. Do you know why the lord's suite is so removed? That seems uncommon."

"I'm afraid I don't, sir. But I believe Mr. Charleton plans on visiting tomorrow, if that is convenient. His family has been managing the property for generations; I'm sure if anyone had any insight on the matter, it would be him."

Finally, they turned one last corner and came to a short corridor. The doors of both rooms on the right side of the hall were open. Apparently his room and Dominick's were not just near, but adjacent.

"Mr. Trent, this first one is yours, and the second is for

you, my lord."

There would be plenty of time to explore Dominick's room later, Alfie reasoned, so he followed Mr. Gibson to his own. The first thing he noticed was the fire burning in the massive stone hearth, casting the worst of the chill to the far corners of the room. The room was large, and the heavy furniture that filled it carved of a wood so dark it was nearly black, but a number of surprisingly bright landscapes hung on the stone walls, lifting some of the gloom.

As Mr. Gibson took his leave with a short bow, Alfie spent a few minutes exploring and was delighted to see that the wall opposite the fireplace held a large bookcase, although it was mostly bare. Two large windows dominated the wall either side of the bed, their diamond panes of glass catching the lamplight and reflecting it merrily. The bed, built of the same dark wood as the rest of the room, had its curtains drawn back to reveal a cascading pile of pillows on top of a thick, heavy-looking quilt. Alfie eyed it the way a wanderer lost in the desert might eye a pitcher of ice water and an eight-course meal.

A knock broke him from his reverie. Moments later, young Jarrett backed through the open doorway carrying one end of Alfie's trunk, Mr. Howe following with the other. Instinctually Alfie stepped forward to help, but hesitated. It was not the done thing for a man of his position to help carry heavy, wet trunks, but it still felt wrong to just watch idly. Fortunately, a crash from the hallway decided the matter for him.

He followed the sound and nearly ran into Dominick as he left his own room to investigate. Just down the hall,

Mr. Gibson was working himself into a fine lather yelling at the two maids. Janie knelt on the floor gathering up pieces of broken crockery with shaking hands, while Moira stood silently by as Mr. Gibson's tirade increased in pitch and anger. At their approach, she lifted her eyes to Alfie's and the coolness of her stare caught him off guard. It didn't seem chilled by malice or dislike, but rather an emptiness. Like her spirit had somehow retreated, leaving only a hollow shell behind to bear Mr. Gibson's wrath.

"What is the meaning of this?" Alfie yelled loudly enough to be heard over the shouting.

Janie immediately burst into tears. "I'm s-sorry, sir! I-I didn't mean to! But you can't stay here!"

In the face of her sudden tears, Alfie found himself at a loss for words, but fortunately Dominick wasn't. He knelt by Janie and took the broken pieces from her hands before she could cut herself. "Surely you're not trying to get rid of Lord Crawford already, are you? I promise his bark is much worse than his bite."

"But that's just it, sir! He can't stay in that room! It isn't safe!"

"Stuff and nonsense," huffed Mr. Gibson. "I will not stand for this sort of behavior! If I—"

"Go on, Janie," Dominick interrupted without so much as a glance at Mr. Gibson. "Why do you think the room is unsafe?"

"I know it is, sir! That's the Wicked Master's room!"

Even Dominick seemed to have no idea what to do with this outburst. "The… Wicked Master?"

She turned beseechingly to Alfie. "He's real, sir! I've heard his footsteps myself, and there's many who've seen him roaming the halls late at night, as evil in death as he was in life. They say those that see him suffer terrible misfortune, if he doesn't kill them himself!"

She nodded tearfully to the doorway of Alfie's room where Jarrett and Mr. Howe stood watching the proceedings. "That was his room, and I wouldn't set foot in there after dark for all the royal jewels themselves. Please, sir, I didn't know we was making it up for you! You can't stay there, you'll be in danger!"

"That is enough!" roared Mr. Gibson. "I will not have you filling Lord Crawford's ears with such haver. If you have nothing better to do than break dishes and spread old wives' tales, then go!"

Janie was on her feet and rushed off without a second glance. Mr. Gibson pulled a handkerchief from his pocket and wiped his red face. "My most sincere apologies, sir. I assure you that Janie will be punished appropriately for the broken tea set and the disturbance."

"No, no," said Alfie quickly. "Really, she meant no harm. It's been a long day for us all I think, and I would hate for her to be punished for a case of nerves. I'm sure Mr. Trent won't mind sharing his teapot with me. Mr. Howe, I'll be ready to turn in as soon as you're able to find a nightshirt. The rest can wait until tomorrow."

❖ ❖ ❖

"From ghoulies and ghosties and long-legged beasties and things that go bump in the night, good Lord deliver us!"

"You're not nearly as funny as you think you are." Alfie poured Dominick a second cup of tea and added two spoonfuls of sugar.

"I disagree."

"Then you're not as clever as you think you are either."

"Ah, well that I agree with," said Dominick, stretching his stockinged feet before the fire. "If I was clever, I would have suggested that you couldn't possibly stay in a haunted room, and should share with me for the foreseeable future."

Alfie couldn't help but smile. "An admirable solution. But alas, I shall just have to brave the horrors of an empty bedchamber. The shock of not being awoken by your snoring or a mouthful of hair will probably be enough to do me in."

Dominick ran a hand over his hair, now cropped à la Brutus. The style suited him disgustingly well and made him look just as devilishly handsome as Alfie feared it might. "You'll miss me."

"Of course I will," Alfie replied, handing Dominick his tea. "But I'm not so far away. We'll figure something out."

Dominick hummed in agreement and they passed a few minutes in companionable silence.

"What do you think of the place?" asked Alfie.

"Well. It's not London."

Alfie snorted, "I'm sure it looks much better in the daylight."

"I'll take that bet. In fairness, it's not a filthy, rat-infested hovel in Spitalfields, but I suppose I can get used to it. All the fine furniture and servants and such." He grinned brightly, but sobered enough to ask, "What do you think though? It's your family home… or close enough."

"I'm not sure yet. I think it'll take some getting used to."

"Mm, you're right. Having to get up to pull the bell for a servant is such a trial."

Alfie rolled his eyes fondly. "If you're going to be ridiculous then I'm for bed."

Dominick waggled his eyebrows, "Sleep tight, don't let the Wicked Master bite!"

The sound of his laughter ended only when Alfie closed the door behind him in disgust.

* * *

It was easy to take the whole story of the Wicked Master as a joke when sitting with Dominick by the fire, but alone in the dark of his room later that night, the presence of some ghastly thing hiding in the darkness seemed almost inevitable. Every sound turned into something sinister. The creaking of the floorboards as the house settled became a phantom roaming the halls for victims. Tree branches brushing against windows were the sounds of something sinister scraping and clawing inside the walls, desperate to find a way out.

He shivered and pulled the blankets higher around his head. Surely everything would look much better in the daylight.

CHAPTER 3

The next day dawned, although Dominick wasn't sure that was what to call it when the sky only changed from a dark grey to a slightly lighter shade. However, with the lighter grey came the arrival of Mr. Howe to help him dress for breakfast.

"Would you prefer the buff or the fawn trousers today, sir? Either will suit the blue coat."

Mr. Howe had out two pairs of trousers draped over a lanky arm for Dominick's inspection. As far as he could tell, they were both just brown.

"Fawn?"

"Excellent choice." Mr. Howe whipped away one of the pairs and laid the other on the bed.

Dominick couldn't help but hesitate, plucking at the hem of his nightshirt as Mr. Howe laid out his wardrobe for the day. Alfie had warned him that all wealthy men had valets, and after he tricked Dominick into accepting half of his fortune in exchange for a sixpence, Dominick was a wealthy man indeed. It was just another one of the strange annoyances he would have to get used to if he was really going to pass as Alfie's cousin.

Still, it was one thing to know he was meant to let another man button his breeches, but it was another to actually stand there and let it happen. He worried his cock might get confused and make associations, but Mr. Howe was strictly professional, both uninterested and uninteresting.

He still felt odd about it by the time he set out for breakfast. He ran a hand over his chin. The part about not having to shave himself was all right, and Mr. Howe had more skill with a blade than most throatslitters he knew, but he still didn't see the need for the rest of it. Alfie had been dressing on his own in London, hadn't he? Perhaps Mr. Howe could be convinced to let Dominick fend for himself. After all, a draughty old pile on the edge of Scotland wasn't exactly Mayfair.

Lost in a daydream about the fancy nobs he'd seen at Alfie's club trying to do for themselves and ending up strangled by their own stockings, he turned first down one hall and then another. He frowned, footsteps slowing. He could have sworn this was the way they'd come last night, but surely he would remember such an ugly statue? Or perhaps they had gone to the left… But no, that didn't look right either.

He heard a rustle behind him and nearly jumped out of his skin.

"Oh dear me, Mr. Trent, I didn't mean to startle you!" The housekeeper, Mrs. Finley, pressed a hand to her ample chest in surprise.

"It's fine, Mrs. Finley. I'm afraid I was just lost in thought. Well, lost in this house is more like. How do you ever find your way around?"

"Oh, you get used to it, sir." She smiled. "I reckon I could find my way around it in the dark by now. I take it it's breakfast you're looking for?"

"It is indeed. And if you could lead me out of the wilds I'd be in your debt."

She laughed and turned back the way she'd come, leaving Dominick no choice but to follow after her like a duckling. Several turns—and not a few more ugly statues later—found him in the doorway of a lavish dining room.

He'd thought that Alfie's townhouse was the fanciest home in the world, but even its rich curtains and fancy chairs looked like Dominick's squalid lodgings compared to this. The room was as imposing as the hall they'd entered through last night, but where the hall reminded him of the castle of a storybook knight, this was more like the realm of a fairy king. The walls were painted a pale green, but layered over and over in white-painted carvings that formed neat frames and arches on every wall. Some of the carvings seemed to have escaped the others and twisted like falling leaves frozen in time. Carved faces peered at him from the mantelpiece and spied down from the ceiling, and stone lions sat sentry just inside the door. Drunkards and beggars by doorways he was used to, but not lions.

The only wall not covered in carvings was made entirely of windows that stretched from floor to ceiling. He'd never seen so much glass in his life; it must have cost a fortune. More astounding, the windows looked like they opened like doors onto a wide stone terrace overlooking a beautiful set of gardens. Even with the plants bare and trimmed back for winter, Dominick could tell they were impressive. In the spring he was sure they would be stunning.

Along the wall opposite the glass stretched a sideboard

loaded with all manner of platters covered by gleaming silver lids. In the center of the room ran a vast table, not only long, but so wide a man on one side would be hard pressed to pass a knife to his friend across the way. Dominick thought of the dining halls at the workhouse. There, a table this size would've sat twenty or more urchins like him. At this one sat only Alfie.

He was at the head of the table with a book open next to him, and Dominick was struck by how at home he looked, surrounded by other beautiful and valuable things. Alfie looked like he belonged. And Dominick himself, he realised with a pang, never would.

He didn't have time to dwell on the thought before Alfie looked up and flashed him a brilliant smile.

"Dominick! Good morning, did you sleep well? Get some breakfast. The eggs should still be warm and I highly recommend the sausage."

Dominick dutifully scooped up some of both. The little jam tarts enticed him, but plain toast would better suit his mood. He sat down cautiously in the chair to Alfie's right, not entirely certain its delicate legs would support him.

Feeling much more settled after filling his belly, he dusted the last few crumbs from his lips and asked, "So. What does a country gent do to fill the hours, then?"

"I can't speak for all country gents, but this one was thinking we could explore the library until Mr. Charleton arrives to call." Alfie tapped the cover of his book. "The selection in my room was somewhat wanting, but where there's one book there's bound to be more. Then perhaps after luncheon we could investigate the grounds and see what we've gotten ourselves into?"

* * *

The library was no less impressive than the dining room. It was smaller, fortunately, but all four walls were filled with books. There were even bookshelves built in between the windows that overlooked the same gardens he'd seen at breakfast. Alfie gasped as they walked in and Dominick smiled indulgently, happier with Alfie's joy than he was with the library itself.

He could read well enough, but rarely had the chance to do so while scrabbling to make a living on the uncaring streets of Spitalfields. Once, an artistic type had paid for the pleasure of Dominick's company for a full night, and Dominick had amused himself while the man slept— drunk on expensive French wines and Dominick's cheap body in equal measure. The books the man had weren't like the few novels he'd come across before. Most weren't in English, but those he could read had been filled with queer notions and stories that made no sense. Aside from the pay, the night had been a disappointment on every front. As far as he was concerned, if a story needed to be written down to be remembered, it wasn't that good in the first place.

But apparently Alfie's fascination with the stories Dominick told him under the blankets at night when they were children had turned into a love of written-down ones as well.

"Dominick look, there's a complete set of Austen! Oh, and Byron! Well, perhaps you shouldn't read those. I don't want you getting ideas. And look at these older ones! Who knows what sort of treasures may lie buried."

Alfie was going from shelf to shelf, running his fingers reverently along the spines, occasionally crooking his head to the side to read a title, then hopping along to the next. The effect was something like an overly endearing owl.

Dominick knelt down by the fire and picked up the tinderbox. It would be faster to light it himself than to ring for one of the servants, and give him something to do while Alfie was in raptures.

Once a nice blaze was going, he settled down in one of the armchairs facing the fire to rest his eyes. Despite the long journey yesterday, he hadn't slept well. His bed was like lying on a cloud, and so cozy he'd expected to fall asleep the moment his head hit the pillow, but every time he started to nod off he'd heard odd noises, sometimes like footsteps, other times like something heavy being shifted.

How quickly he'd gone soft. This time a year ago, he was going without more often than not, falling asleep on his cot with nothing to keep him warm except a blanket so worn as to be near invisible. Back then, if all he'd heard in the night was a few footsteps and things being moved about, he'd have counted himself lucky, but could have slept just as soundly through screaming matches and street fights.

Dominick dozed to the much more reassuring sounds of Alfie's footsteps as he pattered around the library, adding books to a growing pile in his arms. Some time later he was awoken by a gentle knock at the door.

"Sorry to disturb you, my lord," said Mr. Gibson with a bow towards Alfie. "But Mr. Gilleasbuig Charleton is here to see you."

"What kind of parent saddles a child with that?" Dominick muttered.

Alfie ignored him, "Thank you, Mr. Gibson. So far, I only know him through our correspondence regarding the property. It will be good to put a face to a name."

"Yes, sir. I've put him in the blue parlour."

"I would've preferred the yellow," whispered Dominick.

"Hush," scolded Alfie as he set his pile of books on a small table beside Dominick's chair. "After you, Mr. Gibson."

As they followed the butler through yet another series of maze-like passages, Dominick amused himself by imagining what sort of man this "Gilleasbuig" would turn out to be. With a name like that, he was certainly old and stuffy. Probably too high in the instep like Mr. Gibson. And a property manager to boot, he'd be sneering up through gold-rimmed spectacles from his wizened frame while clutching his precious ledgers in gnarled hands. Stooped and shrivelled from too much time behind a desk recording land titles or rent payments or whatever it was property managers did.

They reached the blue parlour, which was just as embellished and overwhelming as the dining room had been, albeit in a different colour.

Mr. Gibson bowed when they entered. "My lord, Mr. Trent, this is Mr. Gilleasbuig Charleton. Mr. Charleton, The Right Honorable Lord Alfred Pennington, Earl of Crawford, and his cousin, Mr. Dominick Trent."

Dominick had been right about the spectacles at least, but horribly wrong about the rest.

Gilleasbuig Charleton was perhaps in his early

twenties, with an energetic bounce in his step he strode over with an outstretched hand and a boyish grin that set off his looks. Not that they needed the help. His sable hair was pulled back in a tail and hazel eyes flecked with amber glowed warmly behind his spectacles. He was of average height, but with a trim figure. Beneath a sensible brown coat, high boots encased muscular legs to the knee. Dominick wondered if they were that high because Charleton spent his days tramping through the mud on the properties he managed, or just to look fashionable while watching others do the tramping.

Taken all together, he had the appearance of a gentleman highwayman and Dominick found himself liking the man against his will.

"Gibs, why must you insist on using my full name? *Gil* Charleton, please. I won't suffer these fine gentlemen to hear the whole thing. They named my brother Robert, after the Bruce, but I ken they had hopes he'd inherit my uncle's barony someday and wanted a suitably noble name. No such concerns though for the *second* son of the second son!"

Damn the man, even his voice was attractive, the brogue that was so harsh to his Londoner's ears softened somehow and made almost musical. As Charleton spoke, Dominick was reminded of a babbling stream he and Alfie had picnicked beside one day on their slow journey up to Scotland. He'd never heard a sound quite like the murmur of clear water tumbling over the rocks. Nothing like the Thames—steady, slow, and stinking. It almost felt disloyal to prefer the little country stream to the river he'd known his entire life.

Dominick shook his head to clear it. He worried for a moment his lapse in attention had been noticed, but Charleton was still in the midst of making his introduction.

"...A pleasure to meet you both finally. I was quite excited to receive the letter informing me of your intention to take up residence, my lord. I've done what I could to keep the place together in your absence, but there really is nothing better for a home than to be *lived* in."

"I agree completely, Mr. Charleton," said Alfie, shaking his hand. "I'm only sorry it took so long for me to make my way up here. My father spoke very fondly of the place."

"I'm only sorry he never had the opportunity to return; my own father spoke very highly of him. His Lordship was very generous when my da suggested some reinforcements on the south wall some years back. That was before I took over the business of course, but considering he had me running up ladders with the rest of the labourers, bucket of mortar in one hand and trowel in the other, you'll forgive me if I take a bit of additional pride in how well it turned out. If you decide to stay, Gibs and I can have a full staff brought in to get it all shined up both inside and out. It will be quite the magnificent sight, as I'm sure you can see."

"I can't actually," Alfie laughed and waved for him to sit. He seemed as drawn in by Charleton's personality as Dominick was.

Dominick felt a brief flare of panic and any positive feelings he might have had for the man immediately turned to dislike. Could he be a rival for Alfie's affections? He was charming, bright, and clearly more at ease with the running of an earldom than Dominick would ever be. And damned attractive to boot.

He shook his head again. The idea was preposterous. Alfie was hardly the sort of man to throw him over for the first pair of well-formed thighs he saw. Still, it couldn't hurt to keep an eye on this Charleton fellow. Just to make sure he didn't take any liberties.

Alfie continued, blithely unaware of Dominick's turmoil. "You see, Mr. Trent and myself arrived well after dark yesterday and could only glean the barest impressions of the house through the rain. And I'm afraid to say, after we both got lost on the way down to breakfast, I haven't been daring enough to explore further than the library, and even that required Mr. Gibson's assistance.

Charleton sprung up out of his seat, even though he'd barely had time to rest his rather shapely backside on it at all.

"Well, no time like the present! I doubt there's a man alive who knows the house better than I do, excepting some of your servants of course." He gave a quick laugh and winked, "For all Mr. Gibson's faults, he and the rest of the staff have kept the house in remarkable condition in your family's absence."

"He did say that you were quite knowledgeable about Balcarres," said Alfie. "I'm sure we'd both appreciate you giving us the full tour."

"Excellent!" Charleton clapped his hands together. "It was still raining when I arrived, so shall we begin with the interior? Right this way, gentlemen."

❊ ❊ ❊

After the eighth or ninth room with a bizarrely specific purpose, Dominick's head began to spin. Men could play cards anywhere there was a table, why did toffs think they needed a whole room dedicated to it?

He used to think his lodgings back in Spitalfields were extravagant. After all, he'd had both a window *and* a fireplace. Not to mention two whole rooms just for himself; he knew whole families that lived in less. He'd *fit* in those rooms, but now, traipsing along as Charleton pointed out endless boudoirs and ballrooms, solars and salons, he felt very small.

Charleton chatted gaily, detailing everything from the history of the wallpaper to which doors caught in the damp and needed a little extra force. All that Dominick could remember from the barrage was that Balcarres was mostly a newer building wrapped around the original manor built nearly three hundred years ago. As such, corridors abruptly shifted from wood to stone and back again as they wove between the two structures, with quite a few hallways ending suddenly in walls which had once been the outer stones of the building.

"Up to three feet wide in some places," Charleton confided, patting one such wall. "They had to knock a few down during the construction and you wouldn't believe what bits and bobs they found. Old coins, a few bottles, even a mummified cat, the poor creature! Imagine, a three-hundred-year-old cat! Oh, here, my lord, I think this will especially interest you."

He opened yet another door, this time to reveal a long gallery. Dominick couldn't help giving a low whistle. The room seemed to stretch at least half a city block. Inside, there was little furniture save for a few cushioned benches placed at intervals down the center of the room. On either wall hung large portraits, starting close to the door they'd come in, though they were spaced further apart as they went along and there was a section of bare wall at the end.

"These are family portraits of every Lord Crawford and his family dating back to the founding of the earldom in the fourteenth century."

Alfie visibly started. Dominick quickly glanced at the nearest few portraits. Hopefully there was not some defining feature common to all that would give Alfie away as not being a true Crawford heir by blood. At first glance there didn't seem to be any reason for concern. Short, tall, fat, thin—all were represented in the men and women whose portraits hung on the walls.

He walked slowly down the gallery, studying the paintings. Out of the corner of his eye he saw Alfie doing the same along the opposite wall. Now that he looked more closely, there were some common elements. Almost all of the Crawfords dating back across the centuries had blue eyes and fair hair.

Dominick ran a hand through his own hair self-consciously. That was what the previous Lord and Lady Crawford had been looking for when they came to the workhouse to find a child to pass off as their own. No wonder he had been their first choice instead of Alfie. While they both had blue eyes, his blond locks were more common in the paintings than Alfie's auburn. Still, there were enough red tresses and ruddy brunettes in the mix that Alfie didn't stand out so completely.

He snorted. That bastard Baz had been right, blast him

to hell. The Crawfords *might* have chosen him, although his fair hair had been lank and his light eyes cruel even then. It was hard to imagine Baz the Badger passing as nobility, unless it was one of a particularly vile set.

Which reminded him, "One of the maids got peculiar last night. Started on about a bloke she called the Wicked Master. Is he up here?"

"Ah!" Charleton said with delight. "He is indeed. A most fascinating story! Although I don't know if it's one the earl would appreciate me bandying about…"

"Trent is family," Alfie said, crossing over to join them. "Cousin something-something-removed on my mother's side. You can say anything to him you would me. That goes in all things."

Alfie nodded solemnly, his word was law in his castle, and Dominick felt a swell of pride.

"Besides," Alfie continued in a lighter tone. "I'm rather interested in the story myself. I'm the one Janie says will be murdered in his sleep by the fellow's ghost after all."

"Right this way then, my lord," said Charleton with a grin. "And allow me to introduce you to your executioner."

He stopped halfway down the hall in front of a portrait of a man in his mid-twenties who'd been painted striding across the manor grounds, one leg forward as if he was about to walk out of the frame. He seemed to be fighting his way through a thicket peppered with small yellow flowers. One hand grasped a fistful of the plants as he forced his way through. In the other he held a small red book, the title—if it had one—covered by his hand. In the distance behind him, the land rose in a wall of rock that jutted up into skies dark with building storm.

"Foreboding, isn't it?" Charleton asked, leaning forward. "The background is the crag beyond the gardens. If you look carefully there's a chapel near the base, although why the artist included that detail when the Wicked Master was hardly a godly man is lost on me. Perhaps it was a rather unsubtle suggestion."

Dominick hadn't noticed the chapel at all. He'd been fixed by the Wicked Master's expression. His blue eyes blazed with anger—a fire made of ice. A snarl fit to match the threatening weather painted above him was set upon his face, and entirely at odds with the bright flowers through which he strode. Wisps of dark blond hair flew around his head in the imagined wind as if the Wicked Master himself was the brewing storm.

"Meet Malcolm Pennington, the Wicked Master," said Charleton.

A shiver ran down Dominick's spine.

"Never an earl, thank God," Charleton continued. "In those days the title "master" was given to the heir-apparent of a noble seat. That's his father in the next painting over, Gordon Pennington, the eighth Earl of Crawford."

Gordon Pennington cut a far less romantic figure than his son. Painted in his later years, he had a strong, almost hulking frame made larger still by the fur-lined cloak he wore, but even a painter's discretion could not conceal his paunch or balding head.

"I vaguely remember my father mentioning this," said Alfie, rubbing his jaw in reflection. "Something about the earldom going to a cousin or nephew? He never told me why though. I assumed the eighth earl had no son. Did

Malcolm die before he could inherit?"

"He did die young, but that's not why he failed to inherit. Therein lies the tale of the Wicked Master."

As he began the story, Charleton's eyes twinkled in a way that Dominick didn't like.

"As they say... Once there lived a young and truly wicked man. The exact details of his villainy have been lost to time, but everyone agrees that he was the most base and vile sort. There is a family history in the library I could show you that has more details. At one point it refers to him as 'The Absalom of the century' which is perhaps not too dramatic for this tale. In any case, Malcolm was a blackguard. They say he rode with thieves and brigands and kept all sorts of low company. It was even whispered that he was responsible for the disappearance of a wealthy farmer. Whether he was or not, all agree that he was a degenerate and a disgrace to the earldom."

Dominick, who was perhaps as low company as could be imagined, and no stranger to thievery and other—even more unscrupulous—means to survive, tried not to take offense. It was just as well Charleton had no idea the sorts of degenerate ways Dominick kept the current earl company.

"But time and again, no matter how far from the path the son strayed, his loving father, the earl, would take him back with open arms. The earl was a living saint, they said, to forgive his son time and time again... All the histories get rather florid here in describing the eighth lord's virtues.

"But despite the earl's kindness, so it was that one night in 1599 during a fierce gale, Malcolm set upon his father as he slept and tried to strangle him with his bare hands.

There was a ferocious struggle, but eventually the earl was able to fight his way free long enough to alert the servants. They subdued the Wicked Master and saved the earl's life. They said the master was like a mad beast that night, howling and baying for his father's blood.

"In time, he was charged with constructive parricide, that is, the intention to murder his father, and tried by no lesser judge than King James VI himself. It had been discovered that sometime before the attack, Malcolm had emptied the manor's coffers, but why he had done such a thing when all would have been his in time, no one knew. Malcolm himself gave no answer, admitting freely to the attempt on his father's life but offering no defense for any of his actions.

"To plead guilty meant death, but the king showed mercy, and spared the Wicked Master's life on the condition that he be thrown from Balcarres House, never to return, disowned by his family and struck from the line of succession. They say it broke his good father's heart to do so, but at the price of his son's life, he had no choice. Yet once again his kindness towards his son was thrown back in his face as Malcolm roamed the countryside like a hungry wolf, waiting for another chance to finish his evil deed.

"The end came swiftly for Malcolm after that. Bad acts have a way of coming back on one, and so it was for the Wicked Master. He died in a street fight in Dundee, beaten to death with his assailant's bare hands, not so very different from the way he tried to end his own father's life. But though his story ends there, ours does not. It is said the Wicked Master continues to stalk the halls of Balcarres

House in death as he did life, searching eternally. Perhaps for his father, to complete his terrible act? Or perhaps for more victims to quench his murderous rage."

Dominick saw Alfie shudder as Charleton finished his ghastly tale. The man was a consummate storyteller. Dominick had chills himself, made of an equal mix of fear and delight at a story well told.

He looked again at the portrait. The cruel eyes of the Wicked Master bore into his, finding him little more than prey for the hunt.

"I'm thankful that the earl's suite wasn't ready for me," said Alfie in a dazed tone. "I'll have trouble enough sleeping in the Wicked Master's room tonight. I'm sure if I was in the earl's chambers, I'd lie awake 'til dawn with the covers over my head, waiting for the ghostly hands around my throat."

"I wouldn't worry overmuch, my lord," said Charleton, clearly pleased with the effect of his tale on his listeners. "It has been over two hundred years and not a single Earl of Crawford has yet to meet his untimely end in a supernatural manner. Perhaps you are insusceptible. After all, the Wicked Master was unable to kill the Earl of Crawford while he was alive, it could be that the same rule applies also in death."

"That still leaves me out in the cold," Dominick muttered.

Charleton laughed, "You seem like a man who can defend himself. Besides, every proper house in Scotland has at least one or two ghosts. In all my years I've never heard the master's spirit being blamed for any more than the usual—strange sounds, missing spoons, hens refusing to lay, that sort of thing."

"Regardless, I appreciate hearing the legend, Charleton," said Alfie. "And for the excellent tour of the house. It will still be some time before I'm confident in finding my way, but you've been a great help. If you guide us back to the dining room, the least we could do would be to repay your services with a spot of luncheon."

"Thank you, I'd be honored," Charleton replied.

"Then lay on, Macduff," said Alfie with a broad smile and theatrical gesture.

Dominick rolled his eyes.

CHAPTER 4

Luncheon was a pleasant affair, Charleton being just as engaging in relaying the news of the village as he was with ghost stories, but Dominick was still glad when he made his excuses to leave, even if it was with a promise to return to sort through the various papers that running an estate entailed. Apparently not having had his fill of exploration for the day, Alfie suggested he and Dominick take advantage of a break in the rain to assess the state of the gardens.

"You know, you'll have to learn how to run your own estates now that you have them. It could be good practice for you to sit in when Charleton returns. I'm sure he's an excellent tutor," Alfie said, leaning more heavily on his cane than usual.

Dominick didn't want to spoil his lover's good mood by mothering him into resting, but Alfie's limp never ceased to remind him of that terrible night, thinking they would both die after only just finding each other once again. He pretended to slip on a wet stone, and took Alfie's arm in his for support. The corner of his lip quirked, but Alfie said nothing and leaned a little of his weight on him, so Dominick considered the victory worth the mild injury to his pride.

In the leaden daylight, the house looked almost as

foreboding as it had the night before. But now that he knew where to look, Dominick could see the seams where the old manor had been swallowed by the new. Stones of different colours met at odd angles, turrets bulging from the walls like growths on a tree. One wing disappeared completely between storeys of the wing beside it, and the countless chimneys and sharp rooflines gnashed at the sky above like broken teeth.

He was happy to turn his back on the house and look out instead over the impressive gardens. They were in better shape than he'd expected considering their years of neglect. Passing pale statues, dry fountains, and rows of bushes now bare in the cold, he and Alfie turned down a tree-lined avenue, the gently waving branches interlocking in an arch above them. Some still clung to the last of their leaves, the bright yellows and reds garishly bright against the grey skies.

Until he'd left London with Alfie, Dominick hadn't known there were so many different trees and plants in the world. He'd spent the first several days of their journey all but hanging out the carriage windows trying to see everything at once. Although these gardens were lovely, there was something about them that seemed insincere, their straight lines and careful tending a corruption of the real nature he now knew existed.

Past the lawn at the end of the garden, he could see rolling hills crashing up against a crag that rose like a rock from the sea. A forest lay around it, and Dominick wondered what sort of mysteries it might contain.

"That was in the painting of Malcolm Pennington wasn't it?" asked Alfie, following Dominick's line of sight.

"Behind the chapel? I wonder if that's still there too."

Dominick shrugged. He was still unsettled by the story, and would probably be even more so once night fell.

"So, now what? Any more corners of the house you want to peek your nose in?" he asked, blatantly changing the topic.

"Actually," said Alfie slowly. "I was thinking we should take advantage of the weather while it's still fair. How do you feel about riding?"

Dominick leered.

✻ ✻ ✻

Alfie was a detestable, tricky little fox and Dominick was going to find a way to punish him thoroughly.

He looked up at the enormous black horse in front of him. It looked fit to be Satan's steed or perhaps a kelpie from the folk tales, just waiting for Dominick to climb aboard so it could drag him off to his doom.

The man holding the creature's reins gestured at Dominick and said... something.

Graham the stablemaster was a giant, with a full beard as impenetrable as his accent. He had a soothing manner and calming hands for the horses, but no time for ill-bred city folk more used to dodging the animals than attempting to *sit* on them.

"He says to go ahead and grab the stirrup and heave yourself up. One smooth motion," called out Alfie.

It was apparent as soon as introductions were made that Graham had as much trouble understanding Dominick's Spitalfields cant as Dominick had trying to understand his thick Scottish burr. Alfie was acting as an interpreter of sorts, but the tour of the house and walk through the gardens had been a bit much for him. He sat on a bench in front of the stables with his leg stretched out in front of him, shouting instructions as Dominick attempted not to embarrass himself, but his directions made little more sense than Graham's.

"Which bit of the horse is the stirrup?" Dominick called back.

"Don't be like that. I know you've seen a horse before. Every good gentleman knows how to ride; you'll love it once you get the hang of it."

Graham raised a bushy eyebrow at the same time Dominick scoffed in disbelief. In this at least the two of them were in understanding. Even the horse shook its massive head, nearly knocking Dominick over.

"Enough dawdling," Alfie tapped his cane against his boot. "Graham has enough to do without playing nursemaid all afternoon. It's just a horse. Hop up and I'm sure I can talk you through the rest."

Dominick took a deep breath. At least if he disgraced himself it was out in the country without any prying eyes.

Or at least, *few* prying eyes. In addition to Alfie and Graham, the footman Jarrett had been leaning against the manor wall, watching the entire time. Dominick caught his eye, meaning to tell him to go find his entertainment somewhere else, but before he could say anything, a sly smile spread over Jarrett's face and he approached.

"Pardon, sir, not to speak out of turn, but my father was a groom all his life and I ken a fair thing or two about horses. I could try?"

He stepped closer and took the reins from Graham. The stablemaster hardly waited for Dominick's nod before hieing off back to the stables, presumably to go deal with beasts he understood. Jarrett ran his hand along the horse's neck in long, firm strokes. It flicked its ears and stamped a bit, but settled quickly, enjoying the touch. Jarrett looked up at Dominick through his eyelashes and dropped his voice.

"See, it's like that, sir. You just have to let them know who's in charge. I'm sure you're good at that."

Dominick bit back a laugh. The boy was *flirting* with him! He wasn't particularly graceful at it, but there was something to be said for a less subtle approach.

He grinned, and looked over at Alfie. His love was clearly too far away to hear, seeing as how he only smiled back, instead of beating Jarrett over the head with his cane or huffing off in a state. He wasn't exactly sure how Alfie would react if jealous, and had no intentions of finding out. He loved Alfie, and although it might be fun to tease the little fiend on occasion, he would never do anything to intentionally hurt him.

Just the idea of it gave him a hard lump in his chest. He swallowed. Alfie was still smiling at him, and making small "up, up" gestures with his hands. Reluctantly, Dominick turned back to the horse. He'd faced greater challenges than a flirtatious footman before. He could handle this as well.

❊ ❊ ❊

An eternity later, Dominick gripped the reins tightly in

his hands and led the horse in an uneven but complete circle around the stable yard at a wavering trot.

"Good," Jarrett said from atop a spirited bay beside him. "Heels down. Steady thrust with the hips, that's what I like to see."

Aside from the occasional coy comment, so far Jarrett was actually quite a good teacher. He'd been patient and explained in simple terms how to get on the horse, and how to keep from falling off again once there.

Dominick risked loosening one hand from the reins to give his horse a quick pat on the neck. The animal, whom he'd expected to have a name like "Lucifer" or "Nightshade" was actually called "Liquorice" and had as sweet a disposition to match. She'd waited docilely while Jarrett fetched the bay to demonstrate the instructions that had seemed so unclear when coming from Graham and Alfie, and didn't seem to mind when Dominick failed to copy Jarrett's graceful motions.

Dominick led Liquorice around again, a little faster this time. He could see how this might be fun with practice. He imagined himself flying across the heath like Dick Turpin, Liquorice his own Black Bess beneath him. Nothing but the sky above him and his sweetheart eagerly awaiting his return.

He spent another hour or so practicing, until Jarrett's anxious looks towards the house became too frequent to ignore.

"I think we're keeping Jarrett from his duties," Alfie said, rising and walking towards them. Dominick led Liquorice over to him, showing off a bit when he brought her to a gentle stop with only the smallest effort.

"I don't mind, milord. There's not much needs doing from me when you're out. Only it's getting close to dinner and Mr. Gibson will be a right devil if I'm not cleaned and ready to serve. Pardon my saying so."

"Quite all right. You were a great help today. If Mr. Trent is interested, would you be willing to continue his education when you have time?"

If it hadn't meant dropping the reins, Dominick would have put his face in his hands.

"Oh, I would be *most* willing, sir. Thank you. If it pleases Mr. Trent, of course."

"Excellent. Then it's settled. I'll leave you to teach him the fine art of the dismount then let you get back to your duties. Please inform Mrs. Finley that we would each like hot water for a bath brought up before dinner."

Alfie patted Liquorice's nose, and stepped to Dominick's side. Out of Jarrett's view, he brushed his fingertips lightly against Dominick's thigh.

"I'll see you later, Mr. Trent," Alfie said with an impish grin before walking back towards the house, leaning less on his cane than before.

Dominick's knees buckled a little when he hit the ground, but Jarrett made no comment. Even more surprising, he didn't use the opportunity to get his hands on Dominick, letting him regain his balance and dignity on his own. Dominick passed off the reins to a boy that appeared blinking from the stables, presumably young Davey. He looked too small to even be around such animals, never mind do the work of the stable lad. Dominick marveled as Davey led both animals at once off to their stalls, seemingly without a care that the beasts were ten times his size and could shake him as easily as a dog shook a flea. Yet the horses did little more than lip at the yellow tufts of his hair as they walked, which they could have understandably mistaken for straw.

It was because of this distraction that he didn't notice Jarrett's approach.

"I did enjoy our time together today, Mr. Trent. I like to go down to the old chapel ruins around midnight. To gaze at the stars, you ken? If you're interested, I'd welcome the company."

With a saucy wink he strode off, head held high and with more than the usual swagger in his hips. The boy was going to be a problem, but damned if Dominick didn't admire his confidence.

But he wouldn't be going to the chapel, that was for certain. Though they hadn't discussed it, Dominick was hoping that by midnight Alfie would have found his way into *his* bed.

He sighed. If Jarrett was going to be on the prowl it would be wiser to keep his door locked lest he mistake an unwelcome visitor for Alfie in the dark. Jarrett might be pleased to find himself mistaken for a lord, but he doubted Alfie would be so forgiving.

CHAPTER 5

Alfie rapped again, glancing down the hall to make sure there was no one to see him.

"Dominick," he hissed. "Open the door. It's me." He tried the doorknob but it rattled in place without opening.

Dominick had locked him out! In fairness, he hadn't mentioned his plan for a midnight rendezvous, hoping to give Dominick a pleasant surprise, but still. Whoever heard of locking one's bedroom unless he had something to hide? What if the servants needed to get in? More importantly, what if Alfie did!

He sighed and pulled his heavy robe tighter around himself with one hand, the other holding the candlestick he'd been too afraid to leave his room without. He hadn't thought Charleton's tale about the Wicked Master had affected him all that much, but after Mr. Howe had left for the night, leaving him in the darkness of the master's room, all alone with the deep shadows and strange night noises of the house... He'd sat for hours wide awake, staying close enough to the fire to be in its circle of cast light, and counting the minutes until the household was asleep and he could risk going the few steps down the hall to Dominick's room.

But now it all appeared to be for nothing. He was loath to return to the Wicked Master's—to *his own* room, but didn't want to risk knocking any louder. These old houses echoed strangely, and he couldn't risk the sound carrying to the servants' quarters and someone coming to investigate. He raised his fist to try one last time, then froze.

There, in the dark at the end of the hall, he could have sworn something moved.

"Hello?" he called out tentatively. "I didn't mean to wake you. I couldn't sleep and was going to borrow a book..."

There was no response. The hairs rose on the back of his neck.

Get a hold of yourself. It was just a trick of the light. There are no murderous spirits, just your own overactive imagination. Go back to bed.

But he couldn't seem to move. He remained fixed in place, squinting down the hall, trying to make out anything in the consuming darkness. He slowly raised the candle, but couldn't see any further into its depths. His blood turned to ice when he realised that he couldn't see who or whatever was there in the dark, but with the candle, they could see him.

He had just about convinced himself there was nothing there, when he saw it again. The figure, for it was a figure, no trick of the light, took off and disappeared around the corner. It was too dark and too quick to make out any details, but Alfie was certain that man or ghost, someone had been there.

He jerked into action, prepared to run back to his room and bolt the door, but found his feet carrying him in the opposite direction instead, after the fleeing phantom. He reached the corner before he even realised what he was doing and took off down it. This hall led right into the heart of the old building, and Alfie's breathing seemed loud in the stony silence. He reached an intersection and looked both ways, holding his breath. He saw nothing, but heard a scrape and the scuffle of footsteps down the hall to the left. He set off at a run, but cursed as the pain in his leg flared and he stumbled.

Damn it, you're not so weak you have to stop already, are you?

He took a moment before tearing off again, his uneven footsteps echoing as he ran. Whatever was there in the dark, he would catch it. But what would happen then he had no idea.

Ahead of him, the darkness solidified into stone. He cried out, his slippered feet sliding as he tried to stop, and crashed into the wall. The candlestick hit the floor with a clatter that reverberated like cannon fire down the silent corridor, but luckily the flame didn't go out. He wheezed, his leg aching with the burst of exertion and sudden impact. He picked up the light and climbed slowly to his feet.

It was impossible. He raised a hand in case it was some strange illusion, but his fingers met cool rock. Slightly damp, but undeniably real. He turned back and in a daze, tried the handles of the only two doors in the hall.

The first was locked, its handle rattling in his hand the same way the one on Dominick's door had. The second door was unlocked and opened onto a room filled with shrouded furniture.

He must have made his way to the part of the house

they hadn't had time to make ready before his arrival. He knelt in the doorway and ran a finger through the dust. It lay thick enough to leave a visible trail, and nowhere else in the room was it disturbed. The figure he'd chased was then either the kind of entity that didn't leave footprints, or the kind that could walk through locked doors or solid walls. Neither of which he wanted to meet.

He shivered, the cold of the house intensifying. This was the wing that the earl's suite was in. Had he just witnessed the spirit of Malcolm Pennington repeating his mad flight towards his father's room? Alfie stood, and staring straight ahead so as not to catch sight of anything unwanted out of the corner of his eye, walked back the way he'd come. Whatever he'd followed here, he wanted no more to do with it.

Which was, of course, when the candle began to splutter.

Trying to keep the building panic at bay, he sheltered the little flame as best he could. There was no way he'd be able to make it back to his room before it went out, and he couldn't remember if he'd seen any other waiting candle sticks or lamps along the disused corridor.

The house yawned around him, a great looming thing. He had to think quickly or he'd be left standing in the pitch black with whatever it was he'd chased and no way of knowing if it was still there.

He ached to go to Dominick, to jump into his bed and pull the covers over his head. Let Dominick coax the story out of him and tell him it was all in his mind, just a terrible tale he'd let get under his skin. Dominick might tease him for it, like he had when they were children and Alfie couldn't sleep because of a ghost story. But even if he could make it that far before the candle went out, Dominick's door was locked and Alfie was even more afraid to knock on it now. Not because he might attract the servants, but because he might attract something else.

The only other place he could think of was the library. It had a fireplace and comfortable chairs. He could spend the night there and if he was seen in the morning, simply say he'd come down to read and fallen asleep. He cradled the candle even closer to keep a stray draught from blowing it out, and hurried in the direction he thought led to the library.

Fortunately, it was not a long journey. If he'd turned right instead of left to follow the spirit, the library would have been the first door he came to. It wasn't far enough for his liking from where the figure had disappeared, but he barely had time to get inside and use the last of the candle to light the tinder in the hearth. If he'd waited any longer he'd have been stuck roaming the halls in complete darkness, but perhaps not completely alone.

Once the fire was burning, he turned back to the library door, thinking to close and lock it. His hand hesitated on the knob. If the figure could walk through walls, then a locked door wouldn't keep it from getting in, but it might keep Alfie from getting out. Reluctantly, he opened the door even wider. It was like staring into the jaws of a predator, but at least if something came for him through the doorway he would have some warning. And if it came any other way, he'd have an escape route.

Feeling foolish, he picked up the fireplace poker and angled one of the leather chairs to face the door. He sat down and rested the poker against the arm of the chair within easy reach. It wouldn't be as good as his sword cane, but it would do in a pinch. He cursed himself for leaving the cane in his room. He hadn't planned on needing it for just a tryst, but by now he should know to have the damned thing with him at all times; he only ever seemed to find trouble when he was without it.

His heart was still racing too quickly for him to even think about sleep. Happily, the pile of books he'd gathered earlier in the day still sat on the small table between the two chairs. He knew there was a collection of poetry in there. Wordsworth had been a fine cure for insomnia when he was a student.

Picking up the top book he frowned, he didn't remember this one.

Neither the spine nor cover bore a title. It didn't look like the ones he'd chosen, those being mostly newer books, and slimmer on the whole. This was a great thing, built more along the lines of a family Bible. Its leather swirled in raised designs across the front, but was badly faded and had a powdery feel along the edges where it would soon crack and peel away.

Perhaps one of the maids had been in here earlier and moved it for cleaning. Curious, he opened to the title page.

A Memoir of Balcarres House;
Being a Complete History of the Earls of Crawford,
to Which are Added
Extracts from Official Correspondence
Together with Personal Narratives

He paged through the book, excited. From the table of contents, it appeared to have been published by his grandfather—or at least at his behest—as his was the name recorded as the current earl. Though he wasn't actually a Pennington by blood, the idea of having a family history was comforting. He was the earl now too, just as all these other men had been, and didn't that make him part of something? One more link in a chain going back for centuries, handed down from father to son.

Although not always to the son.

He ran his finger along the contents, then flipped to the chapter titled "The Eighth Earl of Crawford, Gordon Pennington". The Wicked Master's father.

The language was old fashioned and the print difficult to read, but from all accounts, Gordon was just as lovingly remembered as Charleton had said. The chapter was filled with glowing praise, calling him "a wise shepherd of his lands" and "ever-vigilant, his eye was everywhere".

Alfie skimmed the pages until he saw the first mention of Gordon's son, Malcolm Pennington. He tucked his feet under himself and angled the book so the light from the fire fell more directly on the page. The story as written was almost identical to Charleton's version, though in truth, he was the better storyteller. The book's account was full of lengthy descriptions of the anguish caused by the upset of the natural order and long moralizing lectures on the duties of the child, with special emphasis on the loyalties due from son to father.

How sharper than a serpent's tooth, he mused as he turned the page.

The book bemoaned the Wicked Master's other crimes, both real and assumed. It discussed the emptied coffers and stolen gold, but also mentioned the disappearance of the wealthy farmer Charleton had referenced, a man by the name of Samuel Whin.

The author had been careful not to directly place blame, but strongly implied that Mr. Whin had been another victim of the Wicked Master, and the only reason he hadn't been tried for that murder in addition to the attempt on his father was that no body had ever been found.

That was when Alfie noticed something odd. Aside from a first use towards the top of the chapter, Malcolm's given name wasn't repeated a single time, with all other mentions only referring to him as "the Wicked Master".

Alfie shivered. *Damnatio memoriae.* To be so vile that one's own name was all but forgotten, to be only remembered through the ages by such a terrible appellation instead. It reminded him of that poem by Shelley that had just come out, the one about stone feet in the sand, boundless and bare.

"Look on my Works, ye Mighty, and despair," indeed!

With that unsettling thought, he closed the book. Reading about the Wicked Master's life hardly took his mind off of his possible encounter with the man's ghost. He set the heavy tome under the chair and reached again for the pile.

Ah, there it was, *Lyrical Ballads* by Wordsworth and Coleridge. If there was anything that could put him to sleep after the night he'd had, it was an extended ode to the Welsh countryside!

CHAPTER 6

In the morning, Alfie successfully evaded any servants between the library and his room, and jumped into bed mere minutes before there was a discreet knock at the door.

"Good morning, sir. You slept well, I trust?" said Mr. Howe as he entered.

Alfie sat up and rubbed the back of his neck. Spending the night in a chair had hardly been the most comfortable, but spending the night with a ghost would have been far worse.

He couldn't help but chuckle. By the light of day his experience the night before seemed silly. He'd had a mind full of ghost stories and flickering candlelight, of course his imagination had conjured all sorts of horrors in the dark. But he was a grown man, not a child cowering under the sheets. Letting those phantasms keep him from his bed had been ridiculous. He couldn't wait to tell Dominick about his foolishness, even if the man would mock him for the rest of their lives.

So resolved, he got out of bed and back into his still-warm robe while Mr. Howe laid out his clothing for the day.

"I can handle myself today, Mr. Howe. I don't believe we'll have any callers, so I promise not to attempt anything too complicated with my cravat. You may go and see to Mr.

Trent if he's awake."

Mr. Howe bowed and headed out into the hall. Moments later he returned. "I beg your pardon, sir. But Mr. Trent's door is locked."

Of course. In all the excitement Alfie had completely forgotten the reason he'd been wandering the halls last night in the first place. Although it wasn't as if he could say, "Yes, I know. I tried to get in for a midnight dalliance last night. Rotten luck for us both." So perhaps it was just as well it had slipped his mind.

"I see. I do believe Mr. Trent is quite a heavy sleeper. Who would have the spare key? Mr. Gibson? Or I'm sure if we both put out shoulders to the door we could bring it down."

"If you say so, my lord," said Mr. Howe with an amused twinkle in his eye. "However, I do not think that will be necessary. If you'll allow me?"

He crossed to the wall closest to Dominick's room and examined one of the bookcases there. To Alfie's eye it looked the same as any of the others, although perhaps more intricately carved, with oak leaves wrapped in delicate scrolls. After a moment, Mr. Howe pressed a wood panel at the back of one of the shelves. There was an audible click and the entire bookcase swung into the room a fraction of an inch. Alfie's mouth dropped open. An actual secret passageway! Balcarres House was turning out to be something straight from an adventure novel.

Heart racing with delight, he moved to join Mr. Howe as the valet swung the hidden door open with ease, revealing a neat archway in the stone wall through which could be seen the back of another bookcase. The panel that acted as a latch was easier to see from this side, and Mr. Howe kindly let Alfie do the honors. With a quick press of his hand, the bookcase swung open and he stepped into the room with a still sleeping Dominick.

Oh, this was going to be *most* convenient.

He corralled his wicked thoughts and put on a suitably blank expression.

"Ingenious, Mr. Howe! Thank you for showing me!" Alfie shouted, and was pleased to see Dominick start awake at the noise, flailing against the bedclothes before collapsing back down with a groan.

"My pleasure, sir," replied Mr. Howe with what appeared to be a barely suppressed smile. "They say most houses of Balcarres' age are riddled with secret ways, although I'm afraid I only know of this house having two. There's the one you've just been through, and another—much longer —leading up from the kitchens to the dining room. Built so dinner could be brought in discreetly without the risk of spilling soup on any priceless rugs, I imagine. And quite useful it is at that."

While Mr. Howe attempted to pry Dominick out of bed and arrange him to some degree of respectability, Alfie examined some of the trinkets and curios on the mantle. Neither man commented on his presence, although Dominick was moving so slowly, Alfie wasn't sure he was aware of much at all.

Having done the best he could with his unwilling subject, Mr. Howe bowed and left the room, unlocking the door to the hall and making his exit that way. Dominick slumped on the bed and blinked owlishly as the door clicked shut behind him.

"I thought I'd locked that." He turned stiffly to Alfie. "I did. How the devil did you get in?"

Alfie rolled his eyes. "Good morning to you too, my love. The hours in which we were parted were as like years for how my heart has suffered your absence."

He dropped a quick kiss on Dominick's lips. "Behind the bookcase there's a secret doorway that connects our rooms."

"Oh? *Oh!* Well," Dominick licked his lips. "That's fortunate."

"It is indeed," Alfie leaned down, attempting to turn his next kiss into something more passionate. He didn't get very far before Dominick winced and pulled away.

"Sorry, Alfie. The spirit is willing, but the flesh feels like it's been rolled back to London in a barrel. Christ, why do people ever get on those infernal animals? I'm sore in places I didn't know I had!"

Alfie laughed, "Wait until you learn to canter! I don't think I sat for a week after my first time! No, don't say anything, I heard it. Wipe that look off your face. I was going to offer to make use of our newly discovered passage to give you a rubdown tonight if you're still in pain—"

"You're going to rub my newly discovered passage? I'm afraid to say it's not that ne—"

"—But just for that," Alfie spoke over him. "I'm going to tell Mrs. Finley how you're feeling and have her do it. Preferably with the most noxious-smelling country remedy she knows."

Dominick lay back gingerly across the width of the bed, his booted feet still on the floor. He muttered something indistinct.

"What was that?"

"I said, you could tell her to send Jarrett to do it. He'd leap at the chance."

At Alfie's frown, Dominick huffed.

"He invited me to go *stargazing*."

An interest in astronomy was an odd pastime for a footman, but he could hardly see how it related to their current discussion. At his confused look, Dominick gave him a fond little smile.

"Stargazing? At midnight? Down at the lonely chapel ruins? Blast, what did you and your school chums call it when you wanted to get at it?"

Alfie's eyes felt like they were about to pop out of his head. "Do you mean to tell me he... he's a..."

"He's one of our sort, yes. And a very unsubtle one at that. Made more than a few comments during the riding lesson yesterday, but the 'stargazing' really was too much. That's why I locked my door last night. I didn't want him to think the cold was the only reason I didn't go out and meet him. Hopefully now he's gotten the message."

Alfie didn't know what to say. The absolute *gall*! How dare Jarrett think he had any right to say such things to Dominick! To assume that he could just saunter over and what? Win Dominick away from Alfie with equestrian knowledge and lewd invitations? Alfie would see him thoroughly corrected on that!

He sat down heavily on the bed. Dominick reached over and took his hand without sitting up.

"I know what you're thinking, but you're not going to have him run out of town or horsewhipped or whatever else you're conjuring up in that devious little brain of yours."

"I was thinking no such thing," Alfie replied absently, wondering if Graham had any skill as a farrier. He must; at least a few of the horses in the stables were geldings.

"Yes, you were. But you're not going to do it."

"I'm not?"

"No, because in about a minute you're going to feel very ashamed for having thought about using your position to ruin a young man's life. And about a minute after that you'll decide you actually admire him for his daring. But right now…"

Dominick squeezed Alfie's hand tightly. "Right now you're going to be told how a thousand footmen could offer me a thousand stars to gaze at, and you'd still be the only man I ever wanted in my bed."

Alfie looked down at Dominick, and his love hit him like a physical blow. His feelings for Dominick were always in the back of his mind, like music playing from a distant room, still audible but not so distracting he couldn't go on with his day. But sometimes he was struck all over again with how much he loved this strong, brave, selfless man, and how lucky he was to be loved by him in return. How sweet it was to feel that way now, in such a peaceful moment, just sitting on a bed and holding hands.

He slowly leaned down, enjoying the look on Dominick's face as he came ever closer. That second where his eyes crossed a little trying to watch all of Alfie at once was just as charming now as it was the first time they'd kissed. Dominick parted his lips as he descended, but at the last moment Alfie veered to the side and whispered in his ear.

"How long do you think until we're missed for breakfast?"

"W-what?"

Alfie grinned and nipped Dominick's ear before sitting upright. Dominick struggled to get up as well, hissing as his sore muscles protested, but Alfie planted a firm hand on his chest and pushed him back down.

"*Stay.*"

Dominick complied and his eyes went dark. Alfie felt him go boneless under his hand, surrendering completely. He pressed down a moment more to ensure his point was made. Then got up, crossing to the door and relocking it.

"I think you were wise to lock your door. I came to *borrow a book from you* last night," he said meaningfully. "And saw someone in the halls."

"Was it Jarrett?"

"I couldn't tell. I gave chase but…"

"But?"

"But I'll tell you over breakfast." Alfie crossed back through the passage into his own room and locked that door as well for good measure. When he came back, Dominick was exactly where he'd left him, splayed out like a sacrificial offering, but he turned his head to track Alfie's progress. His parted knees were bent to let his feet rest on the floor and Alfie could look up the entire delicious length of him. Under his gaze, Dominick's chest rose and fell with quick breaths and his tight buckskin breeches did little to hide his growing excitement.

He walked to the bed and stood between Dominick's legs, giving each of his boots a light kick to open him up even further to Alfie's perusal. Though still fully clothed,

Dominick looked a wanton mess, his cock now straining against his breeches and tongue peeking out to wet his open lips. There was such power in knowing that he was the one who could do this to Dominick. That he alone could make the fierce fighter turn docile and compliant. It was enough to make him dizzy, so he put his hands on Dominick's thighs and slowly lowered himself to his knees.

Once kneeling, he made quick work of the placket of Dominick's breeches, letting out a pleased hum when his magnificent cock sprang free. He shifted, getting more comfortable.

Before Dominick came back into his life, Alfie had only done this act, and had it done to him, once before at university. He'd had ample opportunity for practice since, Dominick being a willing, though less-than-patient, subject for his explorations.

However, in the months they'd been together, there were still a few things they hadn't done. Although Dominick had taken him—frequently and to great mutual pleasure—Alfie had yet to take him in return.

He was unsure of how to broach the subject, and Dominick never had. He'd wondered at first whether Dominick only enjoyed the more active role, but the more he'd considered it, the more he worried Dominick might associate being taken with his days of selling his body to survive. As such, Alfie hadn't raised the matter for fear of reviving painful memories that were best left forgotten.

As much as he might be curious, he would never do anything to hurt Dominick. Besides, what they did together already brought him greater joy than he'd ever believed possible.

With that joy in mind, he leaned in and pressed a kiss to the head of Dominick's cock, before running a gentle tongue down its length. Dominick hissed at the teasing and twitched under him, but other than clenching in hands in the bedspread, he stayed exactly as Alfie had put him. Alfie rewarded him with a series of firmer licks, before burying his nose in the crisp hair at the base. Dominick's scent was thickest there and most intoxicating, the raw masculinity of sweat and desire overwhelming his senses.

He took Dominick's cock in hand, giving it long lazy strokes as he kissed his way sideways to the delicate place where thigh met groin. He had to nose the buckskins open wider to reach, but the reward was worth it. Such a tender and vulnerable spot, bared so trustingly that he couldn't help but take advantage. He sucked down hard and Dominick let out a yelp, one hand flying up to cover his mouth and smother his moans. Alfie sucked harder, and worried the pale skin with his teeth until a dark red mark rose up.

He licked the mark and hummed, pleased with his results. Let that rascal Jarrett try anything now and he'd see that Dominick wasn't his to have.

He let go of Dominick's cock and raised his head. Dominick whined and wiped his hand over his mouth, teeth marks visible in the meat of his palm.

"Visiting the library."

"What?" said Dominick, more of a wheeze than an actual question.

"That's what we called it. At university. You didn't ask if another boy wanted to go stargazing, you asked if he wanted to visit the library."

"I don't give a fuck if you asked him to dine with Napoleon! If you don't—" Dominick's tirade was cut short by a deep groan as Alfie pressed his hands down hard on his thighs and pushed upwards, rolling the overexerted muscles under his palms. He drew his hands back down slowly, fingertips leaving faint trails against the grain of the leather, then pressed up again with his knuckles down, digging deep into the meat of Dominick's legs.

Dominick cursed. Alfie knew his muscles would feel better afterwards, but decided it was time to let pleasure overwhelm his pain. He dipped down, taking as much of Dominick's cock into his mouth as he comfortably could, then just a bit more. Dominick could swallow him all the way to the root, and though Alfie wasn't there yet, he was determined to one day match his lover in skill. He called it "being considerate". Dominick called it "being a competitive little bugger".

He drew back, and took to sucking Dominick's cock in earnest, still treating his legs to the firm caresses that would prove beneficial, for all that they hurt now. Dominick thrashed above him, his shouts muffled again by his fist in his mouth, before forcibly trying to make himself lay still on the bed as Alfie wanted. Alfie thrummed with desire, his own neglected cock pressing painfully against his breeches, but there would be time for that later. For now, he hollowed his cheeks as he took Dominick in deeper. At the same time he wrapped his arms around Dominick's thighs, simultaneously pulling him closer to Alfie while also pinning him to the bed. He slid his hands under the breeches just enough to grasp the lush swell of Dominick's firm buttocks and dug his fingers in *hard*.

His howl of pleasure only barely muffled, Dominick's hips flew up as he came, nearly bucking Alfie off him. Alfie choked momentarily, but recovered quickly, uncommonly proud of himself for not spilling a single drop.

Eventually, Dominick's cock began to soften, and Alfie released him before the sensitivity became painful, gently tucking him back in and setting him to rights. Dominick did nothing to help the process, just lay on the bed with his eyes closed, panting weakly. Under the circumstances, Alfie decided to forgive him.

He leaned over and kissed him deeply, a dark thrill running through him knowing Dominick would taste his own essence in his mouth.

When Dominick finally gathered wits enough to try to pull Alfie down, he leaned back, laughing. "Later. We have to go now or there will be questions as to why our breakfast is growing cold."

Dominick looked at him in disbelief. "I could barely walk before and you want me to attempt stairs *now*?"

"Up, up," Alfie took his hands and pulled his groaning lover to his feet. He took advantage of their closeness to give him a last teasing kiss. "Perhaps if you successfully navigate the stairs, then later we can make a *visit to the library*."

CHAPTER 7

Dominick made his way to the dining room mostly under his own power, although the stairwell banister was an invaluable ally on the way down. Between the effects of his riding lesson yesterday and Alfie's ministrations this morning, he felt as ragged as a three-legged dog and about as stable as one, too.

As they slowly descended to breakfast, Alfie took Dominick's mind off his discomfort by regaling him with the tale of his adventure the night before. While his grin at Alfie spending the night *in the library* out of fear of an imagined spirit earned him only an eye roll and a swat on the arm, he couldn't help but laugh out loud at the description of Alfie chasing the nocturnal visitor through the house. If it had been Jarrett, as it probably was, the poor boy must have been out of his mind with terror of nearly being caught breaking into his room by an *earl*. Doubtless he would make no further attempts on Dominick's person, and would go looking for more amenable, and available, pastures.

He suppressed a groan as he finally sank into his seat at the table. He'd worried that Alfie was going to feel hurt or, even more foolishly, insecure when he told him about Jarrett's attempted seduction. But apparently his concerns about Alfie's reactions were unfounded. His lover wasn't upset, he was downright *possessive*.

In the process of placing his napkin in his lap, his hand brushed over the spot where Alfie had bitten him. He could almost feel the heat of the mark through the fabric. It would be a spectacular bruise when he undressed this evening. If asked, he was sure Alfie would claim he had no particular designs in mind and had only meant it as a bit of play. But he didn't believe that for an instant. Alfie had claimed him, as surely as if he had put a collar around Dominick's neck with his name on it in big brass letters.

Dominick flushed at the idea. He'd always thought of himself as independent, beholden to no man, but if Alfie wanted to call Dominick "his"? Well. There were worse fates.

Although he'd like it better if Alfie kept those sharp teeth of his further away from delicate parts of his anatomy. But if he did, he would be unable to suck Dominick's cock as devastatingly as he had this morning. A tricky problem.

"What's got you thinking so hard?" Alfie asked, toying with a fork. The table had been set but the sideboard was still bare.

"Just a mathematical problem. I'm sure it's far too complicated for you."

Alfie opened his mouth to deliver a no doubt devastating retort when Mrs. Finley, looking distinctly out of sorts, came in without knocking.

"Beg your pardons, sirs, but I'm afraid we're all rather at sixes and sevens this morning. Mrs. Buie in the kitchen thought you were breakfasting later because Mr. Gibson hadn't told her you were up, and the rest of us assumed you were still eating since he hadn't informed us it was time to clear the tables. It was only just now when Mr. Howe asked about having your rooms made up that we realised no one had spoken to Mr. Gibson at all this morning! I had Jarrett run up and check his room to see if he was unwell, but it's empty!"

"Did he say anything to the staff about leaving, perhaps on an errand? He didn't mention anything to me yesterday," said Alfie. "Mr. Trent?"

Dominick shook his head, "Not a word."

"Nor to any of us as far as I ken. Oh, it's just like Lily all over again, poor dear. Mrs. Buie's daughter she is, and the kitchen maid she used to be, until we woke up one morning and she'd disappeared into the night, run off without a word!"

Mrs. Finley shook her head. "But she always was a flighty thing with her head in the clouds. Her, I would expect to pack up her bags without notice, thinking it some grand adventure. But Mr. Gibson? At his age?"

"Are Mr. Gibson's things missing?" Dominick interrupted, sensing an oncoming lecture on the follies of youth and the worse follies of those well past youth.

"No, sir," Mrs. Finley replied, collecting herself. "Jarrett says everything is still accounted for, like he just vanished into thin air."

"Gather the staff if you will, Mrs. Finley," said Alfie, rising from the table. "And tell Mrs. Buie to wait on breakfast. Mr. Gibson may be somewhere injured or otherwise unwell, and we'll need all hands on deck to find him."

*   *   *

A short while later, the servants had been dispersed in pairs to go searching. If any pair found him, and he was incapacitated in some way, one could stay with him while the other ran for help.

Graham acknowledged his assignment to begin searching the grounds with a short nod, while young Davey bounded after him, giddy with adventure in the way of all small boys. Mr. Howe and Jarrett gave much more courteous bows before heading off to look through the men's quarters and Mr. Gibson's room in particular for any clues. If they found nothing, they would assist Graham and Davey outside. Mrs. Buie and Mrs. Finley would start with the women's quarters and the attics and spiral downwards through the central body of the house, while Moira and Janie started by the earl's suite in the east wing and worked their way west.

This left Alfie and Dominick to start in the west wing and work their way east. There would be some overlap of areas, but as Alfie had pointed out to his concerned audience, it was better to be over-thorough than for Mr. Gibson to be overlooked. If all went to plan, he would quickly be found, but if he hadn't been by the time the indoor parties met in the grand hall at the center of the manor, the alarm would be raised in the village.

Dominick marveled at the speed with which Alfie organised everyone and how quickly they all jumped to follow his orders. They too must sense the nobility Dominick saw in him, the one that had nothing to do with

Alfie's blood, but everything to do with his character.

"One more thing, Mrs. Finley," Alfie pulled the woman aside as the other groups fanned out. "Is there a spare set of keys to Balcarres? I don't have a set and want to make sure I can conduct a thorough search."

"Take mine, sir," she replied, unhooking a large ring with at least a dozen keys from her apron. "Mrs. Buie and I can fetch her set from the kitchen. If Mr. Gibson has locked himself away somewhere, you'll be able to find him with these."

Alfie thanked her and the search began. He and Dominick began in the portrait hall at the far end of the house and slowly worked their way inwards and downwards, opening every room and cupboard they could find. Charleton's tour the day before helped, but Dominick still felt as if he was walking in circles in some enormous maze.

"I know I'm a heavy sleeper, but I still think I'd have noticed if Mr. Gibson was locked in with me," Dominick said with only a cursory glance into his room, hoping the jest might ease the worried wrinkle in Alfie's brow. "Do you think it was him you saw last night?"

Alfie gave one of his considering little hums. "It might have been. I honestly couldn't see much more than movement in the dark. If it was though, he's got more speed on him than I would've guessed. But that still doesn't answer the question of where he disappeared to."

"What about that locked room? You said there were two rooms in that hall, one dusty and one locked. If it was Mr. Gibson you were chasing, he would have had a key."

"He still would have had to be damned quick about it,

but it's not impossible. I was thinking of that room when I asked Mrs. Finley for these." Alfie held up the set of keys. "Shall we go there now?"

"No, we should stick to your plan. 'An orderly fashion' and all that."

Alfie huffed. "Why must you pick now to be sensible?"

Dominick plucked the keys from his hand, "We'll be there soon enough. If we are where I think we are in this warren, the hallway with your library is next. It's not far from there."

He was pleased to discover he was right when the next corner led them to the far end of the hall containing the library, but there were several other rooms that had to be checked first. By the time they'd checked the first few, Mrs. Finley came into view with a curtsey.

"No luck, Mrs. Finley?" asked Alfie.

"None, sir. Mrs. Buie went off to join the lasses but I'm beginning to worry that this is a matter for the magistrate. It wouldn't be like Mr. Gibson to just leave."

"I'm afraid you may be right, but let's finish up here first. Just this hallway and the ground floor and we'll be done. If you want to start at the other end, we'll meet you in the middle."

"Very good, sir."

"Oh, I believe one of those doors may be locked, just shout out if you need the key."

Alfie went into the next room on their side, which left the library to Dominick. He'd been thinking up several bawdy jokes about "visiting the library" with Alfie, but Mrs. Finley's presence made him reconsider.

He eyed the room warily. Perhaps there was a secret

passage hidden behind one of these bookcases as well. Even if Mr. Howe didn't know about it, Mr. Gibson might. But without knowing which panel was the trigger mechanism, it would be almost impossible to discover. Reaching as best he could over the neatly ordered books, he started pressing the back panels of each shelf just to be safe. He was stretching to reach the top row of a bookshelf when he heard a scream of terror.

He ran out into the hall, his aching muscles forgotten, and barely avoided colliding with Alfie. As one, they turned and ran in the direction of the scream. Mrs. Finley stood at the end of the hallway before an open doorway, her hands covering her eyes and sobbing. All the other doors along the corridor were open as well.

"Oh, it's horrible! Horrible! Oh, poor Mr. Gibson!" she wailed.

Dominick reached her first, and put an arm around her, drawing her away. As he did, he glanced over his shoulder into the room behind her and let out a curse.

On the other side of the doorway, he caught a glimpse of a man's legs clad in a servant's formal black socks and knee breeches.

"Mr. Gibson?" he mouthed at Alfie over Mrs. Finley's bobbing cap.

Alfie stepped into the room out of Dominick's sightline, before returning quickly. The sorrow on his face was a clear answer.

"This was the locked room..." he said so quietly that Dominick barely heard it.

He glanced at the door. If it was locked last night, it hadn't been a minute ago when Mrs. Finley opened it. That was worrying, but he had more immediate concerns. He left Alfie with the body as he escorted Mrs. Finley down the hall, trying to murmur comforting nothings as she clung to his shirt and wept.

He was rescued by the arrival of Mrs. Buie and the two maids. Mrs. Buie took one look at the housekeeper and an air of grim understanding came over her. She stopped in place, while the younger women ran to Mrs. Finley.

"Oh my dears!" she cried, as Dominick gratefully released her into their care. "Mr. Gibson is dead! It was so awful!"

"There, there," said Moira in her soft voice. "We're here now. No more tears for him."

"Mrs. Buie," Dominick said, "You can tell the others to call off the search. And have someone send for... for whoever should handle this."

Mrs. Buie nodded, but did not have the chance to reply before Mrs. Finley cried out again.

"But his face! It was so—I can't even say, it's too terrible! And the marks on his neck, like black handprints!"

Janie gasped. "Lord save us! The Wicked Master is back!"

CHAPTER 8

Within a few hours, the doctor arrived, bringing with him the minister and the magistrate as well.

Alfie had sent Moira to escort Mrs. Finley to her room and keep her company while she rested. He'd send the doctor up to see her later to ensure the shock hadn't done any permanent damage. Janie he'd deemed far too excitable to be of assistance, but Mrs. Buie had stepped in and was keeping the girl busy running endless trays of fortifying tea and cakes up to the assembled party. This however, meant that Mr. Howe was required to be on interception duty, to keep the girl from "accidentally" catching a glimpse of the corpse and going into hysterics about the ghost of the Wicked Master come to kill them all in their beds.

Alfie rubbed a hand over his face. It was barely past noon and had already been a very long day.

The doctor, a small man by the name of Mills, knelt over the body, checking the eyes and joints and performing whatever other tests he seemed to require to prove what they all knew; Mr. Gibson was dead, and had been for some time. They'd covered the body with a sheet while they waited for Doctor Mills to arrive, but that did little to mitigate the horror.

As the doctor poked and prodded, Mr. Gibson stared

unseeing at the ceiling of the room with his blood-flecked eyes. Dominick had tried to close them, but they flicked back open eerily and remained that way, as if even in death they were locked on his murderer.

For there was no question in Alfie's mind that he'd been murdered. Around Mr. Gibson's neck were dark bruises, clearly made by fingers gripping tight and crushing until all life was choked from the man. They weren't quite the "black handprints" that Mrs. Finley had wailed about, but they weren't far off either.

While Doctor Mills examined the body, Laird Carnbee, a portly and heavily mustachioed man who also served as the local magistrate, ambled around the room picking up this and that. In between replenishing his plate of teacakes and tartlets, he made a show of testing the lock on the window and examining the width of the chimney. The minister, Mr. Bisset, stood at the head of the body, praying loudly and generally getting in the way of both the magistrate and the doctor.

"Well, doctor, what can you tell us?" bristled Carnbee.

"Not much more than the obvious, I'm afraid," said Doctor Mills.

He was a meek little man with all the presence of a coney hiding in a hedge, but Alfie was still wary. He'd trusted Doctor Barlowe for years, and where had it gotten him? Both his parents dead and his London townhouse burned to ash with Dominick and himself nearly gone with it. A nervous glance over at Dominick told him he was thinking the same.

He had worried, given Dominick's past, that the presence of the magistrate would make him nervous, but after the briefest of introductions, Carnbee had completely ignored him. After all, what importance was a mere *Mister* Trent, when there was an *earl* to impress with his so far non-existent investigatory abilities.

Carnbee had been quick to stress the *laird* in his title, patronisingly explaining that it was Scottish word for "lord". After the man's haughty dismissal of Dominick, Alfie had to bite his tongue to point out that that wasn't exactly true. After all, the address of "Lord" only applied to barons and above, and a laird ranked much, much further down the list, somewhere between a baronet and a knight. If Alfie's memory of Debrett's was accurate, even addressing him as "*Sir* Carnbee" wasn't strictly correct. Had Carnbee not been harrumphing all over the manor as if it was his own, Alfie might have done so anyway as a courtesy to his neighbor, but he was not inclined to now.

From the corner of the room, arms crossed against his chest, Dominick rolled his eyes. He probably wasn't aware of all the finer points of the situation, but he knew a braggart when he saw one. Still, he was clearly keeping an eye on Carnbee. It would be just their luck if the old bull was actually good at his job.

Doctor Mills continued, "As you can see, it is obvious this man has been strangled. It would have taken great strength, although if you see by the bruising here, the killer—by accident or intention—pressed directly on the arteries on both sides of the unfortunate Mr. Gibson's neck, killing him by cutting off blood flow to the brain, rather than air to the lungs. It would have been a faster death, but still not a pleasant one."

"Any idea when the murder was committed?"

"From what the staff have said, I would assume sometime in the night, but I have no way to be certain. You'll notice the body is peculiarly rigid, which I have observed to generally happen several hours after death."

"The poor man," intoned Mr. Bisset solemnly. "For the wages of sin is death, but the gift of God is eternal life in Christ Jesus our Lord."

Carnbee cleared his throat. "Well, it's clear to me what happened here".

"Is it?" Alfie asked, surprised. Perhaps he'd been mistaken and the magistrate had a far keener eye than he'd perceived, picking up the most minute clues from the room and discerning the culprit without even conducting a single interview of potential suspects.

"Indeed. Clearly Mr. Gibson, in his nightly locking up of the house, happened upon some would-be burglar and caught him in the act. The thief then strangled Mr. Gibson and fled out the window by which he had entered, using a penknife or some such to relock it just as he had unlocked it when he came in."

"Bollocks," Dominick snorted.

All eyes in the room turned to him, startled at his language, the minister visibly jerking in surprise.

Alfie pressed his lips together firmly, although to stifle a grin or a grimace he couldn't say. Dominick now dressed and looked the part of a wealthy man of ease, but he spoke and acted like the Spitalfields tough he was. That they both were, until Alfie had it trained out of him by his adoptive parents. They would have to work on that if Dominick was ever going to pass in society without suspicion, although Alfie was sure he could find much more pleasant incentives for improving his behavior than he'd endured himself.

But all that would only be necessary around others. He wouldn't have Dominick change the way he was when they were together for anything.

"I beg your pardon?" asked Carnbee snidely, intruding on Alfie's thoughts.

Dominick shrugged. "I'd wager every sneaksman and housecracker in a hundred miles knows Balcarres doesn't have enough servants to post a night guard, and you're saying what? A professional jumper thought that rather than trying any of the doors or lower windows, he'd bring a ladder all the way from home to force one on the second storey? Then he had the sheer bad fortune to pick the window to the locked room Mr. Gibson was in—during the middle of the night for no good reason—strangled him and left, not taking anything with him, but being kind enough to unlock the door before he went so we'd have an easier time finding the corpse?"

"What are you, a thief-taker?" Carnbee sneered.

"No. But I do know you can't relatch a window lock with a penknife from the outside, and that's a fact."

"Gentlemen!" Alfie interrupted, before the magistrate had time to consider how Dominick might have come by such information. He might guess that it was through personal experience house cracking, and he would be correct. "I appreciate that a crime as severe as this likely cannot be solved by such a brief investigation. Carnbee, would you care to interview any of my staff to see if they saw or heard anything suspicious?"

Please don't ask me, he thought. *I don't know whether it would be more difficult to admit to seeing a ghost or to explain why I was about at that hour to begin with.*

"Not necessary," Carnbee huffed, obviously noting the lack of title in Alfie's address. "I'll send word around. I wouldn't be surprised if there've been similar burglaries at other estates in the nearby counties. These sorts tend to move around, you see. Could even be a pack of them. You'd be wise to ensure the manor is shut up tight until the ruffians are securely locked away."

"Unless they have penknives of course," Dominick muttered.

"Thank you, magistrate," Alfie said loudly, "We'll take that under advisement."

He turned to the minister. "Shall I have Mr. Gibson brought to the church or—"

"Oh goodness, no!" cried Mr. Bisset. His ginger beard, which rivaled Graham's in size if not in colour, flew back and forth violently as he shook his head. "I will of course ensure that all of Mr. Gibson's spiritual needs are met, but the earthly ones I leave in the hands of the good doctor."

"Oh, I see," said Alfie, taken aback. "I just assumed if there was to be a viewing…"

"I hardly think that will be necessary. We can have everything sorted by Sunday, but best to have the doctor take him for now. Like myself, Mr. Gibson had no family in the village."

In the corner, Carnbee choked on his third piece of shortbread in as many minutes.

That should teach you, Alfie thought. *Perhaps the minister will see fit to do a sermon on gluttony soon.*

Aloud he said, "Of course, whatever you think best. Doctor Mills, I can have Graham take you back to town in the cart with Mr. Gibson's remains then?"

"That will be fine."

* * *

Carnbee left quickly after that, with one last glare at Dominick on his way out. Doctor Mills followed shortly thereafter, escorted by Mr. Howe down to the stables to make arrangements with Graham.

Alfie assumed Mr. Bisset would be eager to leave behind the scene of a murder and return to his flock in the village proper, but unfortunately was incorrect. The minister seemed inclined to make up for his earlier curtness by waxing eloquent over every aspect of Balcarres House. Alfie had at least been able to escort him as far as the hallway, fearing the minister might shove poor Mr. Gibson aside so as to better praise the carpet he was lying on, but no further.

He glanced back into the room, hoping Dominick would save him, but Dominick was paying them no attention at all. He was kneeling by the body and after a long look, started patting it around the chest and torso. To Alfie's shock, he then started rifling through the corpse's jacket like a looter picking the pockets of the dead after a battle. Finally, Dominick ceased his search and sat back on his heels. He regarded the body for another long moment, then drew the sheet back over it and rose to his feet.

At Alfie's confused look, he shook his head and put a finger to his lips.

Say nothing now in front of the minister, we'll discuss it later.

Mr. Bisset, his back to the door and unaware of Dominick's strange actions, continued to drone. Good Lord, no wonder the Scots were so dour; if Alfie had to listen to a sermon like this every week, he'd be grim too. A horrific thought dawned on him. Surely the lord of the manor would not be required to attend services? Perhaps he could buy his way out. A new roof for the church perhaps? Churches always needed new roofs. Or an organ? The congregation might appreciate that, especially if it was an exceptionally loud one.

Eventually Mr. Bisset noticed Dominick's presence.

"...and I'm sure you agree with me, Mr. Trent. I can tell you are a man of fine tastes."

"Only the finest, for sure. That's why I never drink French beer or English champagne."

The minister laughed, a tittering nasal sound. "Then as a man of refinement, I'm certain you appreciate the blending of styles present in the house, the architecture is exquisite."

"Oh yes, and I've heard a trip to the chapel ruins is quite enjoyable, though I've yet to have the pleasure myself."

Alfie interrupted, before Dominick could make any more uncouth references. "Mr. Bisset, it's been good to meet you, albeit under such terrible circumstances, but I'm afraid Mr. Gibson's untimely passing has put the household quite out of sorts. I do look forward to continuing our acquaintance in future."

He hoped it wasn't too great a sin to lie to a man of God.

"Of course, of course. When should I bring the missus then?"

"Bring her to...?"

"To the dinner party. Of course once everything is put to rights, you'll be having an introductory dinner for the local persons of quality. We need to celebrate the Earl of Crawford returning to his seat at last!"

Alfie wanted nothing more than to return to a seat, preferably on a large, overstuffed couch where he could sleep for a week.

"Of course, Mr. Bisset," he sighed. "We'll let you know."

* * *

Once the minister was finally convinced to leave, the rest of the day passed in something of a haze. Alfie had no time for his own list of concerns amongst overseeing Graham and Jarrett wrapping Mr. Gibson up and taking him out to the cart, realising he'd forgotten to have Doctor Mills check on Mrs. Finley, and dealing with the numerous fears of those under his roof. The list began with a murderer on the loose and ended with how he was going to make Dominick ready for a dinner party, even a country one, in such a short amount of time. To top it all off, the constant running around on his feet all day had set his injured leg aching as it hadn't in months.

In short, he was tired, scared, lonely, and in pain.

"That will be all, Mr. Howe," he said wearily, tying his robe around him. "Be sure to lock your door tonight, and remind everyone else to do the same. After the day we've had, I think I'll sleep in tomorrow, or try to anyway. I'll ring for you when need be, no reason to come by before then."

"Very good, my lord. Sleep well, or as well as you can at least."

"You as well, Mr. Howe."

Alfie locked the door behind the valet and didn't even wait for his footsteps to disappear down the hall before going to the bookshelf and opening the passage to Dominick's room. The bookcase on Dominick's side was already open, the small gesture bringing a flicker of happiness despite everything. Dominick was already in bed, the ring he wore on a chain around his neck glinting in the lamplight. He wordlessly held up the covers for Alfie to crawl under.

He had to lean heavily on his cane to make even the short journey across the room, but the moment he was in bed, Dominick was pulling him closer, his hands gentle but arms so strong as they wrapped around him and held him safe. Alfie closed his eyes and just enjoyed the moment. Here was where he belonged.

"I told Mr. Howe not to come by in the morning," Alfie said finally. "He'll get suspicious if I do it often, but after the day we've had… Christ, what a mess."

"Hush now," Dominick said, pulling off Alfie's nightshirt. "You've already got the worst of it handled. We'll figure out the rest later."

He carefully tilted Alfie's head up from where it was pillowed on his chest, and kissed him once gently, then again. Alfie broke away from the second kiss with a sigh.

"I'm sorry, Nick, I don't think I can tonight. I'm just so tired."

"I know, love. I only wanted a kiss, was all."

Alfie drifted as Dominick tucked him against himself more securely, Alfie's head under his chin and his injured leg resting on top of Dominick's own. Alfie drew his fingertips over the face of this dear, dear man and Dominick nipped them lightly as they went by.

"I love you, you know," Alfie said sleepily. "Even when you're alluding to obscene acts in front of a minister."

"I know. I love you too. Now sleep well, everything will look better in the morning."

CHAPTER 9

The Wicked Master lashed out again, trying to escape. Dominick clung tighter, wrestling the evil spirit back as it tried to break free. If Dominick let him go, the ghost would kill again. Locked rooms were no barrier to it, and Alfie lay sleeping and vulnerable right next door. The spirit flailed out, one surprisingly solid hand connecting with Dominick's face, knocking him into consciousness.

"Let go!" hissed the body struggling in his arms.

Dominick shook the confusion from his mind as he eased his grip. "...Alfie?"

"No, the other naked man in your bed," Alfie gripped the far end of the mattress and pulled himself free. "Christ, you're like an iron octopus."

"Are you all right?" asked Dominick guiltily, sitting up.

Alfie flopped onto his back. "A bit tenderised, but I'll mend."

He smiled up at Dominick and canted his head to the side. His auburn curls, free from pomade, twisted in a riotous halo around his head, and his bright eyes sparkled in the morning light. "Hello, there. Good morning to you too."

"Good morning," Dominick leaned over and kissed him, before collecting him back into his arms, much more gently this time. They lay together, just enjoying the peace and comfort that came from one another's presence, until the sounds of a household stirring at the start of another day came drifting up to them.

Alfie sighed, and Dominick let him pull away with great reluctance. "Shall we go for a walk after breakfast? I need to get outside these walls."

"As long as your leg is all right."

"I think so." Alfie took a few steps back and forth, even balancing on one leg while he bent down to pick up his discarded nightshirt and sword cane. The view made Dominick growl.

Alfie winked at him cheekily. He stepped forward, pressing the tip of his cane against Dominick's chest and pushing him back against the bed. Dominick couldn't help letting out another growl as he fell back against the pillows. There were worse ways to start the morning than at the mercy of a beautiful man.

Alfie held the pressure for a long moment, then tapped his cane against Dominick's chest once before tucking it under his arm with a jaunty flourish, as if he was in fancy dress at the opera instead of naked in another man's bedchamber.

"Tonight," Alfie grinned. "Give us both something to look forward to. But first: breakfast, a walk, and whatever fresh horrors the day decides to throw at us."

❋ ❋ ❋

They passed through the gate at the top of the garden and followed a little path that led across the fields that spread up the gently sloping hill behind the house.

Dominick kept a watch on Alfie out of the corner of his eye, hands ready to steady him. But while Alfie was clearly using his cane for more than just the sake of fashion, his steps seemed relatively even and pain-free, so he allowed himself to relax.

"What were you dreaming about this morning that meant I should be popped like a grape?"

Dominick kicked a pebble and watched it bounce along their path. "I thought you were the Wicked Master and if I let you go, you'd be free to kill again."

Alfie grimaced, and they walked in silence for a bit before he asked, "Do you think that's our killer? A ghost who can walk through walls?"

"No, but I almost wish it were," said Dominick, meaning every word. "Then we could hope that Mr. Gibson was just facing supernatural punishment for some wicked deed and the rest of us could sleep peacefully. But if the killer is flesh and blood, then it means it's someone in the house who might strike again."

"You don't believe Carnbee's theory about a band of roving burglars?"

Dominick let an inelegant snort be his only response.

Alfie sighed, "Nor I. On the upside at least, a ghost can walk through walls, our murderer cannot."

"I wouldn't count on that," said Dominick. "Yesterday, while you were entertaining the minister, I checked Mr. Gibson's pockets. His keys were gone. I think that's how your ghost disappeared. Whoever it was had already killed Mr. Gibson and left, but you caught him returning to the body for some reason, and when you gave chase he quickly locked himself in using Mr. Gibson's keys. Then sometime later he let himself out, leaving the door unlocked behind him."

Alfie visibly shuddered. "I'm not sure which is worse, the idea that a murderer snuck past the library while I was asleep with the door open, or the thought that he stayed in a room with his dead victim all night."

They reached a low stone wall where the field met the forest surrounding the crag and stopped to rest against it. Beyond the wall, the gorse bushes grew thick and wild, free from man's attempts to tame them. The land turned much steeper from this point, and Dominick didn't think Alfie's leg could bear such strain today. But it was pleasant enough to enjoy the crisp air, and the rare patch of sunshine that broke through the clouds warmed the stones beneath their hands.

Looking back past the manor, Dominick could follow the gentle slope of the hillside through farmers' fields all the way to the nearby village and beyond, where it dropped from cliffs into the sea.

"Beautiful, isn't it? My father used to say you could see all the way across the bay to Edinburgh on a clear day. But I imagine we won't get too many of those this time of year."

Dominick could believe it. In the patchy sunlight, even Balcarres House itself looked touched by a bit of magic. The grey stones were soaking up the last bit of light before winter set in, the windows glittering and flashing as the sun passed through wisps of cloud. The many chimneys and strange roofs that reflected the warren of passages almost made sense, as if Dominick just looked at it the right way, the house would unfold like a child's doll house, revealing all the secrets that lay within.

Thoughts of secrets must have been on Alfie's mind as well, "You think the murderer must be one of the staff then?"

Dominick nodded. "It seems likely. If it's someone else, it has to be someone who knows the house, to make their way in and up all those stairs undetected. I certainly don't believe they brought a ladder."

"Charleton matches that description I suppose," said Alfie. "Although he seemed begrudgingly fond of Mr. Gibson. 'Gibs' I think he called him."

Now that was a thought. Could the charming Mr. Charleton be a killer? He didn't seem the type, but it would at least mean Dominick's dislike of him wasn't unfounded.

"He's strong enough, I'm sure." Dominick said slowly. "But you're right, I don't see a motive. One of the servants looking to move up in the ranks now that there's a lord around to take notice, perhaps?"

"That sounds like your Jarrett," Alfie sniffed. "A footman has few opportunities for advancement, and we already know he's willing to go after the things he wants."

"Even if he's never going to get them." Dominick bumped his shoulder against Alfie's, but his lover remained unmoved. "And we know he was up and about that night. If nothing else, he might have seen something."

"I suppose we should tell Carnbee then, though I'm loathed to do it. I wouldn't trust the man to find the bean in a Twelfth Night cake, never mind a murderer."

"True. And we can hardly say, 'Oh yes, magistrate, we think the boy has information. You see, he was awake at the time to arrange a different hanging offense between me and him, but please don't hang him for murder unless you're sure.' "

Hidden between their coats and the wall, Alfie took Dominick's hand and squeezed it gently. Dominick knew he worried about the possible penalties their love carried. As an earl, Alfie would likely face little more than public censure if they were caught. But that would certainly not be the case for dirty, rough Dominick Tripner, even if he had gotten himself a fancy new surname and the clothes to match.

Still, it was a risk he would gladly take, because the alternative was a life without Alfie. Dominick had lived that way for the thirteen years between that last day at the workhouse and the boxing match at The Red Dog, and he didn't have the strength to do it again.

He ran his thumb over Alfie's knuckles. "It might not be Jarrett. Mr. Howe could have done it?"

Alfie let out a soft laugh, "If you're trying to cheer me up, you're not very good at it."

"All right. I still say it could be him, but if you don't want to think about someone with access to your drawers being a killer, what about Graham? He'd make a fine murderer. Probably wouldn't even need both hands to strangle a man, he could just reach out and..." Dominick made a claw with his free hand and snapped it shut before shaking it at the sky like a villain in a pantomime.

"Yes, what a blessing to be so surrounded by potential suspects," said Alfie dryly. "Anyone else you'd care to blame? Moira the maid perhaps, or Davey the stable boy? I suppose Mrs. Finley's fit of sobbing could have been an act, although if it was then she should be on Drury Lane."

"I wouldn't let her hear you say that. I suppose it could

have been Mrs. Buie… If looks could kill."

Dominick looked up at the sky. A few light drops of rain had begun to fall, but he didn't want to go back.

"I suppose, based on how he died, we can exclude Davey and the womenfolk," he said soberly, his humour fading with the sunlight. A man had been strangled to death, and they had no idea who had done it, or even why. "But that still leaves too many men in the house who could've left those bruises."

"Or it's still possible that it's someone else entirely unknown."

Dominick sighed. "I don't like this, Alfie. I don't like not knowing you're safe."

"Nor I you," Alfie said. He dropped Dominick's hand and stepped away, pacing out a few feet in thought before returning. "You know what this means, don't you? If we leave it up to Carnbee, who knows if the murderer will ever face justice, or how many others he may kill before that happens. We're going to have to investigate it ourselves."

Dominick could do nothing but look at him in shock.

"You've already done a fine job, searching Mr. Gibson and pointing out the locked window," said Alfie. "And we did it before when I was being blackmailed."

"Yes, and we nearly died because we were too distracted by your damned cousin to see who the real villain was!"

"So we'll learn from our mistakes. Assume no one is safe."

"You're right, no one *is* safe! Did you forget the killer has Mr. Gibson's keys?"

"So what would you have us do?"

"Leave!" shouted Dominick.

He hadn't considered the idea before, but now that he said it, it sounded better and better. "Go to one of your many other houses, or one of mine. What about that hunting lodge in Yorkshire? You liked it there. Or we could go to the continent even, finally have those adventures you used to want so much!"

Alfie's cheeks reddened, but his voice when he spoke was quiet. "That won't protect anyone else."

The words landed like stones, dragging Dominick's hopes of escape down with them. Alfie was right. Of course he was right. Dominick would never forgive himself if he took the easy way out and left others behind to suffer. But the thought of doing anything that might draw the killer's eye to them, to put Alfie in more danger...

The rain, that had only been a few drops before, started in earnest. Dominick ran his hands through his wet hair in frustration.

"Curse you and your damned heroic nature. I should have told you more stories where the white knight gets eaten by the dragon. Come on then. Let's get back to the palace of death before we catch colds."

Changed into dry clothes and ensconced besides a fire in one of Balcarres' many parlours, Dominick relaxed a bit. That banyan of Alfie's he had such fond memories of had been lost with the townhouse, but seeing Alfie wrapped up in a new one, a much warmer quilted damask that Dominick had convinced him to buy, was almost as good. He ran a hand down the sleeve of his own and propped his feet up closer to the fire. It was hard to worry about much when one was wearing silk slippers. By the look on his face, Alfie was making an awfully good stab at it though.

"Immediate tragedy aside, Mr. Gibson's death poses a number of other problems. The house finances will have to be looked over, especially if he was not one for note taking. I'll have to have Charleton go over them with me on his next visit, since I've no idea what the figures for running a house like this *should* look like, or how to transfer that responsibility to someone new. I'd hoped Mr. Gibson could interview more staff as well, but of course his position will have to be filled first… And then there's the whole problem of this damned dinner party."

Dominick, whose mind had been wandering, came back at the sound of Alfie swearing. "Dinner party?"

"Yes, while you were picking Mr. Gibson's pockets, I let that blasted minister talk me into hosting a dinner party for the county 'persons of quality'. Whatever that means. God, a man was lying dead at his feet and all he could think of was social climbing!"

"Perhaps a party would be a good thing," Dominick said. "Give people something to look forward to, take their minds off the murder. Might even be a chance to do some investigating. I admit, I'm not sure where to start with that."

Alfie collapsed down in his chair. "A party might. But this is a *dinner* party. You remember when I took you to the club and there were four different spoons?"

"It's that bad?"

"Bad? No, that was just a casual luncheon. This is going to be much worse."

He turned to Dominick and his face bore a look of concern different to the one he'd been slipping into since Mr. Gibson's death. "Please don't take this the wrong way, but I don't think you'll make it through."

Dominick was stung, "Without embarrassing myself, you mean?"

"Without giving away that you're not used to such things. There are so many rules, Dominick. So many stupid little things that people born into society know how to do instinctually, but make no goddamned sense to anyone else. It took me years to learn all the different codes! Years!

"If you lay your cutlery on the right of your plate it means one thing, the left another. There's a dozen different ways to unfold your napkin incorrectly, and God forbid you drink your wine with the wrong hand! Every time I'm dragged to anything more formal than an evening of cards, I still worry I'll make some basic mistake and everyone will realise I don't belong and it will all just unravel. I was planning to teach you with time, but I can only put the minister off for so long before that becomes suspicious in itself."

A thought occurred to Dominick and he turned it over carefully. "Is that the reason you wanted to get out of London? To keep me away from society until I... could act like one of them?"

"No," said Alfie with a pout. "We left because I'm a selfish man and wanted to keep you all to myself for as long as possible. I haven't started teaching you formal manners yet because I wanted to keep you just as you are, which is even more selfish."

Dominick laughed loudly. "You don't need to worry

about that, then! If dressing like a fop hasn't turned me into one, then feeding me like one won't either. Go on. Let's bring in some plates and you can show me how it's done. If you could learn it, it can't be that hard."

"You're not angry?"

Dominick shrugged. "I'm not best pleased, but I understand. We're like spies, sneaking into the land of nobs and eating up all their goodies with our oyster forks."

He laughed again, but Alfie's stricken expression stopped him.

"Christ, really? Oyster forks?"

CHAPTER 10

Alfie bit back a comment as the sugar bowl upended and soaked into the tea already puddled in great quantities on the tray.

It was astonishing how a man who was so precise when picking a lock or bringing Alfie to climax could be undone by a simple tea set. They should have begun training for this as soon as he decided to pass Dominick off as his cousin, but there was something endearing about the way Dominick cradled his teacup in the morning in both his great hands, and Alfie hadn't wanted to make him feel self-conscious.

Dominick let out a growl of frustration.

"Remember, keep your hand relaxed and your little finger—"

"I'll tell you what you can do with your little finger." Dominick picked up the teacup and saucer with exaggerated care before carefully adding in one spoonful of sugar and a societally acceptable amount of cream. He picked the cup off the saucer by the handle with two fingers and took a successful sip. He then placed the whole setup back on the table with only the faintest clink.

"Very good!" praised Alfie.

"I feel like a trained bear. 'Gather 'round morts and coves! He sits upright and drinks, just like a real man!' "

"Perhaps that's enough for today," Alfie said diplomatically. "Want to go look at the portraits and come up with more scandals for my forebearers?"

Dominick perked up immediately at the suggestion, as Alfie thought he might. Making up outlandish stories about passersby was a favorite pastime of theirs while out in public, and Alfie had been wracking his brains trying to think up a way to continue the game in their more secluded environs.

And ending the etiquette lesson early seemed prudent for the sake of the crockery, if nothing else.

✳   ✳   ✳

"...great-great-great-grandmother Edith was never the same again after, but in all fairness, neither was the dog."

Dominick roared with laughter and Alfie, equally pleased with his own joke, joined in. Each time one of them calmed down, the other began snickering and set them both off again. They sat on the floor of the portrait hall, leaning against one of the padded benches, and Alfie felt truly happy for the first time since coming to Balcarres. He wiped the tears of mirth from his eyes and leaned his head back against the bench.

"I suppose I'll have to have one of myself commissioned at some point, though it feels like cheating somehow, not really being one of them."

"Bollocks," said Dominick. "You still call them your ma and pa, don't you? That seems good enough for me. Besides, the way I think about it, all these ladies going back all these years? You think every one of them's been faithful? I wouldn't be surprised if the last real Earl of Crawford was the first one. And the rest of the noble lot's been descended from some lucky stablehand ever since. Hell, think about Grannie Edith! They were lucky the next earl didn't come out with paws and a tail!"

Alfie collapsed in laughter once again. He couldn't seem to stop while the portrait of the much-maligned woman frowned down on him, so he crawled to his feet and staggered off down the hall. He finally came to himself towards the end of the room, and went the few feet further to look at the portraits of his parents.

Dominick was right, he did think of them as his parents, for all that he clearly knew they were not. But they had been kind to him, treated him as best they knew how, and called him their son in public. Perhaps that was all it really took.

Dominick's voice drifted from behind him, "Do you miss them?"

"Sometimes," Alfie admitted. "My mother especially. We lived together in Bedford Square after father died. Neither of us was much for going out, so we spent a great deal of time with one another those last few years. I don't know if they ever really thought of me as their child— they never were particularly loving. But neither were the parents of the other noble sons I went to university with, so perhaps that's just the lot of the rich."

Alfie brushed a speck of dust off the gilt frame of his mother's portrait. She was much younger in it than he had ever known her. It must have been painted shortly after her wedding, decades before they decided to bring an orphan into their lives to be their mock heir. She looked happy.

"You know, I did forget sometimes," he admitted. "I spent half my life in that workhouse. But after a year or two of being in their home, I would wake up some mornings in my own bed, in my own room, and wonder if it hadn't all just been a strange dream. And the longer I lived like this..."

He waved a hand to encompass not only the whole room, but the whole manor, and all the other manors and houses and wealth that came with his title.

"The less and less real my childhood felt. It was as if I actually *had* been born into it all—that I really was their son and heir. And then something would happen and I would remember that it was all a lie, none of it was really mine. I was playing a part and if I slipped up, even just a little, everything would come tumbling down and I'd be back out on the streets. And this time I wouldn't even have you to protect me."

"Is that why you're so worried about this dinner?"

Alfie shook his head. "I don't know. Perhaps. Or perhaps it's just that I didn't really feel like the Earl of Crawford until we came here, but now with a murder, a possible ghost, and all the rest of it, at least teaching you the proper way to hold a spoon is something *real* that I can do to prove I belong myself. Does that make any sense?"

Dominick draped a heavy arm over his shoulder and Alfie leaned back into him. He trusted Dominick to be on the lookout for prying eyes. He wouldn't have made such a clear gesture of affection if they weren't alone.

"Perfect sense."

They stayed like that a while, looking at the portraits of Alfie's parents—the parents Dominick could have had.

Dominick didn't say anything, but he didn't have to. Alfie imagined he could feel the ring on its chain around Dominick's neck pressed against his back, even through their many layers of shirts and coats. It was Dominick's only link to his family.

Would it be worse, Alfie wondered, *to have just a scrap of something or to have nothing at all?* Dominick would likely never know anything about his own family; did he envy Alfie for having such a well-recorded adoptive one?

He toyed with how to ask, but couldn't think of the right way to do so. Eventually, the matters of the estate he'd been putting off all day finally became too pressing for him to ignore any longer.

"I suppose I'd best work on some of the 'all the rest of it' before dinner."

"Do you want me to keep you company?"

Alfie shook his head. A quick look out the window confirmed that the rain had stopped, and the weather was uncommonly bright and still. "There won't be many more fine days like this until spring. You should go enjoy it while you can. See if Jarrett is free to give you another riding lesson."

Dominick looked down at him with a distinctly unimpressed look.

"I mean it. It's plain to see you have the makings of a fine horseman. You shouldn't let some lusty little footman frighten you off."

"I'm not frightened of him," Dominick's chest puffed out in offense. Alfie tried not to smile. "I just don't want you to worry is all. You've got no reason to be jealous of the likes of him."

Empty hall or no, Alfie didn't dare risk kissing Dominick, despite how much he wanted to in that moment.

"I will be jealous, bitterly so," he said. "But only of you getting to go out and ride while I'm cooped inside looking at roofer's bills and the like."

He dropped his voice. "I trust you, Dominick. If Jarrett really makes you uncomfortable, that's fine. We can get Graham to teach you. Or hell, we'll hire someone just for the purpose. But for all the spoons and dinners and frustrating parts of this life, I want there to be parts of it you enjoy too. Learning to fence was what kept me sane all these years; it's clear horse riding suits you just as well. And once this blasted leg is healed up, I can think of nothing I'd like to do more than go out riding with you across the countryside, as free as if we were flying."

"If you're sure," Dominick said, still sounding uncertain.

"I am. If nothing else, think of it as a chance to interrogate a suspect. See if Jarrett had any reason to want Mr. Gibson dead, aside from potential career advancement."

"*That* I can do!"

Dominick sounded like he was looking forward to prying into the affairs of a potential murderer more than he ought. He took his arm off Alfie with a last quick squeeze, and they walked back down the long gallery to the main part of the house. As they passed the portrait of the Wicked Master, Alfie paused to look at it more carefully.

"Does he look like the person you saw the other night?" asked Dominick.

"You can quit that any time. I already told you, I realised there were no such things as ghosts as soon as the sun was up. No, it's something else."

Alfie squinted at the painting. There was something there that he knew he was looking right at, but somehow couldn't see.

"Never mind. I'm sure I'll figure it out eventually."

* * *

The afternoon was just as tortuous as Alfie feared it would be. The study Mr. Howe led him to was clearly designed to intimidate visitors, and it did a fine job on Alfie as well. He finally got settled behind the large oak desk, but no sooner had he cracked open one of the many account books than he heard voices from outside the window. Curious, he gazed out.

Just his luck, the study overlooked the yard where Dominick and Jarrett were working with the horses. Dominick really did look magnificent astride that beautiful black mare, like a dashing hero from a lurid novel. And that was just while walking the animal around in circles. Once he found his seat and grew comfortable in the saddle, he would be breathtaking.

Alfie turned his eyes back to the books and was able to focus on them, completely ignoring what was going on outside and not even looking over more than once or twice —a minute.

Shaking his head, he added up the line of numbers again. It was honestly embarrassing that he was so besotted he couldn't even do simple addition. Between glances out the window, he added the column three times before sitting back in disbelief. He wasn't the one in error, the numbers themselves did not add up. The correct amount should be just over five shillings more than the written total.

It might just be an innocent mistake, he reasoned. After all, he wasn't always perfect with his sums either. But this was one of the books Mr. Gibson had kept. What if there were more mistakes like this? Only a few shillings at a time, but those shillings would quickly add up. If Mr. Gibson had been skimming funds and someone else found out about it, would that be reason enough to commit murder? Surely it would've made Mr. Gibson more likely to kill the person who found out, instead of the other way around. Unless he was taking the money for a reason. Blackmail perhaps?

Alfie shivered. Whatever it was, it was all speculation for now. He couldn't even be certain anything untoward was happening unless he found more instances of missing money. He flipped to the next page, and began to add again.

❊ ❊ ❊

Alfie was in a right foul mood by the time Mr. Howe arrived to help him undress after dinner. He'd found several more mathematical errors, all that vanished money from the Balcarres house funds. Only small amounts each time but still, how quickly pence became shillings became pounds.

His other torments hadn't ceased either. Dominick kept

at his riding lesson until he had barely enough time to get changed for dinner, not even giving Alfie a moment to speak to him in person and perhaps vent some of his frustrations at how dare Dominick look so delectable when there was nothing Alfie could do about it. Not that he could say such things over dinner either as Dominick, glowing with happiness as he told Alfie all about the lesson, only made it worse.

If he had to hear one more breathless syllable about what a lovely creature Liquorice was, how quick to obey, or how Jarrett said Dominick was a natural horseman and would be cantering in no time, Alfie was going to do something extremely unfortunate. Like demand Dominick take him right there between the trifle bowl and the clotted cream.

By the time Mr. Howe arrived to help him prepare for bed, Alfie would have happily taken scissors to his blasted clothes and told the man to be on his way, but he clung to his propriety with the last ounces of effort.

"Did you have a pleasant day, my lord?"

"Fine," Alfie gritted out.

"I'm pleased to hear that. Is there anything else—"

"No, that's all. Thank you. Sleep well."

"You too, sir," Mr. Howe bowed and Alfie's eyes flicked to the clock, mentally calculating how long it would take Mr. Howe to set Dominick to rights, and how much later he should wait to ensure everyone else was settled for the night. Two hours perhaps. He could wait two hours.

"Sir, if you don't mind, there is one more thing…"

One hour then.

"Yes, Mr. Howe?"

"Well, Mr. Gibson's tragic passing has left the role of butler unfilled. I'm sure you must have someone in London who would suit, but I would be honored, sir, if you would give me the opportunity to take on the position in the interim."

Alfie did not, in fact, have anyone in London who would suit. All of the staff from his townhouse either being long since placed in new households, or pensioned comfortably like Mrs. Hirkins. He hadn't really considered this problem amongst all the other more pressing concerns, but if Mr. Howe wanted the job, then it was one less decision he had to make.

Unless Mr. Howe had killed Mr. Gibson for just such an opportunity, but one crisis at a time.

"I think that will do very well, Mr. Howe. Your valeting duties will still need to be completed until that position can be filled, but I trust you to find a solution."

"Of course," said Mr. Howe brightly. "Thank you, sir!"

"My pleasure. Now if that will be all?"

"Indeed. Good night, sir."

"Good night."

After the door clicked shut, Alfie sat in a chair by the fireplace, counting the seconds on the mantel clock. Half an hour should suffice.

CHAPTER 11

Dominick barely had time to lock the door behind Mr. Howe before he heard the latch on the bookcase door click open.

He bit his lip to hide a smile. Alfie had been noticeably agitated all through dinner, a fact Dominick had pretended not to notice. It was no wonder—while Alfie had sucked him off so wonderfully and unexpectedly yesterday morning, it had been days since Dominick had attended to *his* needs. Add to that a great deal of stress and a rather unhealthy dollop of jealousy, and his lover must be near climbing out of his skin for it now. Especially considering how regular their love-making had been recently.

Regular in frequency at least, spectacular in practice.

Still, Alfie was so fun to tease, and Dominick never missed an opportunity to wind him up further. He jumped when he turned around and saw Alfie, acting as if he hadn't heard him enter the room.

"My God, you gave me a shock! What do you think you're doing sneaking around like that? I might have knocked your block off!"

"Couldn't wait, I needed you." Alfie said plainly. If he was so far gone already as to be that blunt in what he wanted, Dominick almost felt bad for what he was about to do to him.

Almost.

"I don't know," he said, stretching one arm over his head and pulling down on it with the other. He knew the move made his chest look even broader than usual, and his robe parted wide at the movement, the cool air prickling across his skin. "It's been such a long day, and I'm sore all over from riding. Another night?"

"I... " Desire and concern warred on Alfie's face. "Of course. I don't want to cause you any further distress, good night."

"Good night, love. Oh, before you go…" Dominick rummaged around in his robe pocket before emerging with an innocuous looking tin. "This works wonders on my muscles. Don't suppose you could give me a quick rubdown, could you?"

Alfie's eyes narrowed in suspicion, and Dominick cursed himself for giving the game away too quickly. He schooled his face into a mask of innocence and it must have worked, because Alfie just took the tin with a nod, and gestured towards the bed.

The moment his back was turned, Dominick grinned. He let his robe fall to the floor and pulled off his nightshirt in one swift movement, padding naked across the room. He climbed slowly onto the bed, pausing with one knee up on the mattress to give Alfie full view of his assets as he pulled the coverlet down, before lying on his stomach, hands tucked under the pillow beneath his head.

"You might want to remove your own clothes," he murmured into the pillow. "Don't want to get them all over with grease."

He listened to the sounds of fabric rustling as Alfie

removed his nightshirt and robe, and felt the bed dip as he joined Dominick. He shifted, spreading his legs wider to give Alfie plenty of room. In all their lovemaking, Alfie hadn't yet done anything to suggest he wanted to be the one on top for a change, although why, Dominick had no idea. He kept meaning to ask, but it wasn't exactly something he could bring up in public, and when he got Alfie alone in private he tended to be somewhat distracted.

Still, perhaps tonight would be the night. He wondered if Alfie would play along with the ruse and actually give him a muscle rub first, or if he would just slick himself up and get straight to the main event. Both approaches had their pleasures.

His body tensed with delicious anticipation and forced himself to relax. As such, he was quite unprepared for the sharp crack of a hand meeting flesh, and the shock of pain that flared on his buttock right after.

He gasped in surprise and reared up on his elbows, but not before there was another crack as Alfie slapped him again, right on the same spot.

"You are a wicked, cruel, unkind villain," Alfie said, punctuating each word with another hit. Dominick didn't even try to hold in his moan. "Teasing me like that. I thought you were actually hurt, but you're just a vile wanton that enjoys toying with me."

That was completely true, but Dominick was hardly going to let it stand. He twisted back to grab at where Alfie kneeled next to him, then used his full bodyweight to throw him towards the center of the bed. Alfie let out a huff of breath as he hit the mattress and Dominick used the moment of weakness to roll them so he ended up on top. This didn't stop Alfie from swatting at him again, so Dominick was forced to grab both his hands and pin them to the pillows above his head.

Alfie's eyes were bright and he writhed under Dominick's grip. Dominick pressed more of his weight down and was pleased to discover Alfie was just as excited by their grappling as he was. He rolled his hips, letting their hard cocks slide together. At Alfie's moan he did it again.

"Wicked am I?" he said. He felt a feral grin steal across his face and did nothing to stop it. "What a cruel villain I am to put you in such a vulnerable position. What will I do with my victim, I wonder?"

Alfie's eyelids fluttered. For all he might enjoy having his way with Dominick, it was clear that nothing pleased him more than to be exactly where he was, completely at Dominick's mercy. Or tonight, to Dominick's lack thereof.

He bent down and took Alfie's mouth in a deep, ravaging kiss. Despite his teasing, he couldn't keep his affection out of it. Perhaps evil villains did not leave lingering little pecks against panting lips, or kiss reverently along high delicate cheekbones... Well. He was only so wicked at heart.

He released Alfie's hands to better touch all of the soft pale skin laid out before him, and immediately felt those hands bury in his hair, twisting and pulling. He kissed his way across Alfie's body, giving extra attention first to the scar on his shoulder, then working his way down to the one on his thigh. The skin there was smooth under his lips, and free of the hair that dusted the rest of Alfie's legs. He couldn't help but linger, but the scar didn't feel any warmer than the rest of him, so Alfie probably hadn't damaged himself too much with all the running around he'd been doing the last few days.

"Don't start that," Alfie said, as he yanked at Dominick's head. "If I start mapping all yours, we'll be here all night."

"Sounds good to me."

"Nick," Alfie panted. "Stop teasing."

Dominick gave him one last kiss, this one to the spot just below the hip bone where he knew Alfie was most sensitive, then sat back on his heels to survey his options. Alfie was beautiful, flushed and splayed with lewd abandon that would have been unthinkable just a few months ago. He looked up under heavy-lidded eyes, and Dominick had to lick his lips at the sight of him. His hands had fallen from Dominick's hair when he sat up, and as Dominick watched, Alfie ran those hands over himself, a pinch at his nipple causing a heated intake of breath, the other hand following the blush that spread down his flat stomach to grip his cock and start stroking it with long, languid pulls.

"And you call me wicked," Dominick muttered.

Sometime, he would enjoy nothing more than to watch Alfie bring himself to pleasure, but right now he ached with want. He fumbled in the sheets, searching for the little tin Alfie had dropped. It wasn't the oil they normally used, but as they'd discovered on one of their stops earlier in the summer, it worked just as well in a pinch.

Finally finding it, had to make a quick decision. He would very much enjoy having Alfie in him. He could just quickly prepare himself and climb on top, although he would most likely ruin the moment with some sort of riding joke. On the other hand, burying himself in Alfie's body and hearing his little gasps and grunts as Dominick hit that perfect spot inside him also had distinct appeal.

"I need you, Nick. Please!" Alfie's hand that had been torturing his own chest flew up to his mouth to stifle a moan.

Well, that certainly made the choice for him.

"Easy, love. I'm here, I'm here."

Dominick wasted no time in slicking up his fingers and preparing Alfie. He opened beautifully, shuddering each time Dominick added another finger, and Dominick couldn't help but lean down and taste his beautiful cock as he worked, Alfie's fist bumping against his chin as he continued to stroke himself. Dominick lapped greedily around the head, intoxicated by the keen saltiness of Alfie's taste. He dipped his tongue into the slit for more, causing Alfie to curse, his hand leaving his cock to push Dominick away.

"Oh, fuck. Now! Fuck me!"

And that was what Dominick had been waiting for, for Alfie to lose himself and shed all those fancy layers, so all that was left was want and lust and hunger. He lined up and slid in slowly, inch by inch, Alfie as hot and perfect around him as always.

He gave Alfie barely enough time to adjust, before he grabbed his hips and drove in hard. Alfie choked, his cry catching in his throat and Dominick leaned down, covering his mouth with his hand. Their rooms were far from the others, but until they knew how well sound echoed around these corridors, it wouldn't do to have Alfie screaming the house down. Having Mr. Howe break down the door brandishing a candlestick would put a damper on their activities.

The moment his hand closed over Alfie's mouth, his lover went wild. No longer having to contain himself, Alfie arched and cried. One hand still worked furiously on his cock, slicked only by his own pre-spend and Dominick's spit. His legs wrapped around Dominick's waist and he lifted himself up with every thrust, hips leaving the bed as he pulled Dominick as deep as he could get.

At Alfie's kicks, Dominick adjusted his angle and had to close his eyes against the overwhelming sensation of Alfie using him for his pleasure. Alfie's wet breaths heated his hand as Dominick tried to give him everything he wanted, and he knew he was doing well when Alfie's teeth sunk into the meat of his palm.

Their pace was impossible to maintain for long, and soon Alfie's whole body went rigid, his head thrown back against the pillows as he came, his body straining upwards until Dominick felt like he was the only thing tying him to the earth at all. He managed two more thrusts before he was overcome as well, wave after wave of bliss rolling through him, and a hiss of Alfie's name on his lips.

He collapsed down onto the bed, not as careful as he could have been to avoid landing on his lover. But Christ, if Alfie wanted courtesy after *that*, he'd have to wait a few minutes.

He reached out blindly and took Alfie's hand, uncaring of the sticky mess, and just lay there a while, recovering.

"I had better head back to my room," Alfie said at last, regret tingeing his voice. "Can't risk staying here two nights in a row."

"Mmm, wait a moment, let me clean you up first."

Dominick gave himself a few more minutes to gather the strength to stand, then crossed over the washbasin and brought back the ewer and a cloth. The water was cold, but he cleaned Alfie up as well as he could, kissing away the chill when it raised the downy hairs on his skin. He gave himself a quick wipedown and—trying to draw out the time before Alfie left as long as possible—picked up the tin of salve.

He pulled Alfie's injured leg across his thighs and began to rub it in. Alfie let out a quizzical noise.

"It really is good for the muscles. You need to take better care with this if you're going to come riding with me one day like you say."

He pressed his thumbs deep, feeling the knots underneath the skin. Alfie hissed at the pressure, but lay back and let Dominick work the salve in and knead the muscles until they began to relax. He kept at it until satisfied, and then circled the gunshot scar carefully with his fingertips.

"Want me to get you now?" Alfie asked sleepily. "You'll be sore in the morning."

"I don't think I'm the only one," said Dominick, allowing one hand to trace up the curve of Alfie's buttocks. "No, best be off. If you stay here any longer I'll decide I have to keep you."

"Mm, sounds nice," Alfie said as he rolled out of bed with a shiver. He plucked his nightshirt and robe off the floor and quickly slid them on.

"It would be," replied Dominick, more softly than he'd intended.

Alfie cupped Dominick's chin in his hand. "It'll be all

right. We'll figure something out, and until then, I'm right through there, safe and close whenever you need me."

Alfie kissed him sweetly before heading back to his own room. "Close this behind me, and double check the lock on your door. I'll see you in the morning."

"In the morning, love."

Dominick closed the bookshelf behind him, and checked the lock as promised. Even knowing their murderer might have keys, it made him feel better hearing the lock click into place. He laid down on sheets that were still warm from Alfie's body and closed his eyes, feeling safe, but lonely.

When he opened his eyes next, the grey light of dawn was sneaking in past the curtains, and Jarrett was standing over him, a razor blade glittering in his hand.

CHAPTER 12

Alfie sat upright in bed, his heart pounding in his chest. He blinked, confused as to what had roused him so suddenly, when he heard Dominick shout. Without thought, he grabbed his cane and pulled off the outer sheath, revealing the sword within. He ran across the room and wrenched open the bookcase door. His momentum sent him stumbling as he pushed open the door on the other side.

In a moment, he took in the scene before him. Dominick was still in bed, fists up to defend himself, while Jarrett loomed over him, a blade flashing bright in his hand.

"Drop it!" barked Alfie, brandishing his sword.

To his surprise, Jarrett immediately complied. Dominick grabbed the knife—no, now Alfie could see it was a razor—up from the bedsheets and held it on his attacker.

"P-Please, sir! Sirs! Milord! I meant to knock, I did! It slipped my mind, please!"

Alfie took in the look of confusion and terror on the young man's face and dipped his sword just the slightest fraction.

"Explain yourself!"

"Sir, I'm sorry! Mr. Howe said I was to help with valeting on account of him being the butler now and perhaps I could learn. But he had to sort things downstairs so he sent me up to wake Mr. Trent and see about a shave, but I forgot to knock and please, I'm sorry! It won't happen again!"

Alfie took a minute to parse through the rush of words that Jarrett, now near tears, had blubbered out.

"You're to be our new valet?"

"Aye, sir. Mr. Howe said so. At least until you can hire someone to fill the position. But I'm so sorry, sir. Please don't turn me out!"

Alfie considered it. It would be a legitimate excuse to dismiss the lad, certainly something better than, "He made advances on the man I love and I didn't like it." But he knew how quickly "out-of-work" became "destitute" and he wasn't sure he could bear to do that, even to Jarrett.

Unless he had hurt Dominick of course. In which case the gates of hell wouldn't be far enough for him to run to escape Alfie's wrath.

"Mr. Trent?" he enquired more lightly than he felt, eyes never wavering from Jarrett. "Are you injured?"

"Only my pride," Dominick replied with a grumble, folding the razor in on itself. "But I think I'll do without a shave today."

* * *

"I don't like it," said Dominick later, during what was quickly becoming their habitual morning stroll.

"Neither do I," said Alfie. "But I couldn't bring myself to let him go for making a single mistake."

"You believe his story then?"

Alfie furrowed his brow, "About forgetting to knock?

Why wouldn't I?"

Dominick picked a stick up off the side of the path, and started breaking it into small pieces as he talked. "I know I locked the door last night. There's a murderer loose with a set of keys. I wake up to Jarrett in my room with a very sharp razor."

Alfie stopped in place, his heart thundering in his chest.

"My God, Dominick, I hadn't even considered... We have to call for the magistrate!"

"And say what? His story is a good one. It may even be the truth. I'm sure Carnbee would take him in on your say so, but..."

"But nothing!" Alfie cried. His reaction to seeing Dominick in danger had been instinctual, but now the terror had died down, replaced with the cold realisation that Jarrett could have been there to do to Dominick what he'd done to Mr. Gibson. He should've run the murderous devil through right there and then.

He grabbed Dominick by the elbow, pulling him behind a large bramble and out of view of the house. "If there's even the slightest chance that Jarrett wants you dead, then that's a risk I'm not going to take. If Carnbee won't take him, I'll bring him to someone who will, even if I have to march him all the way to Calton Hill Gaol at swordpoint to do it!"

Dominick put a big hand over the one clutching his arm and gave it a fond squeeze.

"I know you would, love. And I'd do the same for you. But we have to think about this careful like."

Alfie gave him a quizzical look.

"Think," said Dominick, flicking the end of the stick like

a lecturing professor. "If Jarrett is our killer, we still don't know his motives nor have any proof. But now he knows we're wary, and won't strike again any time soon. Far too suspicious, you see. He and I go out riding and I happen to ride off a cliff—"

Alfie's stomach knotted.

"—and you're going to remember him with the razor. And now my death doesn't seem so accidental, does it?"

"You don't think—"

"*But*," Dominick interrupted, tapping Alfie lightly with the stick. "If we raise hue and cry and he's not our killer, then the real murderer finds out we know about Mr. Gibson's keys being missing, because we've just raised hell about Jarrett entering a locked room, when really Mr. Howe lent him his keys and he just left that bit out. Christ, I should've thought to say something then."

"I didn't think of it either," said Alfie. "Give me a moment to make sure I understand. What you're saying is, if Jarrett's *not* our killer, tipping our hand will make the actual killer go to ground and we'll never catch him."

"At best. At worst, he decides we know too much already and goes after us both."

Alfie shuddered, "And if Jarrett *is* our killer, he'll be too skittish from his close call today to do anything, giving us time to prove it was him."

"Exactly. I wonder though…" Dominick frowned and absently tapped the stick against his leg like a riding crop.

"Wonder what?"

"Why he would want me dead, is all. I mean, I had good reason to think he liked me, or parts of me anyway. Seems strange to get the keys to the room of the man you've been trying to fuck and your first thought is to kill him."

"You don't think it was jealousy do you?" Alfie said, now even more worried than before. "If he's guessed, or seen us somehow, it could be a case of, 'If I can't have him, no one can.'"

Dominick let go of Alfie to run a hand through his hair in thought, tousling it just past the point of respectability.

"Could be," he said at last. "But Jarrett strikes me as more the type to just shrug and move on to the next warm body. He still made comments last lesson, but hasn't pushed me to meet him again. I think if he found someone willing to bend him over a stile, he'd forget me in an instant. Much as my pride hates to admit it."

Alfie scrubbed his face with his hands. "Your pride is the last thing I'm worried about at the moment."

Dominick nodded, conceding the point. "Fair, but even if he's not our murderer, this is still bad news for us."

"Oh wonderful. As if we didn't have enough of that already. No please, do tell."

"Well, Jarrett might be as lacking in wit as he is in tact, but he made me as a... *man's man* pretty quick. If he's working as our valet, he's going to notice things an ordinary bloke might not. Suspiciously mussed sheets, damp towels every morning, a hidden tin of salve or oil? Of course that's assuming he doesn't just try to crawl into my bed one night and find you in it!"

Dominick laughed at his own joke, but Alfie wasn't finding it particularly humourous.

"I'm glad you find it all so amusing," he sniffed, crossing his arms. "You must forgive me if I'm rather more concerned instead."

"Hey, now," Dominick tossed the stick into the briar that seemed to be closing in on them. With a quick glance back towards the house, he wrapped his arms around Alfie and pulled him in. Alfie tried to stand firm, but he'd never been able to resist Dominick for long, and melted into him, clutching him tightly in return. Dominick rested his head on Alfie's shoulder, and his breath was a warm current caught on the brisk November wind.

"I'm worried too. But keep our wits about us and everything will be fine. I'll watch your back and you'll watch mine, just like always, right?"

"Right."

"Good." Dominick gave Alfie a quick kiss just below his jaw. The spot was the only bit of his neck visible above his overcoat, but it also happened to be a highly sensitive part of his body, and Dominick—the utter cad—knew it.

He stepped back before Alfie could say anything—or get him to do it again, this time with teeth. He chapped his bare hands together and breathed on them, his breath forming clouds in the morning air. "All right, I know you said the fawning—I mean, *charming* Mr. Charleton would be by today. Best head back if you're not going to keep him waiting."

Alfie frowned, "You're not coming back with me?"

"And listen to the two of you go on and on about the price of wool or taxes or that sort of thing? I'd rather take my chances with the murderous strangler, thank you."

Alfie shook his head. "Take these then; you can't strangle him back if you can't feel your fingers." He handed over his gloves. "Try not to stretch the seams."

Dominick winked, "Thanks. If I'm not back by supper,

send someone out to look for me. You could tell Jarrett to start by the chapel."

Alfie turned and headed back to the house, ignoring Dominick's hearty guffaws behind him.

✻ ✻ ✻

"Charleton, if I look at any more numbers, my head will spin. Allow me to beg a retreat now, and we can return to the field after some tea and sandwiches?"

"A strategic withdrawal if ever I heard one," Charleton laughed, pulling off his spectacles and rubbing the bridge of his nose.

Alfie pulled the bell and requested some light refreshments from a very formal Mr. Howe.

Charleton had brought with him a large bag filled with various ledgers and papers and had spent the last few hours educating Alfie on the basics of the property surrounding Balcarres, as well other land in the nearby area that belonged to the Crawford title. Everything seemed to be remarkably well-run, both by Charleton and his father before him. It shamed Alfie to think of how his father had mostly ignored his holdings outside of London, aside from the required signature if something needed his approval, and was determined to be more involved in the care of his earldom in future.

Charleton returned to the bag now and retrieved a squat bottle sealed with wax but bearing no label. He held it up to the light, and the rich amber of its contents seemed to glow with promised warmth.

"If you don't mind, my lord. I thought this might warm

us a little better than tea. It's just the thing for these grey November days, although at least it isn't raining for the moment."

Alfie thought about Dominick off exploring on his own and echoed the sentiment.

"Indeed, and perhaps…" He hesitated, but if he was going to be more involved in his properties around Balcarres, then he and Charleton would be seeing quite a bit of each other, and it seemed churlish to keep him at a distance. "Perhaps you would do me the honor of calling me Pennington. Or no, if I'm honest, so few people call me that, I probably wouldn't remember to answer. Would Alfie be too informal?"

"Not if you concede to calling me Gil," the grinning man responded. "And seal the contract with a glass of this."

Alfie fetched a pair of glasses from the sideboard.

"What exactly are we drinking, *Gil*?"

"Ah, *Alfie*, it's a local vintage. The finest scotch south of Aberdeen, although I am perhaps biased. Strictly speaking though, you might be obliged to not ask too many questions regarding the distiller's license."

After one sip, Alfie was ready to ignore men rolling barrels of the stuff down the street as long as he was offered a taste. Perhaps he could make discrete inquiries about obtaining a ready supply for the manor. Although it was early, he had Dominick's Christmas present to think of, and keeping them both well-stocked throughout the long winter months seemed a fine gift indeed.

"May I propose a toast?" Gil raised his glass. "To Gibs. I knew him long, but I did not know him well. May his rest be quieter than his passing was."

"To Mr. Gibson." Alfie echoed.

Along with the bag of papers, Gil brought with him the townspeople's condolences and word from the minister that the funeral would indeed be ready to proceed on Sunday. Alfie had hoped to witness Charleton's reaction when he broke the news of the murder to see if he reacted suspiciously, but clearly word traveled quickly in the country. Besides, it was hard to believe such a cheerful man could have murder in his heart. Although he might have said the same of Doctor Barlowe. Alfie's hand tightened around his glass in alarm.

Calm yourself. He drank from the same bottle. Besides surely two different murderers aren't going to try to kill you in the same manner.

He deliberately took another sip and gestured to the two chairs by the fire. No sooner had they settled than there was a soft rap at the door. Moira and Janie entered with trays laden with not only the requested tea and sandwiches, but also a pot of coffee, several miniature cakes, and other tasty morsels. For a woman as pinched as Mrs. Buie, she certainly wasn't stingy when it came to her kitchen's output.

"Oh! Dear, let me help you with that!" Gil immediately leapt up and took the tray from a blushing Janie.

"Thank you, sir," the girl giggled. She all but melted as Gil took the tray from her with a winning smile and an overdone exclamation at its heaviness.

Feeling rather awkward just sitting there, Alfie rose to take the other tray from Moira.

"That's quite all right, milord. I've got it," she said softly but firmly, eyes downcast.

Alfie, somewhat taken aback, complied, but hastily cleared a space on the desk of papers, so she could more easily set it down. Moira gave him the briskest nod of thanks and waited silently to be dismissed. He couldn't help but notice that in contrast, Janie was working on an increasingly absurd list of things that she would be more than happy to fetch should Gil require them. A small grin curved the corner of Gil's full lips and his eyes flashed behind his spectacles. Apparently his new friend's charms were not only noticed by women, but downright lethal to them.

Odd choice of words when there's a murderer about.

Alfie frowned to himself as his doubts began to resurface. But Gil couldn't be the murderer, could he? He'd been nowhere near Balcarres House that night.

As far as you know, the worried voice in his mind piped up again. *He did say that no one knew the house better than he did. What if there's another secret passage, one that runs from outside to somewhere in the building? He could have crept in, killed Mr. Gibson, and left the same way, with none of us the wiser.*

The idea seemed absurd, but still left him uneasy.

"Thank you, Janie, Moira," he said brusquely. "That will be all."

The two women curtseyed and left. Janie seemed to be furiously trying to think of an excuse to stay, but Moira shuffled out quickly and with a distinct air of misery. Perhaps she was still in mourning for Mr. Gibson. Or just mourning the attention the other, prettier girl received from their handsome guest. It must be difficult for a plain girl to find suitors in such an isolated location. Although perhaps she had a beau in the town, some young farmer's son or shopkeep or the like. Alfie really didn't know what all the town had to offer in any sense. They'd been so focused on reaching the house that first night, and hadn't had the time or a good reason to visit it since.

"How is the town? Colinsburgh, I believe? Is there much trade and the like?"

"I like it well enough of course," said Gil as he loaded up a plate. "Born and bred. But 'town' is a generous term. 'Village' is more the like. That is one problem we've always had with this place, anything needed special you've got to get sent in from Kirkcaldy, or even Perth. That's where I'd send notices for more staff, if that's what you're thinking. Could try Edinburgh too, but I don't think you'll need to resort to bringing any useless city folk out here. Present company excluded of course."

"Of course, and I shall ignore any country mouse and city mouse jokes, no matter how tempting they may be," replied Alfie, bemused. His earlier concerns about Gil being a murderer were slowly being pushed aside by the man's irrepressible good humor. "That is good advice, however. I've left the increased staffing in the hands of Mr. Howe, thinking he will know best what we need. Is good help another thing you can't find locally?"

"I wouldn't say it like that, the people around here are good folk and hard working. It's just they all already have their own trades or haven't the skill or well... don't turn out to be as reliable as one would think."

"Oh?"

"Aye, up until shortly before you arrived, Mrs. Buie had help in the kitchen, a lass by the name of Lily, her daughter."

"Moira's sister." Alfie remembered his faux pas the night of his arrival with a grimace.

"Exactly. The two sisters are close as could be, even though they're about as alike as chalk and cheese. Moira being the chalk, poor thing, and Lily being the cheese." Gil winked conspiratorially and snapped up a bite of ginger biscuit.

"Now, the Buies have worked in Balcarres for as far back as anyone can remember, and everyone assumes they'll be here until the place crumbles back into the earth, so you can't imagine how surprised we all were when one day Lily just disappeared! There's all sorts of rumors in town of her having run off with a secret admirer, or gone to try to make her fortune in London or America, all sorts of silly things."

"Isn't anyone concerned she met with foul play? Especially considering recent events?"

Gil waved a hand. "Oh no. The postmaster says he's gotten a few letters for the remaining Buie women from her, all marked Edinburgh for the return. So we know she's made it there at least. That's another thing I should mention, if you're writing to anyone and don't want the whole village to know about it, send someone to mail it elsewhere. The postmaster's not to the point of opening the mail to see what's inside just yet, but I've met fishwives who gossip less than that man."

Alfie laughed and let the conversation drift to the other inhabitants of Colinsburgh and their antics. So engrossed was he in Gil's tale about the ongoing feud between the baker's wife and the wheelwright that he didn't notice the skies begin to darken. Light drops of rain against the windows grew more frequent and clinked as their icy centers struck the pane. Alfie poured them both another round of scotch, warmed by the drink and the company alike.

Somewhere outside, Dominick shivered alone in the dark.

CHAPTER 13

As he watched Alfie walk back towards the house, Dominick pulled on the gloves still warm from his lover's hands and flexed his fingers. Alfie's hands were narrower than his own, so they were a bit tight, but better that than frozen. He turned and surveyed the land before him with excitement.

He picked a direction at random and set out on an adventure.

* * *

Less than an hour later found him back where he'd started.

He knew now why it was called the *blasted* heath. The scrubland had looked exactly like the Scotland he'd envisioned; bare rock showing through the ground in patches like the bones of a giant, but those bones had proven deceptively difficult to cross. His coat quickly became tangled in the thick gorse bushes, and trying to free himself led to the discovery that their evergreen leaves hid long thorns that tore at him as he struggled.

He fared little better trying to stick to the bare rocks. They were covered in lichens and moss that had grown impossibly slick in the rain or flaked off in large plates beneath his boots, knocking him flat on the ground. He finally admitted defeat when he realised he couldn't remember if the stories had ever made clear the difference between a heath and a moor. In one a man could drown on land that looked completely solid, he knew. It wasn't worth the risk. Dirty and disheveled, he turned back in defeat. But when he reached the garden wall, he found he couldn't bring himself to head back to the manor without something to show for it, so instead followed the sedate little path beyond.

After some time, the path wound through the wood and led him to a small clearing in the trees. He stopped in his tracks.

In the center of the clearing stood a stone building with walls that stretched up towards a sharply pointed roofline, but no roof to be had. A step closer revealed that the windows were empty of glass, their high arches like yawning mouths. It was a small church, or had been. The gorse grew thick around its base and spread in rolling waves across the clearing. But at second look, the swells that he at first mistook for thicker clumps of the stuff were actually tombstones, tilting at wild angles and almost completely grown over.

He picked his way closer in a hushed silence. The land itself knew there was something reverent about this place. He shivered despite himself and ran a hand over a cornerstone carved into the shape of an angel.

This must be the chapel where Jarrett had wanted them to meet. Hopefully he only used it as a meeting point and had a more comfortable spot nearby, otherwise anyone the poor boy invited here was likely to turn tail and run from such an eerie spot at night.

He quirked a grin. *And any man brave enough—or amorous enough—to stick around is going to end up with thorns in some very unfortunate places.*

A quick glance upwards revealed what he already knew to be true: the reaching branches of the trees blocked any sight of the sky. *Stargazing indeed.*

He walked to the front of the chapel with a small smile on his face, excited to relay *this* part of his adventure to Alfie. Built into the stone above the open doorway was a weathered crest. Even in its worn and crumbling state, Dominick had seen it enough in the last few months to recognise it as belonging to the house of Crawford. Intrigued, he stepped inside.

The gorse had not yet made its way into what had once been the interior, but the pavers were cracked and buried under thick grass that had pushed up through the stones and reclaimed the chapel for the woods. It was a strange feeling, to be facing where the altar once stood, and have only a floor of grass beneath his boots and a ceiling of branches and rolling sky. Built high into the far wall was a circular window, divided into three teardrop shapes like a wheel in motion. As the trees beyond swayed in the wind, he could almost swear the stone began to turn.

Shaking himself, he looked away. He'd allowed his imagination too much free rein. In search of distraction, he examined the memorials carved into the stone of the nearest wall. All Penningtons, unsurprisingly. He stopped when he came across a name he recognised. Much of it was faded, but clearly carved into one of the largest and most ornate memorials was the name:

Gordon Pennington
Eighth Earl of Crawford
1548 - 1607

The Wicked Master's saintly father. Right enough that he should be memorialised so prominently in the chapel, at least for as long as it had been in use. Most men got far less, regardless of their piety. Dominick glanced down. If the eighth earl's memorial was in the chapel, that probably meant he'd been buried there as well. Those stones were now long gone, and who knew how deeply he'd been planted beneath them. Dominick's toes could be moments away from cracking through his devout skull. He took a step back and then another until he was outside the arched entrance of the chapel once again.

Looking at the overgrown graveyard behind him, he shivered and tucked his hands—now growing cold despite Alfie's gloves—into his pockets. He ought to turn back, but the earl's memorial raised an interesting question.

If you bury the sainted father in the chapel, then where do you bury the bedeviled son?

A rustling noise came from the woods. He stood still and listened. Nothing.

He scoffed at himself. "Now who's been listening to too many ghost stories? Got yourself worked into a fright by the wind and your own imaginings."

He turned to leave, then faintly heard it again. Less of a rustle that could have been mistaken for leaves or other sounds of the forest, but more like a quiet voice whispering to him.

The hairs on the back of his neck rose.

"Who's there?" Dominick called out, fearing a response.

"Jarrett? Is that you?"

There was no reply, but when he stood still, he could still hear the voice, a quiet yet unrelenting murmur that drew him. *Like a rat to the piper.*

He walked around the chapel towards the noise. Some distant part of himself screamed that he was being every fool in the stories that scoffs at the monster and goes out to prove it doesn't exist, then has his soul dragged down to hell by the beast. Still, he'd faced worse on the streets of Spitalfields than strange sounds.

He left the clearing and stepped into the woods. Ahead, the ground at the end of the clearing sloped sharply down into a ravine that cut through the trees. At the bottom of it, clogged with fallen leaves, a little stream burbled sluggishly, the water lapping over pebbles and sticks in an inconstant melody.

He barked out a relieved laugh. So much for the strange voice calling from the woods. Alfie would be delighted when Dominick told him that he was such a city boy he hadn't even recognised the sound of fresh running water when he heard it!

He rolled his eyes at himself. A city boy he might be, but one look at the heavy clouds brushing the treetops was enough to tell him it was time to head back to the house before he got a thorough drenching.

As he turned, his foot caught on something and he fell. His palms hit the ground hard and the impact jarred up his arms and through his jaw, clacking his teeth together painfully. His knees landed in a great puddle, splashing mud up around him, soaking his already torn clothes. Trying to stand, he lost his footing again and began to slide down the hill into the ravine. He scrabbled for purchase, but his hands found only soft earth and dead plants that tore away under his grasp.

At the last moment, his hand caught hold of a tree root. He gripped it with all his strength and pulled himself back up to the top of the hill.

He knelt there gasping and staring at his hands in the mud, Alfie's fine gloves now irreparably destroyed. A hot rush of anger flooded him and he swore, kicking out in his rage, shouting as his foot connected with something unexpectedly solid, toppling him over yet again. Near blind with fury, he tore at whatever it was that had tripped him, pulling away the thick gorse in handfuls, heedless of the thorns that cut into his skin through the ruined gloves. The rain began in earnest, the heavy patter of it on the leaves like the rushing of a carriage on a cobbled street, drowning out the sound of the stream below.

The frigid water seeping into his skin cooled some of Dominick's rage, leaving him feeling drained and sore. He could do nothing but sit back on his heels, panting as he caught his breath. Wiping the water from his eyes, he looked at the object his frenzied attack had revealed. It was a stone the length of his forearm across and at least as tall, but it had been buried under so much debris it was no wonder he hadn't seen it.

Perfectly circular, with strange fluting around the edges, it was clearly no natural stone. It reminded him of something he'd seen in London in the weeks they'd been waiting for Alfie's leg to heal enough to travel. They'd been staying in a rental property not far from the remains of the townhome, and each day they'd walk the few blocks to the British Museum in Montagu House and marvel at the objects on display until Alfie's leg could take no more. He remembered the temple there, brought back block-by-block from Greece, and this stone looked like a part of it.

A broken column.

On instinct, Dominick dug his hand into the thick mat of rotted leaves around its base until he felt a flat area. Brushing the leaves aside revealed a nameplate carved into the stone.

Malcolm Pennington

He reared back in surprise. Here he was, the Wicked Master of Balcarres House. No date, no summation of his life or words of remembrance, just a stone left to be reclaimed by the forest and forgotten. Dominick looked back towards the chapel. The little grave seemed a long way away, and all the other tombstones were in front.

"Unconsecrated ground, eh? You really must have been a bastard for them to hate you that much." He gave the stone a fond pat. "That's all right. Sounds like you wouldn't have made the cut anyway, even if you were buried under a pew in Westminster itself."

He used the stone to lever himself to his feet. "I'll likely see you there eventually. I'd rather it not be today, though a nice bit of hellfire sounds damned tempting right about now."

He grinned and felt his teeth chatter. The rain was coming down even harder, and the open roof of the chapel was the closest thing to shelter between him and the house. With a sigh, he buried himself as deeply as he could into his soaked coat and began the long walk back, the lonely tombstone fading into the forest behind him.

❈　❈　❈

It was a thoroughly bedraggled and miserable creature who banged on the kitchen door of Balcarres House some hour or more later.

After a few moments, the door cracked ajar and Mrs. Buie peered through the opening, her lips pursed in displeasure.

"Away with you! We've no food nor alms for—Mr. Trent!"

"Forgive the intrusion, Mrs. Buie. I don't need food, but some tea would be appreciated, and perhaps a towel if you've one to spare. I didn't want to risk Mrs. Finley chasing me out with a mop if I dripped all over the front hall."

Mrs. Buie ushered him in with a snort that might have generously been considered a laugh. "Janie, fetch Mr. Trent something to dry himself. Moira, inform Mr. Howe of his return. I suppose you'll be wanting hot water for a bath as well?"

"If it's not too much trouble," said Dominick, easing himself down into a chair at the kitchen table.

"It is, but we'll manage."

Dominick was taken aback by her tone. He hadn't been on this side of the divide for long, but he'd have been in for a lashing if he'd spoken to gentry that way before.

"Can I help you with your boots, sir?"

He hadn't noticed Jarrett lounging in the corner. Wonderful. Fending off a flirtatious footman in front of the mutinous cook what was just what he needed to make this day even worse. He frowned at Jarrett and cut his eyes over to Mrs. Buie, hoping the little trollop would take the hint.

Jarrett rolled his eyes. "I *am* training to be a valet. Sir."

Dominick slouched back in the chair. His feet were numb, and he was too cold and exhausted to refuse. At least if Jarrett tried anything, he'd be in easy kicking distance.

To the boy's credit, he seemed to recognise Dominick's poor state and made no ribald comments and even kept his hands to himself. Mostly. As the two maids returned with an aghast Mr. Howe in tow, a cup of tea was pressed into Dominick's hand. He tossed it back, grimacing as the liquid burned his tongue even as it thawed his frozen core. The cup was immediately replaced, and this he sipped more slowly. By the time he was finished, he had a blanket draped around his shoulders, and Mr. Howe promising a hot bath to be ready in his room shortly.

"Thank you," said Dominick, warmed a little by the very idea. "If Janie or Moira could drop by with something sweet, that would make the evening perfect."

Silence fell over the kitchen.

"Oh! I meant—" Dominick flushed. "Not while I was in the bath or for... unsavory purposes. Just... cakes?"

"I'm sure *Mrs. Finley* would be willing to bring you something." Mrs. Buie's eyes were like ice, and her hands too close to the knives for Dominick's comfort. He wouldn't be eating a bite of whatever was sent up. Arsenic was flavorless, after all.

Flustered as he was, he recognised that this place

was not the relaxed, comforting space of Mrs. Hirkin's kitchen where—even though she might bluster—she was always happy for the company and another set of strong hands. From Moira's nervous glances to Mrs. Buie's outright hostility, he knew that he wasn't welcome. With a mumbled thanks and the blanket clasped tightly around him, he plodded out in wet stocking feet in search of the route back to his room.

What a strange thought, that he should now make servants nervous, not because he was beneath them, but because he was so far above. Most of his life, if he'd turned up at a kitchen door, he'd have been greeted exactly the same way Mrs. Buie had at first, but instead of ending up with a hot drink and a seat at the table, he'd have been shooed back out into the rain with brooms and pans raised against him like weapons of war.

Now he was shooed along in precisely the opposite direction, still out of the kitchen, but this time towards the eventual comfort of his own room and a roaring fire. And yet, he didn't really belong there either.

He thought of gleaming rows of cutlery to be held and used and placed just so. The difference between a show at a theatre and one at an opera, and what clothes were appropriate for one but not the other. The seemingly endless ways to tie a cravat. All the great unwritten rules of a society that had taken Alfie years to adjust to, yet he expected Dominick to pick up immediately.

He might as well be asking you to learn to fly over the dinner party rather than just attend it.

As if he wasn't miserable enough without the voice of all his doubts echoing through his head. The hall was bitterly cold, most of the great fireplaces lying unlit. He pulled the blanket tighter around his shoulders and tried to walk on the rugs wherever possible, but where the floor was bare he had no choice, the icy pavers cut his aching feet like knives.

Suddenly, he heard a burst of laughter from ahead, followed by voices raised in mirth. As he'd done in the woods, he followed the sound. This time he found himself led to the door of Alfie's study.

"Nick!" Alfie cried out happily as he opened the door.

Dominick smiled to see him. Alfie was sitting on the floor in front of the fire in his waistcoat and shirtsleeves, his face flushed from the heat of the blaze, and probably also from whatever was in the glass he held aloft in greeting. All kinds of comments were on the tip of Dominick's tongue, but he faltered. Gil Charleton was sitting cross-legged on the rug in an equal state of semi-undress. On the floor between them were several stacks of playing cards in various configurations and a half-empty bottle.

"Please, do come in," said Charleton warmly, as if it was his home and Dominick the one merely visiting. "I was just teaching Alfie here this new card game I picked up on my most recent trip to Edinburgh. It's all the rage in the hells, of course. I'm surprised you don't know it."

Any response he might have had died on his lips. Charleton had called Alfie by his first name. Dominick might not understand all the rules of high society, but he knew that a man calling another by his first name was a sign of the most intimate friendship.

Or intimate something else, that damned voice added,

taking in Alfie's state of undress and the blush high on his cheeks. Dominick knew all too well how soft and open Alfie became with drink, and how irresistible he looked in such a state. He was seeing it now.

But no. He might not trust this oily little charmer as far as he could throw him—which was probably quite a ways based on their difference in stature—but he trusted Alfie. And that was what mattered. Besides, it would be good for Alfie to have a friend who wasn't him. From things he'd said, there'd been precious few of those over the years. If the bespectacled rogue made him happy, then so be it.

He tried to paste a more pleasant expression on his face and stepped forward.

"Wait," said Alfie, squinting up at him. "You're dripping wet!"

Dominick grinned wryly, ready to regale them with the tale of his misadventures, but Alfie cut him off.

"Don't stand on the carpet, you'll just muddy it up."

Dominick turned on a socked heel and left.

CHAPTER 14

Supper that evening was a quiet affair. Taking advantage of a break in the downpour, Gil had begged off, claiming other business that needed to be done, so it was just the two of them at the table.

Dominick had relayed a clipped version of his discovery in the wood and resulting misfortune, so perhaps the irritability that came of being caught in foul weather was the reason for his ill mood. Alfie'd thought he was going to come back to play cards with them after he'd gotten clean and dry, and had a glass of the excellent scotch ready to warm his bones, but Dominick had never returned.

Jarrett cleared the table and set a bowl of frothy syllabub in front of each of them before exiting the room with a brisk bow. The dessert was one of Alfie's favorites. He really would have to find a way to thank Mrs. Buie, although she might view any praise from him with the same suspicion with which she'd treated all of their limited interactions so far.

He lifted his spoon delicately and dipped the tip of it into the syllabub, drawing it away from himself in a motion that caught only the smallest morsel of the treat. He looked over at Dominick to see if he had copied Alfie's actions, but his lover was just staring down at the bowl glumly.

"I learned an interesting tidbit today," Alfie tried, hoping to draw Dominick out. "Apparently until very recently, Mrs. Buie's other daughter—a Miss Lily—used to work at Balcarres as well, until she mysteriously disappeared one night."

Dominick grunted and picked up his spoon in his fist. Alfie tried not to wince as he dug into the dessert, scooping a large portion towards himself and swallowing it down.

"Yes, I know you already knew that. But what you don't know is that while there's all sorts of stories about her running away with her mystery lover or haring off after adventure, what's certain is she's sent her mother letters from Edinburgh, though no one knows what they contain. I wonder why she would choose to vanish so suddenly, only to keep her mother abreast of her whereabouts."

Alfie brightened, thinking of how quickly Dominick had won over Mrs. Hirkins. If he could charm her, then surely Mrs. Buie would melt in his hands. "Perhaps you could convey my appreciation to Mrs. Buie for her excellent fare and see what morsels you can tease out? Both culinary and informational bites would be welcome."

Dominick paused for just a moment, then brought another heaping spoonful of syllabub up to his mouth.

"Why? You think she'll trust me more because I'm common?"

"Said the pot to the kettle," Alfie hissed. "Although, I see why she'd think it. My God, are you trying to eat that or tunnel through it?"

Dominick threw his spoon down. It clattered across the white tablecloth, leaving wet spatters in its wake.

"What is it?" Alfie bit out. "You've been a miserable rip

all through supper."

"Oh forgive me. Did I forget to use the soup fork this time? Or insult someone's mother with my arraignment of the chicken bones?"

"I know it's difficult, but I'm trying to help so that you —"

"So that I what? Don't embarrass you in front of *Gil*? Or any other quality friends you might have?"

Alfie grit his teeth. His eyes darted over to the partially hidden door that led from the dining room to the kitchen. "So that no one will ever question your place next to me, you fat-headed lout."

Dominick's eyes blazed, but when he replied his voice was dark and low. "That's right, I am a lout. How could I forget? Also a thief and a bruiser and a whore."

"Well, if that's all you are, then you're the most expensive whore I've ever seen," snapped Alfie. "Half my assets. I could have bought a damned duchess for less."

As soon as the words were out of his mouth, he regretted them. He hadn't meant it like that, like Dominick was something he'd bought and owned. The idea that he could have anything in common with those men who'd paid for and abused Dominick turned his stomach. He'd tried to be so careful with Dominick's body, to make sure he only did the things he wanted, and nothing that would bring back memories of dark times, but now he'd gone and thrown it all in his face. It would have been kinder if Alfie had struck him.

But before he could marshal any of that into speech, Dominick stormed out of the dining room and slammed the door behind him.

Alfie put his elbows on the table and buried his face in his hands. He couldn't have handled that worse.

* * *

Alfie put off going to bed for as long as possible. He wanted Dominick to have time for his anger to cool, and more than that, Alfie needed the time to compose an appropriate apology. He still wasn't sure he had it right, but the longer he waited, the more guilty he felt. He stood in front of the bookcase that connected their rooms, hand wavering over the panel that opened it, nervous that he still hadn't found the exact words he needed. But the sooner he apologised to Dominick, the sooner he could go about making it up to him.

Strengthened by that thought, he opened his bookcase and pushed the panel on the back of Dominick's. It clicked, but the bookcase didn't move. He tried again, then tried pushing the bookcase itself to force it open. It rocked a little, then stopped.

Oh.

It wasn't stuck. Dominick had put something heavy in front of it to keep Alfie out of his room.

Alfie slid down to the floor, crestfallen. Dominick didn't want to hear his apologies, didn't want to see him at all. And why would he? He knew how ashamed Dominick was of his past, and yet he'd still said those terrible things. If only he could make Dominick see that he didn't care that he used to sell his body to survive, only that he'd survived. But no, Alfie had felt attacked and he'd lashed out, aiming for the soft spots where he could do the most damage.

The irony that Dominick was the one who taught him to fight that way wasn't lost on him. He let his head fall back against his bookcase with a heavy thud. The bookcase shook, and a moment later something cracked him on the skull.

"Ow!" He rubbed the spot where whatever it was had struck him, hoping it wouldn't bruise.

On his lap lay a small red book, its cover faded and covered in dust. Wrapped around the book was a blue ribbon with red trim, the bow that tied it pressed flat, its edges frayed with time.

He looked up. There, on the back of his bookcase, was a narrow slot no wider than his thumb, running just beneath the top shelf. The book must have been hidden away in there for who knew how long before being jostled free by Alfie in his misery.

He carefully pulled on one end of the bow, expecting the silk to dissolve beneath his fingers. To his surprise it held. The ribbon unwound from the book with a whisper, revealing bands of brighter red where it had protected the leather from fading. As with the book he'd found in the library, there was no inscription on the cover, so he carefully opened it. He was surprised to find it wasn't a printed book at all, but instead filled with sloping handwriting in ink gone brown with time.

Heart racing at his find, he clambered to his feet and crossed to the candle burning low beside his bed. As he held the book open to the light, his breath caught as he slowly deciphered the faded words. Scrawled across the top of the first page, in larger letters than the rest, read:

Property of Malcolm Pennington

My Account of Days

Alfie could hardly contain his excitement. Centuries ago, the Wicked Master had written a secret journal and hidden it away behind the bookcase where no one could find it. His hands were the last to have touched this book before Alfie's. What would he find inside? The rantings of a madman? The vile musings of the worst kind of villain? Had the Wicked Master written in this very diary the night he'd meant to murder his father before being cast out for good?

Alfie's hands trembled as he closed the book. He spun around; he had to show this to Dominick, he would—

The back of Dominick's bookcase loomed in the darkness. Though only wood, it felt as impassable as the Alps in winter, to be breached only with great force and terrific loss.

Looking down at the little book in his hands, he tucked the ribbon into the cover and set it on one of the bare shelves. He then slid the bookcase back into place, concealing the connection to Dominick's room beyond. At the last moment, he left it cracked open just a hair. Not enough to be noticed, but enough that if Dominick changed his mind and wanted to come to him, he wouldn't have to fumble for the latch in the dark.

Buoyed by that bit of hope, he got into bed and blew out the candle. He stared at the outline of the bookcase in the dark for a long time before he fell asleep.

CHAPTER 15

"...And so does that bring me back to Ecclesiastes, 'For the living know that they will die, but the dead know nothing, and they have no more reward, for the memory of them is forgotten.' Words we should all take care to remember. I am reminded, in fact, of a most illuminating story I once heard, the moral of which will no doubt be apparent to all here..."

But that's not going to stop you from explaining it anyway, Alfie thought bitterly. He attempted to school his face into a look of thoughtful contemplation even as he resigned himself to at least another half hour of torture.

From the pulpit, Mr. Bisset continued his sermon with the sort of rambling pleasure one expected of an especially long-winded professor of some obscure interest, not a minister delivering a eulogy for one of his congregants.

Alfie eyed Mr. Gibson's coffin with some envy. At least there was one member of the village who didn't have to listen to it. Or be stuck sitting on these damned pews for God knew how long. He tried to stretch his stiff leg as discreetly as he could, which wasn't much.

The curse of being so bloody important, they stick you in the front pew.

Before the service began, he'd been pleased to see how many of the locals had turned up to honor Mr. Gibson, but if the whispers and looks he'd caught were anything to go by, the reason for the high attendance was less a dead butler, and more a living earl. At least for once it was his station drawing attention rather than his appearance. As a child, his auburn hair had been close enough to red to earn him all sorts of unwanted looks and cruel taunts, but Colinsburgh had more than its share of red-haired congregants, varying in colour from the ginger of the minister himself, through Janie's fox-coloured curls, all the way to shades of red so bright Alfie couldn't believe they existed in nature.

He shifted again as Mr. Bisset continued to drone. Would falling asleep in front of everyone really be so bad? The social gaffe might be enough to let him cancel the dinner party, at least for a while, but he would probably end up guilted into donating more than just a new roof. Alfie had no doubt that if Mr. Bisset talked long enough, he'd end up offering to rebuild the church completely just to escape. From the looks of the place, with its stones worn black from candlelight and the assorted grime of centuries of congregations all crammed in together on the worn pews, it might be worth it.

He bit back a smile and turned his head instinctively to share the thought with Dominick, but Dominick just stared straight ahead, back straight. Even in the press of the packed space, he'd managed to keep several inches of space between them.

In the days since their argument, Alfie still hadn't thought of the right words to apologise. He'd kept the bookshelf between their rooms cracked open on his side, hoping Dominick would come to him and tell him what he needed to do to fix this, but he hadn't.

The thought was gloomy enough that he almost missed the end of Mr. Bisset's eulogy.

"...the point of which is to say, 'so shall the sin be returned unto the sinner.' And may all of us, including Mr. Gibson, have our sins be forgiven by the good grace of Jesus our Saviour. And may the presence of the Holy Spirit be will you all, for this day and all your rest. Amen."

"Amen," Alfie repeated, feeling blessed indeed as the congregation finally got to its feet and began to mill slowly out the doors to freedom. Being in the front pew was again a disadvantage as they were some of the last to escape, but not once during the long wait did Dominick even look at him, or acknowledge Alfie's presence more than to pass him his cane from where it leaned against the wall on Dominick's other side. Even then, he didn't check to see if Alfie wanted it, just passed it over before he even thought to ask.

Whether it was just desperation to find someone to converse with or some more impish impulse Alfie couldn't say, but the moment he emerged into the courtyard and spotted Gil, he called out to him.

"Gil! How good to see you, despite the tragic circumstances."

He felt more than saw Dominick stiffen at his side as Gil approached with a beaming smile.

"Alfie! Mr. Trent! A pleasure indeed. I'm sure Gibs wouldn't mind our finding some joy on this day. I know he seemed quite a dour chap, but he was not without his charms."

"I'm glad to hear it," Alfie said earnestly. "Are you free?

I see Graham coming with the carriage. You're welcome to join us for luncheon if you haven't plans."

"That sounds splendid, thank you."

Alfie wanted to weep with gratitude, he wasn't sure he could take another carriage ride in silence, never mind the prospect of the rest of the day spent the same way. He had to apologise as soon as he could.

He suddenly regretted his rash invitation. If he hadn't invited Gil he could have apologised on the way home and been laughing with Dominick by dinner. Who cared if he didn't have the right words. He fully regretted being such a beast to the man he loved. They'd muddle through the rest of it together like they always had.

He nodded his head, determined, as Graham pulled the carriage to a stop in front of him.

I'll make it the quickest luncheon possible and with any luck, I'll be begging Dominick's forgiveness within the hour, he decided as he climbed onto his seat with rather more pain and less dignity than he'd prefer. Gil swung up onto the seat opposite, and Alfie slid over to give Dominick room.

Dominick made no move towards the carriage. "I think I'll walk."

"What?"

"I said, 'I think I'll walk.' It's not too far, and I might as well, since I can. Stretch my legs that is."

Alfie felt his cheeks flame at the words. His injured leg, held rigidly at a diagonal across the carriage to keep it from hurting, seemed horribly conspicuous and the cane in his hand was twice as heavy. He'd been trying not to focus on his limitations, but here Dominick was, throwing them back in his face.

"Are you sure?" he gritted out.

"Very."

"It's not so far from the kirk to Balcarres as the crow flies," said Gil cheerily. "We'll hardly have to hold luncheon at all for you. You might even beat us back!"

"I'm not hungry." Dominick finally looked at Alfie, but the momentary relief was cut short by his next words. "I think I'll see if Jarrett has time to give me another riding lesson."

Alfie bit back his first several replies on account of their still being on holy ground. "It's a Sunday. You shouldn't intrude on the staff's leisure time."

"Oh don't worry," said Dominick with a grin that was all teeth. "I'm sure he'll enjoy it."

❋ ❋ ❋

"It's hardly my business, but I couldn't help but notice a certain tension between you and your cousin. Is everything all right?"

Alfie sighed. After eating a luncheon that tasted like ash, he'd suggested they retire to his study instead of the library. That his study overlooked the stables and training yard while the library did not was pure coincidence. He looked down as Dominick's black horse took another turn about the yard, Jarrett's bay trotting along beside him.

"Mr. Trent and I had a disagreement. I thought I was the only one handling it poorly, but apparently I was mistaken. I apologise if we made you uncomfortable."

Gil joined him by the window and passed over a glass of scotch with a shrug. "I understand. Family. Even when you love them, you hate them. And even when you hate them, you love them. Isn't that right?"

Alfie laughed. "Something like that."

"Well, I'm sure you'll work it out then. If I can be of assistance in any way, let me know."

"Thank you," Alfie said, and meant it. He toyed with the glass. The sound of laughter drifted up from the yard below. Dominick *was* his family. Alfie loved him and knew he was loved in return. He didn't actually think Dominick was going to leave him after one little spat, but it didn't make the jealousy sting any less.

"Mr. Trent..." Alfie chose his words carefully. He couldn't trust Gil with the whole truth of course, but the urge to unburden himself was overwhelming. "He did not expect to come into his fortune, and was not raised to move in the circles he now finds himself. I've been trying to show him there are benefits as well as burdens, but he's found it frustrating. We argued, I said some things I shouldn't have and now..."

He waved a hand, gesturing to the room, the training yard, and the entire blasted house.

"I see. Well, I can't help much with society, I barely make the cut around here; being the nephew of a minor baron isn't quite so impressive suddenly when you choose to make your own money instead of starve genteelly. But I'd be happy to go over his assets with him if it would help."

"Thank you. He needs to know to run an estate as well, but all I've been able to get him interested in so far is the damned horses!"

Gil laughed, and crowded closer for a better view. "He's quite good for a beginner. Who's that with him though? I don't recognise him."

"You don't?" Alfie frowned. It wasn't possible for Gil to know everyone in the area of course, but with how friendly he'd been with the rest of the staff at Balcarres, surely he'd at least met Jarrett. "That's Jarrett, he was the footman until Mr. Gibson was killed, now he's training to be our valet."

He couldn't help but shudder at the thought. Still, perhaps this was an opportunity to collect some information on Jarrett as a suspect. A nice juicy clue would be a perfect reconciliation gift for Dominick. "You really don't know him?"

Gil stared out the glass for another long moment before shaking his head. "No, he's not from the village, I'd remember him. Gibs would have hired him though, so wherever he came from, he must have passed muster."

Just what we need. A footman with a mysterious past, and the only man who knows where he came from is dead.

One problem at a time.

"Would you mind showing me that card game again from the other night?" Alfie raised his glass. "I'm afraid I had too many of these to remember it properly."

Gil grinned and stepped away from the window. "Of course. I'll shuffle while you pour us another round."

Alfie glanced out the window one last time in time to see Jarrett point at something that made Dominick throw his head back with laughter. Then he turned his raised face towards Balcarres House, almost as if he was searching for something.

Heart pounding, Alfie stepped back from the window before he could be seen, and went to pour himself another glass.

CHAPTER 16

Dominick cupped his hands to the window and stared out into the night. There was nothing to see, not that he'd expected much. He could still hear the rain lashing the earth outside and sighed. Even if it abated by morning, the ground would still be far too muddy for riding or walks. He was trapped inside for another blasted interminable day.

The days since his argument with Alfie had passed grey, silent, and wretched. The ones since his antics the day of the funeral even more so. He saw Alfie at meals, but their conversations were brief and mostly to do with the rain which had continued to fall unabated for almost a week and only deepened the gloom surrounding them.

After he'd had time to calm down and think about it, Dominick looked back on the way he'd acted with sheepish regret. He'd been as moody as a child who saw another playing with his favorite toy, and reacted poorly. He was still hurt by what Alfie had said, but he could see now he'd been needling Alfie, trying to goad him into a row. So he couldn't be surprised when the man gave him what he wanted. Compounding his bad behaviour by taunting Alfie about both his leg and Jarrett when they were in public and Alfie unable to respond had been especially cruel.

He was tired of their silent war. He'd moved the chest blocking the passage between their rooms that first morning, feeling like a hysterical maiden who'd barricaded herself in to protect her virtue. But in all the days since, Alfie hadn't tried to come through to his room again, and Dominick hadn't had the courage to try to get into his either. He knew it made him a coward, but he was terrified that if he tried, he'd discover that Alfie had blocked his side as well.

He didn't know what to say to make it right between them, and any time he tried, all the important words fled from his mind and those that were left were so meaningless as to be embarrassing. There was only so much that could be said about the weather!

He turned away from the window. Somewhere in the house, Alfie was sure to be curled up with a book by a fire. A hollow ache echoed in his chest at the image. He couldn't seem to find his way back to that. He missed Alfie. Not just his beautiful body or whip-crack mind, but just the simple comfort of being close to him.

He shook himself. Right, this was getting ridiculous. Sighing and moaning never got anything done. He could either continue to mope around like a pathetic character from a melodrama, or he could take action and fix things. But how? He had no idea how to get Alfie talking to him again.

So find something interesting to say.

He considered it. Discussing the rain for the thousandth time was obviously out. The bawdy joke he'd learned from Jarrett was also out, for obvious reasons. Perhaps if he had some interesting piece of news or gossip?

He remembered Alfie telling him about the second Buie sister and her mysterious flight into the night. Perhaps if he could tease out more of the story, he'd have bait enough to entice Alfie into conversation and they could go from there. He slapped his leg, resolved, and set out in what he hoped was the direction of the kitchens.

❉   ❉   ❉

Eventually, he gave up on trying to find the path from the kitchens he'd taken the day he'd come in like a half-drowned cat. Finding himself in the dining room somehow for the third time, he cut his losses and pried open the panel Jarrett came through at meals with their dishes, and took the hidden passage that led down from there.

The Buie mother and daughter were sitting at the kitchen table, a mug of warm milk in front of each of them. At his entrance, they startled, Moira pushing her chair back, eyes wide, and Mrs. Buie setting down her mug with a very unimpressed thump.

"My apologies," Dominick said, putting on his most winning air. "I didn't mean to interrupt you ladies so soon before bed."

"Mean to interrupt us after bed then, aye?" Mrs. Buie snapped.

"No, not at all! Nothing of the sort!" Dominick couldn't help the tinge of red that lit his cheeks at the thought. Moira was barely more than a girl, and he'd rather lie with an asp than Mrs. Buie—it was probably the safer option. "I merely meant that Al-Lord Pennington has been after me for some days to convey his thanks for such fine vittles. He'd do it himself I'm sure, but you know how that sort are, a bit high in the instep."

" 'Vittles'," said Mrs. Buie flatly.

Dominick had snapped at Alfie for wanting him to play the commoner, but here he was doing just that. He'd hoped using the sort of language he was used to would win the prickly woman over, show her he was more like them and could be safely taken into confidence, but he began to suspect he'd badly overplayed his hand.

" 'That sort'," Moira piped up, her soft voice thin and squeaky with disuse. "Oh we know all about 'that sort', don't we?"

"Moira."

The maid ignored her mother. "Your sort, you mean, don't you, *sir*? Happy to be giving orders all day long, running us to and fro until we can barely think straight, then at night come crawling down the stairs, all honeyed words and apologies. Trying to charm your way into our beds, or even a dark pantry would do. Then daylight comes again and you act like all them sweetnesses and promises never happened! Who's got to deal with what happens then? Not your fucking sort!"

"Moira!" Mrs. Buie shouted. Moira ran from the room, her apron hem raised to her mouth but doing nothing to muffle the sounds of her sobbing.

Dominick was fixed in place, unsure of how things had gone so badly so quickly.

"I think you should go, sir." Mrs. Buie said. She hadn't even risen from her seat but her eyes burned with a fury as threatening in its power as if she held a knife to his throat.

He ducked a quick nod at the suggestion that was clearly an order, and all but fled back up the way he'd come, his shoes clattering on the bare stone stairs. He walked the halls briskly but unseeing, trying to focus on acting natural, unbothered, like he hadn't just been shouted at by the quietest of maids and sent running back above-stairs by her mother. As he walked, picking a direction at random, he tried to process everything that had been said.

It was clear that Moira had not been speaking in generalities, but with painfully personal experience. Had some man charmed her and mistreated her after? Someone with some power from the sounds of it—a guest to the house? Or was it not herself her tears were for, but for her missing sister?

Of course.

It was as if a shuttered lantern that had only illuminated the smallest fraction of the story finally opened, throwing its full light on the tale. The poor girl, Lily, must have been charmed by someone above her in station, and then when the cad refused to acknowledge their liaison, had fled to avoid the scandal of a ruined reputation. In a big city like Edinburgh, she could start again, with no one asking too many questions.

Had the girl been carrying the consequences of her actions in her belly? That could be the reason for her sudden flight; she had told her lover about the child, only to be rejected. She would have had to leave before the results of her indiscretion became too obvious. There were plenty of women in London who pretended to have dead husbands and plenty others who made no excuse at all, just raised their children as they were. And still others...

Dominick stopped. *And still others who left their babies at workhouses and went back to their old lives.*

He put his hand to his chest, feeling his ring on its

chain press into his skin. Had his mother been like poor Lily? A maid deceived by some man and forced to give up his bastard just to be able to return to work and provide for herself?

The ring his mother had left with him was sized for a man's finger. He'd told himself it was a token of affection, proof his parents had loved each other, even if they couldn't love him. But perhaps it was just the opposite, some damning clue as to who his father was, so that one day when Dominick grew up, he could uncover the truth and deliver her vengeance. Would Lily return alone in a month or two, tight-lipped about the reason for her vanishing? Was there a man out there now, cursing some small object that he thought misplaced, not knowing it had been wrapped in blankets and delivered to the workhouse along with a squalling babe?

But if so, which man?

One name came immediately to mind. He tried to dismiss it as prejudice and his own personal dislike, but it was the only one that made sense.

Gil Charleton.

He was the only one who could be what Moira called "your sort", well above her in station and to be treated like the gentleman he was—in name at least. Charleton would be able to give orders to the maids, and at the house frequently enough to notice them individually. Had Lily caught his eye? Dominick didn't remember him noticing Moira at all when their paths had crossed, but perhaps one sister was fairer than the other. Had he dallied with Lily and then abandoned her when he found out she was in the family way? Even the second son of a second son could never marry a housemaid, but he could charm her.

And that was the word he kept coming back to. Charm. Moira had used it herself to describe the mystery man, and how many times had Dominick sneered at how charming Charleton was, and how easily... certain people fell for it.

Christ. What was he going to tell Alfie? He could hardly go to him waving the olive branch, then accuse his new friend of being a lecherous cove.

Or of being something even worse. He wouldn't be surprised if at some point Mr. Gibson had stumbled into one of those dark pantries and seen Charleton and Lily together. Had he said something to Charleton? Threatened to tell the new earl when he arrived about the sorts of things his overseer got up to with the staff? Charleton said himself that no one knew the house better than he. Had he snuck in that night and permanently silenced his blackmailer?

Dominick shivered. He knew it was all conjecture, but he still thought he was onto something. But without any proof, there was nothing he could do about it. And even if he told Alfie, there was no reason for him to believe a word Dominick said, especially with the way things now stood between them. He sighed and looked up.

The corridor he was in seemed familiar. After a moment's thought he turned right and headed for bed. There was no reason to stay up any later. He would not be having his reconciliation with Alfie tonight, if the only things he had to offer were accusations that would drive them further apart. Perhaps in the morning he would figure out a way to bring Alfie back to him.

❋ ❋ ❋

When he heard the knocking, Dominick stretched. It felt like he'd barely fallen asleep, but already Jarrett or Mr. Howe was at his door to help him prepare for the new day. He opened his eyes and was about to bid them enter when he realised something was wrong. Instead of the watery light of another rainy dawn, his room was pitch black with only the faintest glow coming from the embers burning low in the grate.

He sat straight up in bed, confused. Could it be Alfie? He never needed to knock before. Dominick would welcome him any time, whether he was awake or not. But perhaps after their row he was uncertain.

Or, Dominick groaned, it was that pest of a footman come to make a more direct attempt at a late night meeting. Jarrett had seemed to accept Dominick's lack of interest with reasonable grace, but apparently he'd just been biding his time.

He reached out in the dark to find a candle when the knocking came again. Directly above his head.

He froze. It sounded like someone was standing beside the bed and rapping on the wall above him, but there was no one there.

Sitting alone in the dark, he tried to tell himself it was some trick of sound, an echo from somewhere else in the house rebounding though the room in an odd way. Heart pounding, held his breath and cautiously pressed his ear against the wall. The stone was cold against the side of his face, the only sound in the room the beating of his heart. It was perfectly silent.

He exhaled. Just a trick then, perhaps a tree branch tapping the window in the adjoining wall.

This is how ghost stories must get started, he laughed softly to himself. *Too many days cooped up inside with nothing to do but listen to your own thoughts swirling around in your head. Of course any perfectly explainable night sound in an old house like this would take on sinister meaning.*

He had the candle in hand, ready to get up, light it off the last remains of the fire, and check that it *had* just been a trick of the senses when he heard it. A low scraping sound, faint, but undeniably real. It was coming from the far corner of the room and dragging itself slowly along the edge of the wall towards the bed. Unable to move, he could do nothing as it drew closer and closer. Faintly, he could make out another sound with it, footsteps between each long scrape.

Step, step, drag. Step, step, drag.

The sound was almost to the edge of his bed, Dominick too petrified to move, when there was a horrendous crash.

CHAPTER 17

Alfie jerked awake, confused and disoriented with no idea what had awoken him.

Moments later he heard a cry coming from Dominick's room. He was out of bed before he fully registered the noise, but his feet barely hit the floor before he heard the sound of Dominick's bookcase being wrenched open. Dominick crashed into the room, stumbling as Alfie's still ajar bookcase gave immediately under his hand, tipping him onto the floor. In mere seconds, Alfie was on him, kneeling beside Dominick and wrapping his arms around him.

"Nick? Nick, what's wrong? Are you hurt? Oh, you're shaking!"

Dominick trembled in Alfie's arms, clutching at him. His iron grip crushed Alfie painfully against his chest, but after so many days without, it was the most welcome feeling in the world. He couldn't enjoy it however, too panicked about what had put Dominick in such a state. He stared at the open passageway between their rooms, prepared to see the hordes of hell come riding out. His fingers twitched. His sword cane was just there, leaning against the bed, but there was no way he could reach it with Dominick wrapped around him.

As minutes passed and nothing more happened, he

realised Dominick held a candlestick tightly in one hand, the candle itself lost somewhere in his flight. Alfie eased it from him, slowly unclenching his fingers one by one. He rubbed Dominick's back soothingly, like he'd done when they were children and he was sick, or Dominick had done for him when the cruelty of the other children had became much to bear. Resting his head against the top of Dominick's, he breathed in the smell of him. Such a simple pleasure, but how sorely missed these last days. The scent made him think of safety and home. He could be that safety for Dominick now. Something had given him a terrible shock and Alfie would be there for him, for as long as he needed.

Long minutes later, Dominick mumbled something into Alfie's nightshirt. His breath was warm and damp where he'd been panting against the material, and Alfie couldn't suppress a shiver.

"What was that?" he asked, carding his fingers through Dominick's hair.

"Said I felt like a damned fool." Dominick mumbled.

"Well, it can't be any worse than that time Matron told me my face would stick that way if the wind changed, and I spent days pulling the worst faces and running in circles to see if it was true."

Dominick snorted, and Alfie cheered silently that he hadn't broken everything between them.

"I like your face the way it is," Dominick said. He lifted his head, and his face was just a breath from Alfie's, tantalizingly close after so many days of distance.

"And I simply adore yours," he murmured, and closed the distance.

It was a deep, rich kiss full of love and apologies. Noses bumping, Alfie turned his head for a better angle and was rewarded by a hot stripe of Dominick's tongue across his bottom lip. He gasped and pulled Dominick impossibly closer, the taste of him intoxicating. Replenished and renewed, he eventually pulled away with one last nip, just to hear Dominick's moan, and rested their foreheads together.

"I'm sorry," said Alfie into the protected space between them. "I was an absolute croaker and said some atrocious things. I said them because I was angry and trying to hurt you, but that was callous of me. Please believe me when I say I don't think of you like that at all. You're the best man I've ever known, and there's no price on my love for you. There couldn't be, because you're the most precious person in the world to me."

"I'm sorry, too," Dominick replied. It was on the tip of Alfie's tongue to tell him he had nothing to be sorry for, just to please accept Alfie's words and let everything go back to normal, but Dominick knew him too well and raised a finger to his lips to silence him.

"I was cold and miserable," Dominick continued. "And then I saw you with Charleton, and he called you Alfie. I was so jealous, not because I thought you had thrown me over or because I was mad you had a new friend, but seeing the two of you sitting there, so comfortable in your fine home, with your fine clothes, you both looked like you *belonged* in a way that I never will. And then it happened again at the funeral, the two of you climbed into a fine carriage—*your* carriage—and I knew I didn't fit, so I lashed out."

Alfie waited to see if Dominick would say more, but he just shook his head.

"My first week at Bedford Square," Alfie said softly. "Mrs. Hirkins was trying to win me over, so she gave me a thruppence and told me to get the order from the cat meat man, and any left over I could keep for sweets. So I asked her if I could keep all the money if I could get the cat into the stewpot myself.

"The idea that someone would buy meat just to feed it to the cat was incomprehensible to me. It made more sense that she wanted something cheap if questionable for the stew. It's a good thing I was such an honest lad, or else I would've done the bloody work first and kept the money without saying anything."

"That's what I would've done."

"No," Alfie corrected, "You would have done the work, then claimed the man had raised the prices on cat meat and gotten another penny out of her. You were always smarter than me. The point though, is that I don't belong here either. I've learned how to be here, and you can too. And please, if you're angry with me in future, *tell* me. I promise to do the same. These last few days have been agony."

"I'll try."

They sat on the floor for some minutes more, taking strength from one another and enjoying the closeness, but eventually Alfie's legs began to tingle and grow numb.

"Not that I want to complain, but why did you come rushing in?"

Dominick sighed. "I heard the ghost."

He told Alfie about hearing knocking on the wall and the ghastly noises that ended with his frantic dash to

Alfie's room.

"But there has to be some other explanation," he finished. "There's no such thing as ghosts."

"I don't know," replied Alfie, dry mouthed. "You hear stories about castles and the like. Think of the Tower of London with poor Anne Boleyn and her missing head."

"Horseshite. There's more people die every day in Spitalfields than ever did in the Tower. If ghosts were real you couldn't take a piss without it splashing on one."

Alfie had to concede Dominick's point. Still, it had been a lot easier to dispute such things before they'd started hearing strange bumps in the night and seeing figures that disappeared into thin air.

"Why don't we investigate, see if we can't find anything to explain it. A particularly friendly rat perhaps?"

"Or the cat, come to get you first," Dominick grinned.

❊ ❊ ❊

The search of Dominick's room revealed nothing out of the ordinary. But with the lack of a natural explanation, the only one left to them was a supernatural one. By unspoken agreement, they trudged back to Alfie's room and cocooned themselves together under the covers. They pulled the bed sheets over their heads and curled close, knees interlocked and hands draped loosely over each other's hips. They were so close their heads shared the same pillow, and their noses brushed when they talked. Alfie closed his eyes to keep from going cross-eyed.

"I was thinking," he said. "About Mrs. Hirkins trying to bribe me into civility with treats."

"Are you going to give me a lemon drop each time I properly carve the wine?"

"If you're carving the wine, I think we have larger concerns. But no, I was thinking of something you might enjoy more. We practice a formal meal in full evening wear, and for each dish that you use all utensils correctly, I will remove an item of clothing. Every dinner-appropriate topic you introduce, the same. *But*, for every mistake or social faux pas, I will put one back on."

"Mmm, I'll have to be a very good student," Dominick growled. He shifted, sliding his thick thigh between Alfie's, his interest in the plan pressing into Alfie's hip. "We'll have to take meals in your room, as much as I love the idea of you sitting at your fancy table, that beautiful arse of yours bare on silk cushions. Squirming and blushing as you sat through course after course, served delicacies on fine plates and surrounded by all your crystal and silver. You'd have to cover yourself with the tablecloth, wouldn't you, to keep the staff from seeing how much you loved it. And me, savoring every last bite."

He snapped his teeth next to Alfie's ear and Alfie involuntarily let out the smallest noise, almost a mew.

"You said these things can last for hours, can't they? I'd make it last that long for you, until you couldn't take it anymore and demand I take you right there on the table for everyone to see."

Alfie gasped, the images Dominick described too similar to fantasies he already had.

"Right," he said hoarsely, licking his lips. "Practice then. Give me an appropriate topic of conversation."

"Rotten weather we've been having." Dominick licked

the shell of his ear.

"Correct," Alfie squeaked. "That's my nightshirt off. What a shame it's all I had. The game's over. I suppose you'd better claim your prize. Quickly."

Dominick grinned against Alfie's jaw, "Have my dessert you mean."

Alfie groaned, although whether it was at the pun or what Dominick did next with his mouth, he was unable to say.

CHAPTER 18

Dominick fussed with his cravat as he examined himself in the mirror. The evening of the accursed dinner party had finally arrived and he still felt woefully inadequate. He couldn't say he was underprepared, Alfie had been thorough in his lessons, and it turned out Dominick was a quick study with the right incentive. But still, this would be the first real test of his ability to pass among the gentry. With a scowl, he pulled the knot out of his cravat and started again.

As the date of the party had grown closer, all of the invitations sent to the highest ranking families in the surrounding area had been declined or returned unopened. He'd been insulted on Alfie's behalf, but his love explained that it was what he'd expected. Most of the great families did not spend the dreary months of the year out on their estates, preferring the lively swirl of the ton, and those that did remain would be such recluses that they wouldn't want to make the journey to meet their new neighbor anyway. As a result, the dinner would be a smaller affair, with only the local figures of prominence.

Alfie seemed to think that would make Dominick less nervous, but it instead had the opposite effect. He cared less about embarrassing himself in front of some paper-skull noble from several counties over who he might never have to see again, but if he and Alfie chose to remain at Balcarres, he would see the people at tonight's dinner frequently—in the case of Charleton, almost daily it seemed—and he did not want them whispering behind their hands about Lord Crawford's idiot cousin who made such a fool of himself at dinner.

In between his "etiquette lessons" and the rest of their reconciliation over the previous days, he'd shared with Alfie all that he'd learned from his ill-fated trip to the kitchen and his concerns about Charleton. He hadn't been completely surprised to hear Alfie's concerns about Jarrett in return. They had found themselves in quite the serpents' lair and would have to be careful not to get bitten.

"May I help you with that, sir?"

A hand snaked towards Dominick's neck and he instinctively slapped it away. The look Jarrett favored him with was so wounded that Dominick had to fight to keep from rolling his eyes. The damned boy belonged on the stage if he was going to be throwing around looks like that.

And that was yet another problem. To his surprise, Jarrett hadn't taken advantage of either their few riding lessons of late or his opportunities when acting as valet to attempt anything further. Even his insinuations had lessened to the point where Dominick felt he was mostly just doing it out of habit. Alfie was pleased at the news, although still deliciously possessive of Dominick's person, but Dominick himself was more hesitant. Sometimes he swore he could see plans and calculations flashing behind Jarrett's eyes. At best, Dominick suspected he was regrouping his forces for a second attempt at seduction, but as they had discovered no further clues to the identity of Mr. Gibson's killer, he worried that the light in Jarrett's eyes might instead be the fire of another impending murder.

"I'm fine, Jarrett, thank you," he said, more steadily than he felt. "That will be all."

"Very well, sir," Jarrett all but sneered, clasping his slapped hand to his chest. "If there's nothing else, perhaps I'll go and see if His Lordship is interested in my services this evening."

"His Lordship is fine without you," Dominick growled.

Jarrett gave him a coy smile as he walked out the door. "If you say so, sir."

Dominick only barely kept from throwing something at the infuriating creature. Whatever game he thought he was playing was a dangerous one. If this was just his way of expressing an unfortunate infatuation with Dominick, he wanted to shake some sense into the little sod. The next man he acted so blatantly towards wasn't likely to be as understanding. Jarrett's cock would cost him his head if he wasn't careful. But if there was something more going on...

Blast it, Dominick couldn't think about it now, he had too many other concerns. He still kept hearing the strange noises in his rooms, not every night, but enough of them, despite Alfie and him turning the whole place inside out. Whatever the ghost wanted, Dominick refused to let it keep him from sleep, but leaving Alfie's warm bed at dawn every morning to sneak back into his own cold one was becoming tiresome. Add to that a murderer, a scoundrel preying on the housemaids, and the impending disaster of a dinner and it was no wonder he was on edge.

He took a deep breath and let it out slowly, hands

dropping from his cravat and flexing at his sides. He'd never loved fighting, only done it because it was something he was good at and it was safer to make a coin with his fists than on his knees. But now he longed for the clear simplicity of a threat that he could face straight on and either pummel into submission, or at least feel better for the attempt.

He looked at himself again. He could face this dinner. It might be a more complicated fight than a simple backroom brawl, but he'd faced down some of the meanest and biggest toughs that the East End had to offer, he wouldn't be intimidated by a minister's wife.

He straightened up and nodded at his reflection. The crisp whites and stark blacks of his evening dress had the sort of elegant simplicity that screamed expense, and though the formal breeches were more uncomfortable than his buckskins, or even his old flea-bitten trousers, he had to admit they showed off his calves to great effect. He felt a touch of pride. As splendid a gentleman as one could hope to find, if he did say so himself. As long as they didn't see the bruiser beneath his fine clothes, he would carry the day.

❊　❊　❊

Two hours later, he was beginning to think he'd underestimated the minister's wife.

"I have always found shallots disagreeable," Mrs. Bisset said, resting her fork on her plate after only the smallest bite.

Dominick was hardly surprised, seeing as how she'd

found the rolls dry and the soup fishy.

The meal so far had been exceptional. Mrs. Buie—who now seemed as giddy as a schoolgirl in contrast—had outdone herself, somehow managing not only a delicate seafood soup accompanied by soft white rolls, but also fresh salad in the midst of November. If the smells drifting up from the kitchen were anything to go by, the following course should prove even more appetizing. To him at least.

Whenever he'd had cause to go down to the London docks, he always used to look out at the prison hulks anchored there and say a quick prayer for the souls on board. Sitting next to Mrs. Bisset gave him the same feeling as being in the shadow of those daunting vessels. She radiated a formidable sense of harsh disapproval that promised only suffering for those doomed to encounter her.

There was no respite on his other side. Doctor Mills, who was meant to have sat at the end of the table, sent a note at the last minute saying he was attending a difficult birth in the village and likely to be there all night. For once, Dominick might have been thankful for Charleton's presence across from him—murderer and defiler of maids though he may be—had he provided any escape at all from the shrewd eye of the minister's wife. However, Charleton was deeply engrossed in conversation with the surprisingly young and buxom Madam Carnbee and seemed unlikely to rejoin the rest of the table any time soon.

"Come now," Dominick said to the frowning Mrs. Bisset with more confidence than he felt. "I'll wager the next round is more to your tastes. At the very least, I've heard rumours of marzipan fruits for dessert."

"I abhor sweets on principle, especially those masquerading as more wholesome foods. In addition, gambling is a sin that I would thank you not to induce at the dining table, no matter what your personal habits may be."

If only you knew, Dominick bit back. "My apologies, ma'am."

He looked up the length of the table to where Alfie was seated at the head and tried to plead for help with his eyes. However, Alfie was unable or unwilling to come to his rescue, trapped as he was with the minister, Mr. Bisset, to his left and the odious magistrate, Carnbee to his right. Snippets of their conversation drifted down the table.

"It is of course unsurprising that the thief or thieves would choose Lord Crawford's home to make their attempt at burglary. It is one of, nay, *the* finest in the county, and for several counties around, if His Lordship will permit me to say so. Wouldn't you agree, magistrate?"

Carnbee harrumphed, although whether the sound was one of approval or disapproval, Dominick was unsure. Perhaps Mrs. Bisset would care to bet on it.

Having now met the woman, he was unsure whether it was the minister or his wife he felt more sorry for in the marriage. Certainly, he was unclear as to how the minister managed to eat, never mind breathe, with the uninterrupted flow of drivel coming from his mouth, but if Dominick had to face Mrs. Bisset across the table at breakfast every morning, he'd try to keep himself distracted as well.

"Indeed," Mr. Bisset droned on, "I have rarely seen its

equal, although it must be said I myself am quite fond of the stonework especially, and I doubt the murderous villains could have meant to depart with that! That would be an uncommonly uncommon crime!"

Carnbee harrumphed again. Alfie laughed politely, but from the way his hand rested on the base of his wine glass, Dominick would guess he was counting down the seconds until he could take the next sip without ending the night foxed as a hare.

Dominick felt little pity. This whole farce had been his idea to begin with; he could suffer the consequences.

"I say, Carnbee," Charleton piped up, momentarily drawn away from Madam Carnbee's fine… accomplishments. "How is that progressing? I expect you have the men responsible for poor Gibs' death in custody already?"

Carnbee harrumphed again, but this time his tone was clearly displeased. "I'm afraid not. I've sent word to nearby counties, but as of yet no word on similar crimes. It's a matter of time though, don't worry. I have my ears open and my eye on a few possibilities."

Dominick sighed. He couldn't stand to listen to much more of Carnbee's incompetence. His belief that Mr. Gibson had been murdered by a gang of thieves who broke into an inconvenient room and took nothing was folly. Housebreakers didn't work like that. And he would know.

Beside him, Mrs. Bisset looked as if she'd found a penny but lost a guinea. He took the chance to win back a few points, as well as end the nonsense.

"Perhaps this is a conversation for another time, when ladies aren't present?"

"Thank you, Mr. Trent," said Mrs. Bisset stiffly.

"Agreed," Mr. Bisset chimed in, having not spoken for at least ten seconds. "You are indeed putting the rest of us to shame, sir. Clearly they place a greater emphasis on decorum where you're from than in Colinsburgh. I thought as much from your accent. Where were you from originally?"

Dominick looked over at Alfie, panicked, but at Alfie's calm smile and small nod, he remembered the lie he was supposed to tell.

"Cornwall."

Mrs. Bisset's mouth dropped open in horror.

"Well, I think it's quite exciting," said Madam Carnbee cheerfully. "I feel sorry for the murdered man, of course. But I'm sure with so many courageous and vigilant men on watch, we're all quite safe. It really does make me shiver though."

"What does, ma'am?" Charleton asked attentively.

"Why, the idea the murderer snuck into the house without anyone being aware! I can't imagine what I would do if I awoke to a strange man standing over me in the middle of the night!"

At the head of the table, Alfie choked on his wine.

Charleton took Madam Carnbee's hand. "I'm sure you have nothing to fear. A clever woman like you would no doubt find a way out of the situation, and probably think up a way to apprehend the villain herself!"

"Oh, Mr. Charleton! You flatter me!"

"Doesn't he just?" Mrs. Bisset muttered. Dominick smothered a grin.

"Nonsense. I only give credit where it is due. I've always

believed that women have far greater powers over men than we give them credit for. Think of Helen, or Cleopatra!"

Dominick didn't know any Cleopatras, but he knew a fellow prostitute back in London named Helen who'd been exceptionally good at separating men from their money. Perhaps Charleton had a point.

Madam Carnbee laughed coquettishly.

"Hear, hear!" Her husband raised a glass. "To the powers of the fairer sex."

They all toasted, Alfie finishing his glass and motioning to Jarrett in the corner for another. Madam Carnbee and Charleton clinked their glasses. Dominick noticed he still hadn't relinquished her hand. If Carnbee was too blind to see his wife blatantly flirting with Charleton the charmer, then no wonder he'd missed so many clues at Mr. Gibson's murder. The criminal element in the area must be delighted.

He snorted at the thought, and Mrs. Bisset wrinkled her nose at the sound.

"Is there something humorous, Mr. Trent?" she asked archly.

Dominick wracked his brains for one of the many appropriate conversational topics he and Alfie had practiced. "I was merely reminded of a moment from Shakespeare. Do you attend much theatre, ma'am?"

"I have attended the theatre twice, and both times found the content to be nothing more than the most base tales of immorality, with no redemptive or improving qualities, presented by the most unspeakable persons for no purpose as far as I can tell, other than the lowering of society as a whole. The fact that it is acceptable for a person of perceived character to admit to enjoying such filth is beyond my faculties to comprehend."

Ah, so you've seen the one about the lonely shepherdess too, Dominick desperately wanted to say, but instead he merely hummed in bland agreement as his salad was taken away and a still-steaming filet of trout with lemon was set before him.

"I believe you'll find that is *not* a fish fork," came her nasal admonishment.

He set the utensil down, as well as the knife in his other hand. The knife was much harder to let go of.

Only four more courses left.

CHAPTER 19

By the time the dessert plates were taken away, Alfie was about ready to weep with relief. They were by no means in the clear yet, with cigars and port still to go, and then rejoining the ladies for conversation or perhaps cards. Although from the scraps he could pick up over Mr. Bisset's monologue, he doubted very much that the missus would allow such frivolity. Still, the bulk of the evening was over, and he had a chance to breathe.

The men all rose as the ladies retired to the parlour.

"Allow me to ring for Mr. Howe to escort you," Alfie offered, already heading towards the bell.

"No need to bother him," said Gil blithely. "I'm sure he's near run off his feet already. I'd be happy to escort the ladies myself. It would be a shame if they ended up somewhere they weren't supposed to."

He winked and Carnbee's wife giggled, although her husband seemed not to have noticed, too interested in the assortment of cigars Alfie had ordered at no small expense. From the look on Mrs. Bisset's face, she was doing a fine job of being scandalised enough for the both of them. He didn't even need to look at Dominick to see the "What did I tell you?" look being sent his way.

After the ladies left—Gil offering an arm to each, but unsurprisingly having only one accepted—Mr. Bisset leaned over.

"Pardon me, but is there a necessary nearby? I often feel the need to stretch my legs after a long meal."

"Of course," Alfie replied. "There's one just at the end of the hall. If you turn to your left just out the door and follow the corridor to the end, I believe it's either the last or second-last door on the right."

The minister clapped him on the shoulder and rose to exit. Left in the room with only Carnbee already happily puffing on his cigar of choice—the outline of another one poorly hidden in his coat pocket—and a haunted looking Dominick, Alfie quickly took the opportunity presented.

"Mr. Howe should be along any moment with a selection of post-prandial drinks, but if I remember correctly, you brought a fine bottle up from Cornwall didn't you, Mr. Trent?"

Dominick jerked at the mention of his name. "Pardon?"

"I was wondering," Alfie said slowly. "If you would mind sharing that bottle you brought with the rest of us. The one you left in the library, I think. Would you *visit the library with me* to help find it?"

Dominick's look of confusion swiftly melted as their conversation about the code used by boys at Alfie's university to schedule an assignation clearly came back to him. He all but leapt from his chair.

"Yes, the library. Of course. I'd be happy to help you search. But I'm afraid I don't remember where exactly in the library I put it."

That's my brilliant love, thought Alfie. "You're right of course. It could take us some minutes. You'll forgive our absence, Carnbee?"

The magistrate waved an indifferent hand.

They strode down the hall side by side without speaking. He didn't even dare glance at Dominick until they were in the library, at which point he locked the door and pushed him up against it with a single motion. Dominick grunted as his back hit the door, but reached for Alfie immediately, pulling him in. Their kiss was a desperate, grasping thing, Alfie delving in for more, only to have Dominick break away to pant in great gulps of air as if he were a drowning man, struggling and struggling, but not getting enough to survive. Alfie's heart wrenched in his chest, and he gentled the kiss to soft swipes of tongue and the faintest press of lips, trying to will Dominick to breathe through him and take whatever strength he needed.

Dominick's hands came up, and while Alfie would love nothing more than to feel them sink deep into his hair as Dominick held him where he wanted him, they had to return to the dining room in the same state they'd left it. He intercepted Dominick's hands with a tender grip around the wrists, rubbing his thumbs back and forth across the delicate skin just under the edge of the sleeve. Dominick sighed against his lips and rested his hands against Alfie's chest, his fingers curled loosely like a child's.

"I'm proud of you," Alfie murmured. "You're doing so well." He punctuated his statement with another kiss.

"No, I'm not," replied Dominick, his voice a study of abject misery. "I thought I had it all down when we practiced, but put me at the table and I can't even make polite conversation with a fucking minister's wife."

"It's your first attempt, of course you're allowed to be nervous. And you're doing fine. The blame is mine. If I'd known what an old battleaxe she was, I would have set you next to someone less…"

"Bloodthirsty?"

"*Difficult*, for your first society dinner."

"You could have sat Charleton next to her. I'd pay good money to watch him try to work his charm there."

"But only imagine if he succeeded," Alfie shuddered, and felt Dominick's huff of laughter against his cheek.

He pulled back and looked his lover in the eye. "You really are spectacular, do you know that? It took me years to even start getting used to any of this, and the way you've taken to it so quickly is just staggering."

"You're just saying that because you love me."

Hearing Dominick acknowledge Alfie's feelings for him without question sent his nerves tingling with delight.

"No, I dragged you off to have my way with you during an important dinner party because I love you. I'm saying you're magnificent because it's true."

His words were rewarded with his favorite kind of smile. The small, crooked one that Dominick only got when he was proud of himself in some quiet little way that he didn't want to draw attention to. Alfie would endure a thousand dinner parties to earn a single one.

"I suppose we should go back soon," Dominick whispered.

"Do we have to?" groaned Alfie, now the one in need of strength at the reminder of all that was still to come. He sunk against Dominick's broad chest, hiding his face against his neck. Dominick had a notch just above his collarbone that had been designed to fit Alfie's nose perfectly.

"It would be a shame to undo all my hard work learning to be an upstanding member of society only to be caught kissing an earl senseless."

"I'm changing all the rules of etiquette. That's the only thing you should be doing."

Dominick obliged him by ducking down for one last fortifying kiss, before carefully setting him back to rights.

"What will we say about the bottle?" He asked as they walked back to the dining room.

Alfie shrugged his shoulders. "Oh, this old house is hiding all sorts of things, it could be anywhere. Besides, I'm sure our guests have already partaken of whatever Mr. Howe brought up. I only hope they left enough for us!"

CHAPTER 20

As they walked back to the dining room, Dominick allowed himself one last brush of his hand against Alfie's to strengthen himself for the remaining ordeal. He had sparred with thugs and madmen, escaped burning houses and dark alleys, lied and cheated and scraped and fought every day of his life. He could do this. To make Alfie proud he could do anything.

He squared his shoulders and opened the door to the dining room. Charleton was pouring himself a glass of something from a decanter and looked up as they entered.

"Sorry, we couldn't wait for whatever elixir it was you went for. Perhaps for the second round?"

"No, no," Dominick said, only gritting his teeth a little. "I'm afraid we couldn't find it."

"Next time then."

Christ. Dominick was just trying to get through tonight and the man was already inviting himself over for more. At least Charleton had sense enough to pour another two glasses. Dominick handed one to Alfie before downing rather more of his than was proper. He would let himself have just this one slip.

They settled back into chairs around the table and Alfie gamely led the polite chatter with Charleton taking up most of the slack. Dominick, slightly more at ease without the presence of the terrifying Mrs. Bisset, was able to get in a few good quips of his own. Carnbee seemed content to take advantage of the complimentary cigars, surrounding them all in a thick cloud of the sweet-smelling smoke.

It wasn't until the clock on the mantle chimed the hour that anyone noticed they were one man short.

"I do hope the minister is all right," said Alfie.

"Perhaps he was being literal when he said he liked a walk after dinner," Dominick offered.

"Perhaps. You didn't happen to see him when you returned from escorting the ladies, did you, Gil?"

"No, I didn't see anyone. Carnbee was here by himself when I returned and Mr. Howe arrived shortly after with the drink selection, but that was all."

"I'll ring for Mr. Howe and see if he wouldn't mind checking the necessary, just in case."

That attended to, they waited with some awkwardness for Mr. Howe's return with a verdict. Dominick knew the rules for the gentlemen's portion of the evening were more relaxed, and was tempted to see if anyone cared to place a wager on whether it was an undercooked bit of lamb or something in the sauce that had been the minister's downfall. Although he honestly wasn't sure if Mr. Bisset had stopped talking long enough to eat either.

It was a long while before Mr. Howe returned, and when he did, his usually jovial face was schooled into a mask of concern.

Dominick couldn't hold back his curiosity, "Well?"

"My apologies, sir, but Mr. Bisset was not making use of the facilities, nor does he appear to be anywhere on this floor. Jarrett informs me that his coat and hat are still in the cloakroom, so the minister is somewhere in the building. I've sent Jarrett to search the upper floors, in case he got a bit turned around."

"Yes, this house is something of a rabbit's warren," said Alfie, but Dominick could hear the unease in his tone. He remembered the last household search in Balcarres and its tragic ending.

When the clock chiming the quarter hour brought no further news, Alfie caught his eye with a worried glance. Dominick nodded. Something was definitely amiss. Alfie stood, his movement rousting Carnbee from his near stupor.

"Gentlemen, I'm concerned something may have happened to Mr. Bisset. I'm sure he is merely exploring the house and will be discovered any moment, but perhaps we should check on the ladies and expand the search ourselves."

❈ ❈ ❈

The search began with an almost festive atmosphere. At the news of his disappearance, Mrs. Bisset merely rebuked her husband's addlepated nature at some length, to the barely disguised amusement of all. The lively Madam Carnbee divided them into teams to search, declaring a half crown for the winner as if it were a children's party game. Since she unsurprisingly paired herself with Charleton, Dominick doubted they would be the ones to claim the prize.

As the minutes stretched, then turned to hours, the mood became much more somber.

"It's far too dark to search outside now," said Carnbee when they reconvened in the parlour. It had finally dawned on him that the minister's disappearance might be serious and as magistrate it was his responsibility to take charge. "I'll have the constables here first thing in the morning, but if he's out there, the best we can hope is that he can either see the lights from the house and make his way back, or has found somewhere out of the wind to bunk down for the night."

Mrs. Bisset, sitting on the settee with Madam Carnbee attempting to comfort her, let out an inconsolable wail, the emotion in it shocking after her demeanor at dinner. Dominick passed her a handkerchief and received a watery smile in return. He'd expected her to be the sort to bear her suffering in stoic silence, but the amount of concern she clearly had for her missing husband had Dominick squeezing her hand gently in sympathy.

"With that in mind," Carnbee continued, "I feel it would be safer for us all to stay here tonight. I am uncomfortable with any of us venturing out in the darkness until Mr. Bisset's well-being can be assured. As I'm sure it will in the morning," he added as an afterthought to the sobbing Mrs. Bisset.

Fortunately, Mr. Howe was shaping up to be the British ideal of a butler; when Alfie rang to see about preparing rooms for the party on such short notice, Mr. Howe informed them that he had already rounded up the staff and had them all working on it. In another stroke of luck, the rooms that could be made ready were in a separate corridor entirely from Dominick and Alfie's.

By the time they were all prepared, it was well

past midnight and Dominick could read the exhaustion on everyone's faces. In a show of unexpected kindness, Madam Carnbee offered to share with Mrs. Bisset and keep her company. Dominick took advantage of the rest of the group getting settled to say his goodnights, with Alfie following almost immediately on his heels.

Reaching their corridor alone, neither of them put up any pretense of going to separate bedrooms. As soon as he had the door open, he pulled Alfie into his room and into his arms. Alfie immediately wrapped his arms around him and buried his face in Dominick's neck in a near-perfect recreation of their position only a few hours earlier in the library. To think, his biggest concern then had been using the wrong fork. He bent down to press a quick kiss to Alfie's temple.

"How are you doing?"

Dominick huffed, smoothing back an auburn curl that had broken free of the Macassar oil. "I feel like I should be asking you that. It was your dinner party."

Alfie groaned, "And I managed to lose the minister. I know, I know, I shouldn't jest. But if I don't, I'm going to start thinking about poor Mr. Gibson staring up from the floor with those terrible bruises, and start waiting for the scream that means Mr. Bisset has been found the same way."

"You think he's dead then?"

"Don't you?"

Dominick didn't respond immediately. He was almost certain the minister had met the same fate, and probably at the same hands of whoever did in Mr. Gibson, but it felt like saying so aloud would make it true.

"I guess it's the same one who killed Mr. Gibson," sighed Alfie, echoing Dominick's thoughts but not his reservations. "Which means we almost certainly have a murderer under our roof tonight. Wonderful."

He stepped away and started undoing his cravat in Dominick's mirror. Dominick helped him slide his arms out of the constricting dinner jacket, and Alfie returned the favor. They took turns playing valet until they were down to only shirts and breeches. Alfie helped himself to a bottle on the side table and poured Dominick a glass as well.

"I told Jarrett we could fend for ourselves tonight. Partially because he'll have enough to do seeing to our guests, but also in part because I was afraid I would look down and see blood on his shoe or something like that. Is that silly?"

"Not at all," said Dominick, fetching his robe out of the wardrobe and tossing it to Alfie, who promptly wrapped himself in it and collapsed in a chair by the fire. Dominick settled for draping a blanket around his own shoulders to keep out the chill. "You're sure it was him?"

"I'm not sure of anything right now. In all the excitement tonight, the whole staff was running amok, fetching this, preparing that. He could have easily slipped away for a few minutes without Mr. Howe noticing. Or Mr. Howe could have done the same. He *was* off fetching the post-prandials when Mr. Bisset went missing. I suppose he could have done him in and stashed him somewhere. Likely with one hand while carrying a tray in the other and not spilling a single drop!"

"Why though?" Dominick chewed the ragged edge of a

nail. "Both Jarrett and Mr. Howe might have had reason to do in Mr. Gibson, but the minister? His sermon was bad, but I don't know it deserved killing over."

"You're terrible," said Alfie, the faintest twitch of a smile on his downturned mouth.

"Or..." Dominick didn't want to say it. Their fight was still too fresh in his mind. He didn't want to risk another, but he couldn't overlook a potential suspect just to keep the peace. He'd rather Alfie be cross with him than dead.

"Or it might have been Gil. Yes, I was thinking the same thing. He knows the house, and was alone after escorting the ladies to the parlour." Alfie pinched his nose. "I can't fathom what his motive might have been, but with village politics, who knows? Perhaps Mr. Bisset's grandfather insulted Gil's great-grandmother and everyone knows about the ensuing feud but us. Or perhaps Gil is as much of a scoundrel as you believe he is, and the vicar's next sermon was going to denounce him. Perhaps... perhaps... perhaps."

He let out a defeated sigh, and Dominick decided the distance between their chairs was too great. He sat down on the rug in front of Alfie and leaned back against his legs. Moments later he was rewarded with long fingers running through his hair and caressing his scalp. He felt like an overgrown housecat and nearly purred at the touch.

"Look on the bright side," he said, butting Alfie's hand when it stilled. He waited until the divine strokes resumed to continue. "It might not have been your friend. You've already listed two other good suspects, and we did leave Carnbee in the dining room by himself when we went to the library. We only have his word he stayed put. Honestly, the only people we can really rule out are the ladies. For obvious reasons."

"Which are?"

"Well, our killer is a strangler. If Madam Carnbee tried to swat a fly she'd probably bounce off it. Mrs. Bisset might kill with a look, but she isn't strong enough either, and did seem truly upset about her husband going missing once she realised he hadn't just wandered off. Besides, they were together the entire time, so neither of them had the chance. Unless it's all an act and they were in it together!"

Dominick grinned, the whole absurd tale unspooling in his mind. "Yes, that's it. The two ladies are secret lovers. Mrs. Bisset being so high in the instep and Madam Carnbee nearly heaving her bosoms right out of her dress and into Charleton's soup... it's all a cover for their forbidden romance. I don't know why they went after Mr. Gibson—perhaps he knew—but the minister obviously had to go and next will be Carnbee. Although frankly I wouldn't blame them for that one. If they need a strangler for him I'd be happy to volunteer."

Alfie flicked his ear. "I don't know why I put up with you, especially when you're being awful."

Dominick tilted his head back so Alfie could see his leer. "They *are* sharing a room tonight."

Alfie flicked him on the ear again.

"You're an absolute beast. A man might be dead and you're being crude."

"Well, if it makes you feel better, we can also rule out you and me. Believe me, I've had my eye on you all night, if you found time to kill the minister between one blink and the next, I'd be far too impressed to turn you in."

"Is that the only reason you wouldn't?" Alfie asked, fondness clear in his tone. He scratched his nails a little harder, right above Dominick's abused ear.

Dominick hissed in pleasure. "Well. I suppose I might want to keep you around for other, selfish reasons. I've never claimed to be a particularly moral man."

"That's all right," said Alfie, leaning over. "Neither have I." The angle of the kiss was awkward, but he tasted of whisky and lingering traces of Dundee cake.

Dominick sighed when they broke apart. "I don't want you to leave, but with a full house I suppose it's too risky for you to stay with me tonight."

Alfie's eyes were sad. "You're right, but let's just have a few more minutes."

Dominick tilted his chin up again, enjoying another soft press of lips, then settled the blanket more firmly over himself. He closed his eyes and leaned his head on Alfie's knee, content to sit and be petted, knowing that as long as he was there, Alfie was safe and sheltered and his.

CHAPTER 21

Alfie watched Dominick prop a chair under his doorknob and climb into bed. Dominick had insisted he do the same, and even tried to open Alfie's door from the outside several times, just in case.

It seemed silly to be closing the bookcase between their rooms with such a safeguard in place, but Dominick was right, with so many people in the house, who knew what could happen. The last thing they needed was for Mr. Bisset's body to be discovered in the night, and Alfie not be alone in bed when someone came to wake him.

He drew Dominick's robe tighter around himself, breathing in the faint scent of him that lingered in the heavy fabric. He was far too on edge to sleep, but none of the novels or books of poetry seemed appropriate for such a dismal night.

As the bookcase clicked shut, his eyes fell upon the little red book on the shelf in front of him. The Wicked Master's diary. He hadn't had a chance to read it since the night he'd found it, being far too engrossed in his nightly "etiquette lessons" with Dominick. But it seemed like the perfect choice for tonight. Perhaps it would even reveal some hidden chamber or secret stair that the murderer used to stash the body of the minister!

Assuming Mr. Bisset is even dead and hasn't just wandered

off into some corner to sleep off his dinner, Alfie told himself sternly.

He picked up the book and settled himself in bed, using his night candle to light the lamp so he had illumination enough to read by.

The diary was delicate in his hands, the red leather flaking at the edges as he opened it and tilted it towards the light. The ribbon he'd tucked into the cover slid out and coiled in his lap, the red and blue bright against the white bed linens.

He set it on the table and turned back to the diary. Few of the entries were dated, but carefully paging through, he caught an occasional month followed by a scrawled 1599. The last year Malcolm Pennington had lived at Balcarres before going mad and attempting to murder his father. Surely if the question of why he had attempted such a heinous act was ever to be answered, it would be within these pages.

Alfie squirmed in excitement and turned to the beginning, wanting to know the tale in full rather than just skipping to its dramatic end. As he slowly made his way through the book, some pages were too faded to read and others crossed out or lost altogether, but there were still enough remaining for him to realise it wasn't just a diary.

It was a love story.

CHAPTER 22

January 1599

Back in the godforsaken house. The old devil, my father, has forced me to withdraw from university and return to this wretched place. To be forced to leave Aberdeen with its books and its parties and its people—God the people!—to return here is akin to leaving life itself for the cold comfort of the crypt. He says it is because he wants me to learn the estate, to be a good lord like himself. Devil take him! His tenants live in fear while his lickspittle friends grow fat with his coin. I think the real reason is that he sensed his control of me weakening. I shall play the doting son in the attempt to regain my freedom, but by God, I fear I shall go mad first!

❋ ❋ ❋

This winter will never end. The old tick grows more bloated while even the servants in the house grow gaunt. I slip them what I can from my own purse, but he watches me. I dare not risk more.

❋ ❋ ❋

I rode out today, though it was bitter cold. I could take

being in the house no longer. Father (wretch that I am to call him such) has had his leeches staying with us for God knows how long. I could take no more of their carousing and the haunted eyes of the maids.

The most odious of these is Old Whin, whose land borders the farm along our western border. He has been at Balcarres House since before my return and I wondered at how he can be away from his lands so long, so I made his empty manor my destination.

To my surprise, all seemed well cared for in his absence. The fields were bare—not surprising for the time of year, but at least no crops lay rotting under the snow. There was also new fencing and repairs made obvious by fresher wood, and I could find not a single stone fallen from the boundary walls—on their side at least. My curiosity whetted, I rode close and found the stock all safe in fresh-smelling barns thick with hay. My hail to the house was answered, and I met the son.

Mr. Samuel Whin appears to be of an age with myself, though unlike his raucous lout of a father, he seems a more quiet, withdrawn sort and had little to say, at least to me. Though I was treated with all courtesy befitting a guest, I must say he regarded me with a most suspicious air. I suppose he thought me emissary from his father, or worse, my own! I would not be surprised if the farm improvements are his own devising. It appears that when the cat's away, the mice will labour! This mouse has his father's dark features, but is fortunately far less rodentiary around the face. A not altogether displeasing visage, though I doubt I will have much call to see it again.

Three more in the village dead of hunger.

*   *   *

Have had the opportunity to call on the younger Mr. Whin again. Our fathers were shooting out the gallery window, and his lost some bet to mine to the tune of a rather staggering sum. The greedy devil would not take a note of promise, and I—called "shiftless"—was still considered more trustworthy than a servant to fetch it.

It was with a heavy heart that I rode to the Whin farm to collect, knowing how much better used the coffers were in the pocket of the son than my father, but with little choice in the matter. I was offered a glass and a chair by the fire. Mr. Whin the younger seemed resigned and unsurprised by his father's excesses. He had hoped, you see, to set aside some funds for the re-thatching of his tenants' homes once the weather clears, but perhaps they could last another year.

When he handed over a small chest with the required coin, those dark eyes were filled with such despair that I could not bear to take it. I will repay his father's debt from the last of my own supply.

He invited me to return for a meal to express his thanks. It is the first thing I have had to look forward to in a very long time.

*   *   *

...was crying... yet another has come for... I cannot bear it.

* * *

Third of April 1599

Samuel's father is dead! I know I ought not rejoice at the passing of my fellow man, but I will not be the only one celebrating tonight. He finally drank himself into such a state as could not be waked and lingered but a few days before passing yesterday night into the arms of the Devil, where I'm sure he was welcomed.

I went today—ostensibly to make inquiries as to his health—and discovered the house in a great state of relief poorly disguised as mourning. Samuel could barely make it through my rote condolences without skipping out of his chair. His smile, that I thought I had seen before on our dinners and rides, has been only the sun viewed through fog compared to the brilliance I saw today. He is beautiful always, but in joy he is sublime. I could barely look directly at him.

My dark sun, my dazzling night. I have said nothing of how I feel, but he must know surely? I am not so good a mummer as to be able to keep my affection from him. Is his silence proof he does not feel the same? Sometimes I think... But I will not act. The risk is too great. I will but observe him as I would a star, and revel in his reflected light.

I asked if he will find the work much harder now his father is gone, and he said the opposite is true. He has had to hide forever and is now free to do as he chooses. Would that I had his freedom.

* * *

Second of May, 1599

Samuel kissed me after the bonfire last night. More I dare not write for fear I will wake from this wonderful dream.

* * *

A day in bed. I defied my father at dinner last night before his friends. When told there was no venison, he claimed a scourge of poachers and swore to have them rounded up. I knew not even a hare had been taken from the forest since his last round of hangings and spoke up, hoping to keep the innocent from being slaughtered on the altar of his vanity yet again.

I knew what the consequences would be. I write this lying on my belly, my back too inflamed even to sit. Forgive also any errors, the swelling makes it hard to see. I will miss riding with my Samuel tomorrow, and for this I hate him more than the rest.

* * *

June 1599

I have done it! My hands shake so with emotion that I almost dare not commit my acts to words. But no, I must! If he found this book, the contents are already such that he would have my head a thousand times over. What is once more? I have not felt so free since the first night my Samuel took me in his arms. There is no bliss that could rival being with him, but the knowledge that I have taken the first step towards our mutual freedom is so like that joy. But I tell the end of my tale first.

The beginning: Knowing that my father's wickedness is surpassed only by his greed, I feared he was planning on increasing the rents for this last quarter day. I let Samuel know of my fears (In truth, I whispered them to him in bed, where we have no secrets from one another) and he suggested that if one was daring enough, what a wonder it would be to rob my father's taxman in the very woods he already claimed filled with thieves and poachers. The money could then be secretly returned to the villagers with none the wiser. I asked, if it would be so terrible if only half the money—still the difference in rent and then some —was returned, and the other half set aside to fund an escape.

He went very quiet then, perhaps remembering the terrible bruising on my face, or the way I cried as he laid wet cloths across my back. My dark star said that no, it would not be such a wicked thing at all, and I was glad. I cannot bear to live in my father's house any longer, yet I have no way to escape it. The last of my own funds were spent those months ago on Samuel's father's behalf and though he has offered to repay me time and time again, his land flourishes and his people are fed because of his money, and I will not take that from them. I will, if my hopes come to fruition, take their master from them, but that is for the future.

We lay together that night, planning and plotting,

bringing paper and quill to bed with us when we could resist no longer and had to see the outline of our dreams made real. His maids are discreet and have said nothing of other things, but what they will think of the ink dotted sheets, I have no idea!

Our plan then, is to raise the funds we need to run away together. To somewhere my vile father cannot reach even with all his well-connected sycophants. So good is my Samuel, that I will not ask him to leave his people to starve, even if it means our flight must be delayed. Such an act would hurt him, although for me he would do it, and for this I love him all the more. His heart ensnared me just as much as his eyes, and I would not have him changed. He is worried though. He said to me, "Mal, swear that you will come to me, the moment your father next raises a hand against you, and we will leave at once, no matter the cost."

I swore so to him but will not do it. If all goes to plan we will have funds enough to escape after the last harvest, before the rain and cold set in and make the roads impassable. We have chosen then as it will give him time to bring up his mother's cousin from Ballingry to learn the running of the land, while still ensuring the harvest is brought in safely under his own eye. The turning of the weather will also make pursuit of us difficult. My father has dragged me home against my will before. I will be dead before he does it again. For my part, I will spend the time collecting the funds we will need. The first step of which I took today!

I claimed an aching head and made my excuses before supper, knowing that the tax collector would be returning to Balcarres House just after nightfall with his ill-gotten spoils, and I would have to act swiftly if I was to catch him in the forest unawares. Though my father has tried to keep them secret from me, I know of several of the tunnels built into the walls of Balcarres, including one that leads to the outside. I escaped the house unseen via this route, and was swiftly masked and lying in wait.

I thought for sure the pistol would fall from my hand when I shouted my "Stand and Deliver!" but for once my father's greed worked to my advantage. He had employed but a single guard to protect the tax collector, and him armed only with a cudgel. No sooner was the bag in my hand than I was away, arriving back in my room in time to hear the alarm raised.

I have hidden the contents for now, but will bring the promised half to Samuel to quietly distribute back to the tenants when it is safe to do so. Each coin in my hand is another day closer to our flight. Soon, my love. Soon!

❊ ❊ ❊

Every opportunity I find, my father's purse lightens. I must be careful and only take what he will not miss for fear he will blame the servants, so I wait until he is in his cups. This is often, and for once I am glad.

❊ ❊ ❊

Another beating, but more easily hidden. Samuel is pleased with the progress of the cousin. He will be a fair landlord in Samuel's absence. The plan continues apace.

❋ ❋ ❋

Twentieth of August 1599

When we made our plan, I asked to have a portrait done. My father was pleased and of course assumed I meant it for the family hall, to show my dedication to the Pennington name. He will have his portrait, though I will be gone by the time it is finished. Let it be something to remember me by. I have asked the artist to include one detail that will likely go unnoticed, but pleases me to know will remain. I will never see it.

I asked to have the grand portrait done so I could have a miniature made without my father's notice or care. It is this one I presented to Samuel today for his feast day. It is small enough for him to carry always, and it comforts me to know that wherever he goes, so will I. I gave him yellow flowers also, thinking to make him laugh, but he said he would cherish them as well.

He then decreed I must have something of his in return. I told him one does not *give* gifts on their feast day, but he could not be persuaded. He untied the ribbon from his hair and handed it to me. A fine thing, in red and blue, but finer still was seeing his dark hair fall free. I hold the ribbon as I write and pretend its smoothness is one of the locks it once held, but in truth nothing could compare to the feel of those tresses beneath my hands!

❋ ❋ ❋

September 1599

Another quarter day. Three guards this time, but still no firearms. The one with the knife seemed willing to chance it, but my father's cruelty is again to my advantage, for I recognised him as a man from the village with a sick child and no money for a doctor, so a small tithe for each of them from my winnings was enough to ensure a peaceful departure. I only hope they are none of them fools enough to speak of it. No matter. The guards next quarter day may ask a king's ransom for their silence, but by then we will be gone. The monies I added to the chest in my room. Added to the coin I have taken from my father directly, I think we have almost enough. We wait now only for the harvest.

* * *

Strange events occurring… …I wonder…

* * *

My father's strangeness continues. He is quiet and at times I feel his eyes on me. I worry he has noticed the decrease in his funds. To stop entirely would only raise further suspicion if he has. I must be careful. We are so close.

* * *

Tenth of October 1599

The house is full again. A feast to celebrate the harvest. Even now I hear the singing and drunken laughter from the hall. My father is himself again, full of the hateful glee of a boy who enjoys pulling the legs off beetles one by one, or throwing a dog in the river to see if it can outswim the current. I loathe him. He is foul. His people starve and he has his magistrate execute any who would steal even an apple. His many bastards run barefoot in the streets behind their ruined mothers as he buys more praises to be sung on Sundays of his virtue. He harassed my mother to her death and treats his only rightful child worse than that dog he would so happily watch drown. I will be glad rid of this place.

The only joy I have is that since his own father is now happily dead, Samuel is invited in his place to stay at Balcarres to celebrate the harvest! His presence is a comfort to me, although seeing him and saying nothing is a torment. Not all is lost however, a quiet word to the housekeeper had him placed in the room next to mine, the one connected by the bookcase! Being with him every night these last few days has given me a taste of what our future will soon hold. I cannot wait. Samuel returns tomorrow to his farm to watch over the last of the harvest.

I go now to spend one more night in my love's arms. Next week is the new moon. Under the cover of darkness he will bring horses. I will meet him with the gold where the secret passage exits this wicked house and we will run. My Samuel is the only light I will need to find my way.

❈ ❈ ❈

tonight new moon. My fathe... all hurts
he ca
so cold

❃ ❃ ❃

Twenty-ninth of November 1599

My fever has broken.
My heart has broken.
No more now.

❃ ❃ ❃

Second of December 1599

This will be the final day I record here and perhaps my final day on earth as well. I know that even if I am successful, I will be remembered as a villain, and if I fail, my father triumphs again. If this record is one day found, perhaps my name will be restored, but I care not. All light has gone from the world. I write these words only so that I know that somewhere will remain the memory of a good man, even if my actions condemn me to be separated from him for eternity. There is no hope other than that he looks down upon me now and understands why I must do this.

My Samuel. My dark star shines no more.

I still do not know how my father found out. Whether it was something he saw in my face during that harvest party, or whether that was merely a test to confirm his suspicions. Would my love still be alive if I had taken less from my father? Or was it my wanting to be free at all that condemned him? I suppose it does not matter now.

The night of the new moon, my father called me to his study. Oh, that night when everything I had dreamed of lay so close at hand! So caught up in my happiness was I, that I never questioned why he wanted to see me. Indeed, it felt my feet hardly touched the ground as I walked to the room. Then I stepped inside.

On my father's desk sat the chest of coins I had hidden in my room.

I tried to run. To save myself but also to warn Samuel. I did not know then if my father only knew about my thefts or if he knew all, but it was a chance I could not take.

In the moment though, my terror froze me before it bid me run. Those scarce seconds were all it took for my father to be upon me. I fought him, God save me, for the first time in my life I fought him instead of giving in and hoping to anger him no further. But for each blow I landed, he had two, my frantic striking no contest to his practiced cruelty. For just a moment, I thought I would break free. Then he grabbed a poker to hand and I remember no more.

The next weeks are lost to me. After my father was done with me, I was taken with such a fever on the brain that I am now told it was a miracle I survived. As I hovered near death, I could have sworn I heard my Samuel crying and calling out to me. It was for his voice alone that I returned to the land of the living.

Just days ago, I awoke, expecting to see his smiling face beside me and feel his lips on mine once more. Instead, there was only the empty ruin of this house, servants who will not meet my eye, and always my father with a satisfied grin upon his face. It was he who told me of the two horses who came walking back alone to the Whin farm the morning after my beating. And he who said how well the man from Ballingry was doing in running the place in the mysterious absence of his cousin.

Despite my pleas, he says nothing of what happened to my love, but the terrible glee upon his face says he knows. Of my crimes, he says only that he is the lord and master of Balcarres House, and those who disobey his wishes will die within its walls.

So be it.

Since I have awoken from my fever, I hear Samuel's voice no longer. I know now that the voice I heard was my Samuel waiting for me on the other side and calling me to join him. And I will, my love. But I cannot rest until I have the truth of your murder from my father. I must know where your body rests so that I may lay down beside you one final time.

I will drag the truth to light with my bare hands. I will not let my father escape from what he has done. I finish here as I go now to do my dark deed. No law of man will forgive a son for killing his father, but Samuel was the best man of any I have ever known, so I only pray God will forgive me, not for my sake, but for his.

I will see you soon my dark star, my waiting angel, my Samuel.

CHAPTER 23

The Wicked Master was back.

Dominick lay in the dark, listening to the scraping and thumping that seemed to come from every corner of his room, sometimes fading until he could almost believe it all a bad dream. Other times the sounds of ghostly footsteps seemed to walk right up to the edge of his bed and stand there, waiting. Watching.

He pulled the covers over his head and told himself he was being foolish. It was just the echo of the servants putting the house to rest, or rats scampering into hidden crannies, or that godbedamned wind howling across the heath, lashing its icy rain against the house, trying to batter its way in.

Then the noises would start again, and he would shiver under his blankets. Why had he insisted on sending Alfie away tonight of all nights? The spectre of death walked the halls of Balcarres. What was the fear of discovery compared to that?

A soft *tap tap tap* came from the side of the room Dominick faced. Against his will, he warily opened an eye and peered into the darkness. The tapping came again, and his heart stuttered as the bookcase connecting his room to Alfie's creaked slowly open. For an agonizing moment, it hung there silent and waiting. Then Alfie popped his head around the corner, auburn curls all askew, and Dominick's heart began to beat again.

"Nick?" Alfie whispered. His voice caught, clicking in his throat at the end.

Dominick couldn't take being in his room a moment longer. He leapt from the bed, tossing the mountain of covers aside. Focusing on the biting chill of the stones beneath his feet, he darted across the room, afraid if he stopped to listen he would hear phantom steps giving chase. He bundled Alfie through the doorway and closed the bookshelf behind them with a firm tug. The sound of the latch dropping into place was a comfort, but he closed the bookshelf on Alfie's side as well, just to be safe.

"Nick, what's wrong?"

Dominick shivered, the excess fear rolling off his spine now that he was out of that cursed room.

"He's back," he said, turning to face Alfie. His love stood in just a nightshirt and Dominick's robe, his arms wrapped around himself, a picture of abject misery. His brow furrowed.

"Mr. Bisset is back?"

"No, not Mr. Bisset," Dominick said, crossing to Alfie almost without thinking and wrapping his arms around him. Whether it was more for his comfort or Alfie's was hard to say. "The Wicked Master. I don't know if it's the mysterious disappearance of the minister or the storm, but he's been rattling his ghostly chains all night. You haven't heard anything?"

He felt Alfie shake his head, the motion brushing his cheek against Dominick's. Dominick took advantage of the moment to give the corner of his jaw a quick kiss.

"Well, believe me when I say it's just as well you came in when you did," Dominick said, trying to put on a brave front, despite the fear that still trembled through him. "I don't know why it's me the Wicked Master wants to haunt. You're the one who's usurped his room."

"I think I know, and I don't think he was. That is... I'm not making any sense," Alfie said brokenly. "I mean, I think I know why he's in your rooms, and I don't think the Wi-*Malcolm*. I don't think Malcolm was wicked at all. Oh Dominick, it's awful."

Alfie pulled away then. The lamp still burned, and by its light Dominick could see that he held a small book. With a sigh, Alfie sat on the bed and looked at it in his hands.

"It's his diary," Alfie said, rubbing a gentle thumb over the cover. "We've gotten the story all wrong. It was the earl, Malcolm's *father*, who was the wicked one. Wicked, cruel, and worse besides. He was the one who killed the farmer who disappeared. Samuel Whin, the man Malcolm loved."

Dominick started. The Wicked Master had a male lover? He took the book from Alfie when he held it out and turned it over in his hands before carefully opening it. The handwriting was faint against the page, it would take him forever to read it in this light. He turned to say as much to Alfie, and was shocked by the sorrow writ across every inch of him.

He set the diary beside the lamp and lay on the bed, pulling Alfie down with him. "Why don't you tell me all about it."

❊ ❊ ❊

Later, curled together under the blankets, Dominick drew comforting circles on Alfie's hip with his thumb while Alfie finished the tragic story.

"...And that's where it ends. Samuel gone, and Malcolm about to confront his father. I suppose we know what happened next."

"I suppose we do. He failed to end that murderous bastard and was cast out. Shamed and shunned for all this time. The poor devil. And no trace of Samuel was ever found?"

Alfie shook his head. His fingers played absently with the ring around Dominick's neck, sliding it back and forth along the chain. More than once in the telling of the tale, he'd had to stop, his throat catching with such pain and compassion for the men long dead that Dominick's heart broke to hear it. He'd had tears in the corners of his own eyes from the first mention of Samuel and Malcolm's plan to run away together, knowing it was doomed. More than one had run down his face when Alfie reached the story's awful climax.

"I think that's why he's haunting your room instead of mine," said Alfie. "In life, that was the room Samuel stayed in. They were together there for a brief time. Together and happy. Perhaps he's trying to relive those memories."

"Or he's trying to find his lost love," Dominick mused. His throat felt hot and swollen. He swallowed roughly to clear it. "I lost you once already. If it ever happened again, I know I'd never stop searching until I found you."

At that, Alfie wrapped his arms around him and squeezed so tightly Dominick could feel his ribs creak.

"I don't know what would happen if I lost you, Nick.

For a while there, I was so scared I would. That you would decide you'd had enough of all the rules and manners and damn fuss of it all and leave me here behind. I was afraid that if I opened the door in the bookcase to come apologise, I'd find your room dark and your bed cold. God knows I would have understood."

Dominick tangled his fingers in Alfie's curls and pulled him close. He held Alfie there, pressed tight against his heart where Dominick could keep him safe. He couldn't put words to all the things he felt—fear, comfort, worry, sorrow, love, love, love, love—all rising together in one overwhelming tide. He could drown in it, and for the man in his arms he would. Just let himself sink below the surface to where everything was still and quiet and let go.

But not right now. Now, he had a sad and worried Alfie in his arms, and that would never do. He tugged the handful of hair playfully and jostled Alfie against his chest.

"Look at us. We've barely been in this country a month and we're as dour as any Scotsman you ever did see. No more of this 'losing me, losing you' rot. It's far too horrid a night for that kind of talk. Besides, I'm like a bur on a curr, you can't shake me now, you're stuck with me for life. If I have to learn the name of every fork in this country and its family connections, I will. And if we—not me, *we*—decide we've had enough of it, I'll teach you to box and we'll be a sensation, the first team fighters in the history of the sport. Or we'll run away to become emperors of the Far East. Or pirate kings, using the same knives to carve through our roast dinners as we do to carve through our enemies."

Alfie lifted his head and wrinkled his nose in disgust. "That's foul. Besides, too much gristle on an enemy, you'll dull the blade."

Dominick shrugged. "Such is the life of a pirate I'm afraid. It's a harsh life, full of filth and unnatural acts. It's a good thing you've been getting so much practice—"

Expecting the assault, Dominick caught Alfie's hand before it could cover his mouth. Tucking his chin down to better see his lover, he caught the tail end of an eye roll. He bit back a smile, glad his distraction from the night's awfulness was working. He pretended to examine the captured hand in some detail. After several moments he tsked, "This will never do."

He shook his head sadly and waited. The trick was to let Alfie's curiosity get the better of him. As long as Dominick could wait it out…

"Go on then," Alfie sighed, no stranger to his antics. "What will never do?"

"These fine hands, of course." Dominick shook his head sadly. Alfie's hands really were quite fine, soft and unblemished from years of genteel living, yet with enough calluses from his fencing training to be interesting. And his fingers, as long and seemingly delicate as the rest of him, but also bearing Alfie's surprising strength, and artful enough to be put to all sorts of exciting uses. "These hands will never take the toil of life on a brig."

"Well, we are to be pirate kings," Alfie reasoned. "Could we not leave all the manual labour to the common sailors while we rule majestically from… whatever part of the ship pirate kings rule from?"

Dominick considered this. In truth, his knowledge of ships amounted to little more than how to avoid being tricked into taking the king's shilling and waking up with a raging headache and a tar brush in hand.

"The captain's cabin?" He ventured hesitantly before grinning. "Yes, wonderful suggestion. I shall keep you in our cabin at all times awaiting my return as I see to the business aboard deck. For practical reasons, you will not be allowed a stitch of clothing."

Alfie squirmed against him, his interest in the idea brushing against Dominick's hip. "Practical reasons?" he breathed.

Dominick lifted Alfie's hand to his lips and pressed a kiss against his wrist, delighting in the full body shudder that earned him. He did it again and Alfie arched against him, his eyes fluttering.

"Practical reasons," Dominick repeated, punctuating each word with a kiss as he moved higher and higher up Alfie's sensitive inner arm. "It's. Quite. Hot. In. The. Indies."

He licked the delicate skin of the inner elbow and bit carefully over the vein. Satisfied with the way it made Alfie gasp and press one of those long legs between his own, he pulled back. "I'm only thinking of your comfort, love. Stuck on a ship full of rough, coarse men, you shouldn't have to suffer the heat as well."

"Mmm, I'm rather partial to rough, coarse men," Alfie hummed. He rubbed his face against Dominick's chest and its thick mat of blond hair. "And a whole shipful, you say?"

Dominick snarled and with a sudden jerk rolled them over so Alfie lay beneath him. He still had one of Alfie's wrists in his hand, and grabbed the other, pinning them to the pillow either side of his head. Alfie just smiled up at him, body completely at ease under Dominick's control. The trust there made his breath catch. He took a moment to simply bask in the beauty of the man beneath him, eyes bright and a laugh bubbling on his lips. Then Alfie raised an eyebrow and Dominick schooled his face into an expression more fitting their current game.

"Listen to you, you trollop," he growled playfully. "What makes you so eager to be a whore?" He punctuated his harsh words with a sharp nip to Alfie's ear, fully anticipating another one of those delightful shivers. Instead Alfie froze in his grasp, body suddenly rigid with tension, and not in a fun way.

"Alfie?" Dominick said, pulling back. "Is something wrong?"

Alfie sat up so quickly his forehead nearly collided with Dominick's nose. Only years of fast reflexes in the ring saving them both from a painful impact.

"I'm sorry," Alfie said quickly, spinning away from Dominick to put his bare feet on the floor, before seeming to realise they were in his room and there was nowhere to flee to. "I didn't mean to remind you. I've tried to be so careful not to."

Dominick's brow wrinkled, "Not to remind me of being a pirate? I'm sorry to say, love, my years without you were not nearly so exciting."

At the mention of their time separated, Alfie's shoulders hunched.

"Ah," Dominick said with sudden understanding. "Of being a whore."

Alfie nodded miserably. "I know I-I treated you rather shamefully when we first met, but I've been trying not to say or do anything to make you feel that way again, especially after the awful things I said when we fought."

"You haven't done anything of the like. This was just a bit of play. Besides, I'm the one who brought it up, so you can hardly blame yourself."

When Alfie didn't respond, Dominick sighed and pulled himself over to sit next to him. With a hiss at the sudden cold, he dragged the coverlet over and wrapped it around both their shoulders.

"It's not something that I'm proud of having done, or care to think too much about, but neither am I going to throw myself upon the floor and sob for my lost virtue. It was unpleasant and degrading, but so was much of living in Spitalfields. And I'm not in that place anymore. I'm here with you, in this dark, haunted, ice block of a house."

Alfie chuckled lightly at that. Dominick smiled, and tapped him lightly under the chin with his knuckle.

"As for anything you said or did before, you must know I forgave you almost immediately? Besides, I learned years ago that you can be an unthinking noddy. If I was to get mad at you each time you did something foolish, my head would have burst before you were even out of leading strings."

Alfie laughed again, a stronger sound this time. "That's true enough. I'm still sorry though."

"I appreciate that," Dominick said sincerely. "But right now the only thing you need to apologise for is dragging me out of a nice warm bed."

He pulled Alfie back down and rearranged them both under the sheets to his satisfaction. Alfie was very obliging, and even raised his hands back up to either side of his head in his earlier position.

"There, everything back as it should be."

He took Alfie's wrists carefully in his hands, and rubbed his thumbs softly over his palms. Perhaps that sort of play was a bit much for tonight. With all the turmoil of the dinner party, the missing minister, ghosts, the terrible truth revealed by the diary, and then the reminder of Dominick's past... Well. Something sweeter was definitely in order to take the taste of all that away.

He had barely finished the thought before Alfie was spreading his legs underneath him and rubbing the backs of his heels against Dominick's calves. Dominick grinned, and leaned down to give him a kiss, before a thought gave him pause.

"Alfie, when you said you didn't want to say or *do* anything that reminded me of being a whore, did that extend to in the bedroom too?"

Alfie tugged at his grip, but Dominick wasn't going to let him get away twice. Alfie pressed his lips together and looked away, but his lack of answer was answer enough.

"Don't misunderstand," Dominick said. He lowered his body down to press more of his weight against Alfie. Their cocks had both softened somewhat during their conversation, but a few rolls of his hips were enough to get things moving back in a more positive direction. "I enjoy what we do very, very much, but it has not escaped me that in certain acts, things always seem to go one way and not the other. I thought it was a personal preference, but now I wonder."

Alfie was still turned away, but his breaths were coming faster and Dominick could feel the rapid beating of his heart against his chest. He took advantage of the situation to lap his way slowly up Alfie's throat. The last remnants of his cologne tickled Dominick's nose with the smell of pepper and fragrant woods.

"What I mean is," he whispered. "Don't you want to fuck me, Alfie?"

Alfie shivered, although whether at Dominick's words of the scrape of his teeth against his jaw, Dominick couldn't say for certain.

"I do," Alfie said with a groan. He turned his head and caught Dominick's lips in a kiss full of passion and tenderness. "God, more than anything, Nick, I do. I just didn't want to make you think of anything awful."

Dominick had to stop a minute and rest his forehead against Alfie's chest. Christ, this wonderful, beautiful, ridiculous man. All these months he'd been holding back because he'd been trying to be careful with Dominick, to treat him like something fragile or important. Dominick would laugh at the idea if it wasn't so tragic. No one but Alfie had ever cared if he was hurt, and certainly no one saw him as valuable.

"Love," he said, the endearment more true than ever. "Remember when I said I couldn't get mad every time you did something foolish? Then let me tell you that you are too sweet for words, and I absolutely cherish you, but I am livid that your being an addlepated cully has cost me months of having your cock in me. *Months*, Alfie!"

"Oh," Alfie breathed. His eyes were blown wide. "Are you going to continue to insult me or would you like me to- to fuck you now?"

Dominick groaned. "Both. You're an absolute menace and a ninny and clearly should not be in charge of something so important."

"I'm an earl," Alfie laughed, hands working their way free of Dominick's grasp to clutch at his back. "Do you have any idea how many acres and people I'm in charge of?"

"And none of them are as important as my arse," Dominick grinned. "Oh course you realise, you need to hush if we do this. Can you be quiet while you fuck me, love?"

Alfie groaned, smothering the sound with his own hand at the last moment. Dominick grinned.

"Well done. Now sit up against the headboard while I find where you've hidden the oil."

"Top drawer, under all the cravats."

Dominick fetched the vial from its hiding spot and returned to bed as quickly as he could, throwing a leg over Alfie's hips so he was sitting in his lap facing him. The position meant they'd be more exposed to the cold air, but no matter, they'd warm up quickly enough, and this way there could be no question in Alfie's mind as to how much Dominick wanted—*needed*—him.

"How's this?" He asked. "Not too much pressure on your leg?"

Alfie leaned forward from the pile of cushions he'd propped up against the headboard behind him, putting his hands on Dominick's thighs and sliding them slowly upwards. The feel of those clever fingers running against the grain of his leg hair tickled and raised goosebumps on his skin.

"My leg is fine, even if you are bloody heavy." Alfie squeezed the muscles at the top of Dominick's thighs almost vengefully. "You're obscene is what you are. Honestly Nick, I think each of these is thicker than my waist." His eyes were large and dark as he squeezed again.

Dominick laughed. "Now you're just fishing for compliments on your figure." He tapped the bottle against the back of Alfie's hand. "Are you going to help me with this, or shall I do it myself?"

He bit his lip to keep from laughing again at the look of pure lust that struck Alfie, stunning him for a moment before being replaced with a nervous flush. Dominick couldn't help but lean in to kiss one pinkening cheek.

"Don't be getting timid on me now, love." Dominick rolled his hips, pleased when he found Alfie gratifyingly hard against him, despite his sudden reservations. "You've been depriving me of more than just your cock, you know. I want to feel those gorgeous fingers in me before you fuck me."

"God, Nick," Alfie swallowed. "The things you say."

Dominick hummed and kissed him again, on the lips this time, before pulling away as Alfie tried to chase the taste. He lifted one of Alfie's hands from his thigh and poured a small pool of oil into his palm. He set the bottle within easy reach on the nightstand then spread the oil along the length of Alfie's fingers, slicking his own hands in the process.

"Go on then. Start with one and I'll tell you when I'm ready for more."

Alfie nodded, sitting up as much as he could with Dominick pinning his hips and rested his dry hand against the small of Dominick's back. Dominick watched the look of fierce concentration on his face as Alfie reached around him. Then a single finger brushed against his entrance. His body twitched at the sensation. Alfie hesitated but after a moment began to push slowly in.

"Is this right?" he asked, brows knit.

"You tell me," replied Dominick, pushing back against his finger in obvious answer. "You do this for yourself all the time when you're impatient."

"Only because you'd take all night with it if given the chance," said Alfie, more snippety than Dominick was used to from a man knuckle-deep inside him. "Besides, it's different when I can only feel ah, one half of the equation."

"It feels lovely. Out and in now. Go on, I won't break."

In this position, the angle was awkward, but what Alfie lacked in maneuverability he made up for in determination. His shallow thrusts were swiftly replaced with longer, surer strokes. Dominick was about to suggest it was time to move on to two, when Alfie crooked his finger unexpectedly, brushing it against that place inside that made Dominick see stars.

He yelped, high and loud, then buried his face against Alfie's neck as the little devil did it again.

"Shh. You're the one who said we need to be quiet."

"Menace," Dominick slurred. He draped his arms over Alfie's shoulders, resting one wrist on the headboard behind him and burying his other hand in the soft hair at Alfie's nape. "Do with me what you will, you corsair. I'm at your mercy."

He felt Alfie's chuckle more than he heard it, but could not take too much offense as Alfie added another finger to the onslaught, twisting and stretching. His rhythm was varied, unpredictable. It was maddening. Dominick found himself rolling his hips against Alfie, trying to get his fingers back to that spot, only to have Alfie seek it out when he was least expecting it.

"Stop playing around and fuck me," he growled.

Alfie grinned. "Who's impatient now? A bit different when you're the one being toyed with, isn't it?"

Dominick responded by twisting his fingers sharply in Alfie's hair, and closing his other hand, still slick with oil, around Alfie's cock. Alfie cried out most satisfactorily and his hips jerked under Dominick.

"Shh," Dominick teased.

"I-I think I should do one more finger," he stuttered.

"No. Now."

Dominick raised up on his knees causing Alfie's fingers to slip from him. He clenched unhappily at the loss, but knew that soon he would have something even better. He shuffled up, positioning himself exactly where he wanted to be, then slowly lowered himself down until he could feel the head of Alfie's cock brushing against him.

"Ready?" he asked.

Alfie nodded, and wrapped his fingers around his cock to guide it. Dominick took a moment to drink him in. Beneath him, Alfie's eyes were glassy and his mouth was open, hot pants of breath escaping with the rapid rise and fall of his chest, drops of sweat beading the hair there despite the chill. Dominick could barely stand to look at him, he was so beautiful. The blush had spread, now running from the tips of his ears all the way down to almost his navel, but any nervousness he'd been feeling was clearly now replaced with excitement. The cords in his neck stood out and Dominick could feel the tension thrumming through his body as he fought to hold back, not taking what he wanted but waiting for Dominick to give it to him. Dominick could taste the anticipation in the air, mixed with their sweat and the herbal bite of the oil.

"Gorgeous."

"Please, Nick," Alfie whispered, and Dominick gave him everything.

He couldn't help the long moan as he slowly sank down, taking Alfie deep, deep, and deeper still. The feeling was exquisite. Having Alfie finally inside him, filling him, felt right, like the last gear in a clock clicking into place, bringing the whole mechanism alive at last.

After an eternity, he finally worked the last inch of Alfie's cock inside him, and sat down on his hip bones, gasping as he adjusted to the stretch. Alfie was probably right; it had been a long time since any man had been inside him, and he should have let Alfie get three fingers in first, but any discomfort was worth finally having Alfie where he belonged.

When he couldn't wait anymore, he rose up on his knees, holding there for a tortuous moment before plunging back down. Alfie gasped and gripped him tightly, his fingernails digging sharp crescents into his back. Dominick did it again, leaning forward a little this time, trying to find the perfect angle.

"Oh fuck, Nick. Fuck," Alfie panted.

Dominick couldn't help but tease.

"How do I feel, Alfie? How does it feel to fuck me at last?"

"God, so good. I can't—oh! Better than anything. I don't, Nick... I can't find words."

"Show me then," Dominick arched his back as he finally found the right angle, lightning racing through him as he worked Alfie's cock into him again and again to hit that perfect spot. "Show me how good it feels to fuck me."

Alfie shivered and jerked up. He started out unevenly, but as the initial shock died down, he was soon thrusting in perfect counterpoint, hips rising just as Dominick came down on the descent. Dominick felt dizzy, overwhelmed, even more so when Alfie recovered his usual confidence and began to explore his favorite parts of Dominick's body with lips and hands.

Their rhythm was too fierce for proper kisses, so Alfie peppered Dominick's shoulders and chest with them instead, those skillful fingers carding through his chest hair and plucking at his nipples. Dominick could do little to return the favor. His arms were draped over Alfie's shoulders again, this time grabbing the headboard fiercely to keep himself upright.

"I'm close, Nick."

Dominick could feel the telltale tingling at the base of his spine as well, but it wasn't going to be enough.

"Hand," he choked out, unable to get out any more than that.

Alfie, clever Alfie, knew exactly what he meant though, and immediately Dominick felt a slick hand wrap around his neglected cock. He jolted at the touch, so focused had he been on the sensations within him that this new external pleasure was almost too much to bear. His pace stuttered wildly as he tried to work himself onto Alfie's cock at the same time as he thrust into his hand, unable to choose between the two delights.

He slammed down one final time as Alfie twisted his palm over the head of his cock and that was it. He bit back the keen that tried to escape as his vision whited out. Distantly he heard Alfie moan his name as his body clamped tight around him. Alfie kept working him, bringing Dominick to peak after peak as his hand grew slick with spend.

Dominick didn't know when his eyes had shut, but he forced them open just in time to see Alfie throw his head back, that long neck on full display and his Adam's apple bobbing as he was struck by his own climax. Dominick leaned forward, covering Alfie's slack lips with his own and smothering his cry of ecstasy with a kiss. At the hot rush of liquid inside him, his softening cock twitched feebly in Alfie's grip.

In that moment, he knew he'd be with Alfie for the rest of his life. Alfie was a part of him, heart, body, and soul. Dominick would never be free of him, and God help him, he never wanted to be.

Alfie groaned, body going limp as the last wave of orgasm washed through him. He began to slump back, and Dominick cradled his head gently to keep it from knocking against the headboard. That sapped the last of his strength as well. He lifted himself free of Alfie with a twinge, before they both collapsed onto the pile of pillows.

They lay there panting, lit only by the lamp on the nightstand and the last few coals glowing in the fireplace. It was more than enough light for Dominick to see the little red book, Malcolm's diary, still sitting on the nightstand next to the bottle of oil. As his breaths began to even out, his eyes wandered to the much more interesting sight of Alfie next to him.

Dominick could have watched him forever. His eyes

were soft and his lips were curved into such a sweet smile that Dominick couldn't help but lean in for a kiss. This one was languid and slow, meant not to excite, but to revel. When Alfie's tongue lapped over his, it felt like a perfect conversation between two bodies, every taste a comfort and every sigh a promise.

Finally, they pulled away, the need to breathe and the chill of the room turning their minds to more practical concerns.

Alfie was the first to break the silence. "That was wonderful. I feel like I should go get the washcloth, since you always do for me, but I'm honestly not sure I could make it that far."

"Leave it," said Dominick, using what little of his energy remained to pull the blankets up from where they'd been kicked to the end of the bed and covering them both. "We'll deal with it in the morning."

Alfie wrinkled his nose, but didn't protest. He wriggled closer, and Dominick raised an arm so Alfie could tuck himself against his side.

"Tell me a story," Alfie yawned.

Dominick huffed out a laugh. He was about three seconds from losing consciousness, but Alfie would be Alfie.

And I love him for it.

"Haven't you had enough tales for one night?"

"Tell me a *happy* story," Alfie said, sounding for all the world like the workhouse urchin Dominick had known all those years ago. "No missing persons or murderers or evil fathers. Or pirate kings gutting people."

Dominick sighed, but it was hard to feel much put out

when he had acres of warm, contented Alfie curled up against him. He ran his hand along the long plane of his side.

"Once upon a time, there were two princes who lived in a draughty old castle. One was very sensible and just wanted to sleep, but the other was foolish and kept him awake."

Alfie huffed, but closed his eyes and let his head drop onto Dominick's shoulder.

"Fortunately the foolish prince was very handsome, so the sensible one forgave him." Dominick conceded. "The princes' lives had been hard at times, full of fear and suffering, but they found their way back to each other, and that was what really mattered. And once they were together again, nothing could tear them apart."

Dominick swallowed back the lump in his throat.

" 'S that it?" murmured Alfie.

"That's all for now. We'll find out the rest tomorrow, and tomorrow's tomorrow, and all the days after."

Alfie hummed and within minutes his breaths had evened into the steady rhythm of sleep.

Dominick lay there just looking at Alfie in the lamplight and feeling at peace for the first time since he'd set foot inside Balcarres. Eventually, he sighed. As right as things felt here in Alfie's bed and in his arms, tomorrow would bring back all the terrors held within the house. He would need his strength to handle them all, and to make sure they couldn't hurt the man he loved.

He reached out to turn off the lamp, but there was no way to reach it without disturbing the man who slept so trustingly in his arms. He looked down at Alfie's peaceful face and settled back down. If he had to squint against the light all night, then so be it.

Just as he had the thought, he felt a gust of freezing air and the lamp spluttered and went out. Surprised, he blinked against the sudden blackness. Outside, the storm still rattled against the windows, but within the room, everything was still. He was just about to chalk it up to a draught, when from the bedside table, he heard the pages of the diary turn and flutter.

A moment later there was silence, but the quiet was no longer oppressive, and the room had lost some of its chill.

"Thank you," he whispered to the dark.

There was no response but the fall of icy rain upon the glass.

CHAPTER 24

Alfie awoke to his fingers being pried up one at a time. Instinctively, he gripped even tighter, unwilling to be deprived of whatever was keeping him so warm and comfortable. He raised his head a fraction and blinked the sleep from his eyes. Ah. Dominick. That made sense. He put his head back down.

"No, no. None of that, you damned limpet. Let me up."

Alfie mumbled something derogatory, content to let Dominick struggle to get out from under him a bit more. It was actually a rather pleasurable sensation. He rolled his hips against Dominick's thigh. Quite pleasurable.

"None of that either," Dominick huffed, but Alfie could hear the fondness in his tone. "That weasel of a valet will be here any minute."

Alfie sighed and loosened his grip. "Be nice. I can't fault him for his taste at least."

He cracked open an eye just in time to take in the delightful view of Dominick making his way fully naked across the room to the chair where he'd tossed his nightshirt, cursing and skipping from rug to rug to avoid the freezing bare floor. The muscles in his arse bunched and flexed with every step, and Alfie bit his lip to keep from groaning at the memory of being buried in that tight heat the night before. He couldn't help a small noise of disappointment from escaping when Dominick pulled the nightshirt over his head and the view was lost.

Dominick looked over his shoulder at him with a wink, as if he knew what he was thinking. He probably did. Alfie wriggled over into the warm spot he'd left behind and pulled the covers tighter around himself. He dozed as he heard Dominick amble about, the hidden passage between their rooms opening as he went back and forth. He was rudely awoken some time later by a nightshirt being flung in his face. He spluttered at the affront but sat up at last.

"Put that on," Dominick said, the handle of a toothbrush sticking out of the corner of his mouth. "I'll be all kinds of jealous if Jarrett gets to see you like that."

He spat into Alfie's washbasin and rinsed.

"How late is it anyway?" mumbled Alfie, pulling on the shirt before tipping his head up and receiving a kiss pleasantly flavored with cloves from Dominick's tooth powder.

"Late enough." Dominick swiped the bottle of oil and Malcolm's diary from the bedside table and tucked them into the hiding place under Alfie's cravats. "I'm starting to wonder if we're on our own for the morning."

"Well, we do have a full house. I imagine our guests are taking advantage of the luxury of having a valet while they have the opportunity. Poor Jarrett and Mr. Howe are probably in a state already. I wouldn't be surprised if they've pressed young Davey into service as well."

"I'd pay money to see them try to do the same with Graham. I doubt he'd be keen to help Carnbee with his socks."

Alfie chuckled, "Indeed not. Poor Mrs. Finley and the

maids though, having double duty of laying out breakfast and assisting the ladies. I can't say I have any idea exactly of what that entails, but I imagine it to be a complicated process."

Alfie rose and limped his way over to the washbasin, his gunshot wound twinging with each step. Country air was supposed to be restorative, but he wasn't healing nearly as quickly as he'd hoped. Perhaps by spring.

He winced as he scrubbed off the evidence of their lovemaking the night before, unable to enjoy the feeling of being clean as the icy water rose pebbles on his skin. Dominick was kind enough to lay out garments for him while he washed, and Alfie jumped into them as quickly as possible after giving his teeth a cursory brush. Dominick, he noticed, was already mostly dressed, though his waistcoat still hung open.

Alfie frowned. "Why do you have your boots on? You don't expect Jarrett to have time to give you a lesson today, do you?"

Dominick glanced out the window where the rain was still coming down in sheets. "No, no riding for me today, I'm afraid. But if I'm going to be tramping around in that mess looking for our wayward minister, I thought these might serve better than evening slippers."

The reminder of the missing Mr. Bisset dampened Alfie's mood, but he couldn't help but try to keep their spirits up. "Well," he leered, "If it's more riding practice you want, then why don't we go back to bed and—"

His words were cut off by a calloused hand over his mouth.

"Alfie, love," Dominick said. Amusement twinkled in

his eyes despite the sternness of his face. "If you ever want a repeat of last night, don't finish that thought."

He frowned and ran the backs of his fingers against Alfie's cheek. "You need a shave. Want me to do it?"

Alfie's eyes fluttered closed. He loved nothing more than the simple domesticity of the act, the inherent trust of baring his throat to Dominick as he held a blade in his hand.

"I'd love you to," he said. "But I think we've been incautious enough for one morning. Go ahead down to breakfast if you're ready, I'll join you shortly. Then I suppose we can tackle the mystery of the missing man of God. With minimal material or mental assistance from the..." He searched for an appropriate word.

"Mutton-headed magistrate?"

"I was going to go with *maladroit*, but yes." He gave Dominick a quick kiss in farewell, stepping back before it could deepen the way they both wanted. "Go. Or we really will give Jarrett quite the shock when he shows up."

"In that case, I'll be off," Dominick said as he unlocked the door and removed the chair from under the handle. He flashed Alfie a cocky grin. "I'd hate to vex the valet."

❉ ❉ ❉

Alfie cursed under his breath and leaned more of his weight on the stairwell banister. His leg had been feeling better for the past several days, but it seemed the persistent damp and cold had finally caught up with him. He grit his teeth as his foot hit the next step down and pain radiated from his wound.

"Can I help you with anything, milord?"

Alfie looked up to see Moira standing at the base of the stairs, a harried look on her face and tired circles under her eyes.

"No, thank you, Moira. I'm almost there." He descended the last few steps under her skeptical gaze, and gave his sword cane a jaunty twirl. "I can usually get about quite well with this, but I'm afraid I still haven't mastered the knack of stairs."

"If you say so, milord." She gave a slight curtsey and glanced down the hall, shifting her weight hesitantly, clearly uncomfortable addressing him without the presence of more senior staff.

"Indeed, I do," Alfie smiled his most disarming smile, but the poor creature still looked ready to bolt at any moment. She held a basket of assorted linens, the wicker creaking as she twisted it in her hands, which looked worn raw. "Forgive me for noticing, but are you quite all right? Your hands look a trifle sore."

She glanced down. "It's from the washing, sir."

Alfie cheered internally, seeing an opportunity to perhaps gain a bit of her trust. "I'm sorry to hear that. I know Mr. Trent has found a balm of arnica to be quite soothing on chapped or bruised skin. If your mother doesn't have the supplies, I'm sure he'd be happy to share."

She stared at him as if he was touched in the head, but he preferred that to her fear.

"Thank you, sir. I'll be sure to ask."

"Excellent! Am I the last down?"

"Aye, sir. The rest are assembled in the dining room."

"Thank you, Moira. I appreciate the warning."

She curtseyed again, and took off at a pace that was barely decorous.

Outside the dining room, he took a moment to brace himself before pushing the doors open. On one side of the room, Gil and Carnbee were having a spirited discussion of the best way to organise the day's search, while on the other side, Madam Carnbee and Mrs. Bisset were clustered together, faces buried in their handkerchiefs.

A loud wail erupted from the cluster, nearly surprising Alfie off his already unsteady feet. To his further surprise, the noise didn't come from the possibly widowed Mrs. Bisset, but from the young Madam Carnbee, who punctuated her sorrow by throwing herself back dramatically in her chair, hand to her forehead. Sarah Siddons as Desdemona could not have done it with a more aggrieved air. The move also exposed the full length of her neck, as well as rather more of her bosom than was entirely appropriate for the breakfast table.

Her antics at least had the effect of halting Gil and Carnbee's argument, distracted as they were by the display. Two seats away from her, Dominick merely reached for another slice of toast.

"Good morning," he said without looking up at Alfie, his attention focused on the selection of jams.

"To you as well, Mr. Trent. Ladies. Gentlemen," Alfie nodded to each group in turn. "Has there been any progress in locating Mr. Bisset?"

Madam Carnbee let out another wail and sank further into her chair, breast noticeably heaving. Mrs. Bisset merely sniffed.

"Unfortunately not," said Carnbee, drawing his eyes

away from his wife's exhibition with difficulty. "I've sent the stable lad down to the village to round up a few men. I was just telling Mr. Charleton that we would be best served waiting for their arrival."

"And I was just informing Carnbee that few will be willing to come out in this weather, and even of those willing, fewer still will be able to make it with the roads in this condition. I wouldn't even rely on poor Davey being able to return, never mind with an army behind him. It would be better to begin the search as soon as possible. Every moment we delay is another that Mr. Bisset is out in this weather without any sort of protection from the elements."

As if to punctuate his point, a curtain of rain took that moment to sweep against the windows, the day outside so dark that nothing could be seen in the glass but their own reflections.

Alfie grimaced. If he was going to be spending the day in that, he was going to need more than just tea. He crossed to the end of the sideboard that held the coffee pot, leaning heavily on his cane with each step.

"Perhaps you should—"

"You oughtn't—"

Gil and Dominick both spoke at once. They stopped and looked at each other in surprise. Alfie rolled his eyes and turned back to the sideboard. If he was going to have to deal with their pissing match, he was going to need some bacon as well.

He loaded a plate and turned back around in time to see Dominick wave his hand at Gil dismissively and return to his toast.

"As I was saying," Gil said, "Perhaps you should remain here, my lord. The captain remaining with his ship, as it were. That way you could coordinate any volunteers who do arrive. And I'm sure the ladies would be comforted by your presence in the house while the rest of us are out in the thick of it."

A hot flush of embarrassment stained Alfie's cheeks. Of course he didn't *want* to go traipsing about in the mud, but just because he was injured didn't mean he was an invalid to be left behind with the women. He looked to Dominick, sure he was about to leap to his defense, but Dominick merely nodded in agreement.

He opened his mouth to give them both a scathing piece of his mind but held his tongue at the last moment. He *was* injured. Dragging himself around all day would only exacerbate his injuries and might set his healing back weeks, if not months. Even worse, he would slow the search party down, perhaps putting the minister's life in further peril. Dominick in particular was sure to be distracted, bless him for the damned mother hen he was. As much as Alfie hated to admit it, they might be right.

He threw back his cup of coffee vindictively, ignoring the burn. He'd liked it better when Dominick and Gil were quarrelling, rather than joining forces against him. Hopefully their treaty would be short-lived. He realised the entire table was quiet, waiting for his decision. No, not just his decision, the Earl of Crawford's decision. These were his lands, and his people. He needed to focus on that, not his own pride.

"Very well," he acquiesced with more grace than he felt. "I'll direct whatever reinforcements arrive, but I agree it's best that the search begin as soon as possible. Gentlemen, when you're ready, I'll have Mr. Howe and Jarrett join us with a selection of coats if you would care for something heavier than your own."

"I think it would be best if Madam Carnbee and I retire," said Mrs. Bisset, rising from the table. The men stood when she did.

"I'll send Mrs. Finley to see if there is anything you require, and remain with you for company, if you'd like."

"Thank you, my lord. Please let me know the moment you have word of my husband. One—" her voice caught, but she continued on, indefatigable. "One way or another."

"Of course, ma'am." Alfie said as she sailed out of the room with her red eyes resolutely forward, a sighing Madam Carnbee trailing in her wake.

❊ ❊ ❊

A short time later, the men were gathered in the hall. Clearly unhappy with Alfie choosing Gil's suggestion over his own, Carnbee was ordering the servants around like his own personal regiment, dispatching Graham and Jarrett to search the land south of the house, while he and Mr. Howe —apparently pressed into service as Carnbee's batman— took the east. This left Gil and Dominick not only in the unpleasant predicament of having to endure each other's company, but also with the even more unpleasant decision of whether to attempt the steep woods to the north, or risk the dangerous and gorse-covered terrain to the west.

"Don't worry," murmured Dominick, joining Alfie at the back of the hall while the others donned thick coats and gloves near the front door. "I won't leave Charleton's body anywhere it will be found."

"That's not funny," hissed Alfie.

He watched as Janie and Moira distributed flasks among the men to keep them warm on their search. As usual, Moira kept her eyes down and stuck only to the task at hand. Janie however, quickly emptied her basket and doubled back to Gil.

"Pardon me, Mr. Charleton, sir," she said, blushing so brightly her face was almost the same colour as her hair. "I thought you might not have had much at breakfast, sir, and didn't want you going hungry, so I collected a few things for you to take."

She handed Gil a small parcel from which drifted the distinct smell of baked goods.

"I suppose the rest of us can just starve then," Dominick muttered under his breath.

Alfie couldn't help but bite his lip as he watched Gil thank Janie, giving her hand a kiss that lingered longer than it should as he gazed up at her over his spectacles, as dashing as any prince. The look wasn't even directed at him and Alfie could feel the force of it; poor Janie was nearly trembling at the onslaught. His unease from before returned.

He glanced over at Dominick and received only a raised eyebrow in response.

Alfie sighed. Dominick was right. As much as he liked Gil and didn't want to think it of him, Moira had all but said *someone* forced himself upon Lily, or at best, seduced her before throwing her aside. And while Alfie hoped his new friend was incapable of either atrocious act, his manner towards Janie was worrying. Was he on the prowl for a new conquest now that the old had fled?

As he looked out on the group of men ready to face the cold, an even more worrying thought struck him. If someone had caused Mr. Bisset to disappear, then the culprit was likely in the room with them now. Presumably the same man had murdered Mr. Gibson. With the group breaking up into teams of two for their search, this meant an innocent man was about to wander into the storm with a killer. With the howl of the wind and the oppressive darkness outside, if the murderer decided to claim another victim, no one would know until it was too late.

Alfie pressed the back of his hand inconspicuously against Dominick's gloved one.

"Be careful."

"I won't take my eyes off him," Dominick whispered back. He inclined his head towards a tittering Janie. "You might have a word with that one. Some truths about the wickedness of man and all that. Put a bit of that nobility and polish to use, I'm sure she'd take a bit of lordly advice as if it were gospel."

"That's me, Earl of Crawford and Defender of Innocence."

Dominick pursed his lips in a sour moue. Alfie would lay good money that he had some rather ribald thoughts he'd like to share about the state of Alfie's innocence, but was thwarted by their being in public.

"Save it for later," Alfie chuckled. "Stay safe out there, and I'll make sure there's hot water waiting in your room when you return."

Dominick pressed his hand back against Alfie's,

intertwining their fingers briefly in a gesture that said, "I love you," as clearly as if he had spoken the words aloud. Then he stepped away, striding across the hall and out into the rain.

✽ ✽ ✽

It took both Janie and Moira to close the door behind the men, a sudden squall pushing back against them and setting the tapestries in the hall fluttering at the edges, shaking off years worth of dust. Firmly shut at last, the door rattled in its frame as the wind whistled around the edges with a haunting, inhuman cry.

Alfie shuddered, the sound enough to bring to mind all the ghosts that haunted Balcarres—those that made their presence known by footsteps in the night, and those that only existed in hushed tones and averted eyes.

The two maids knelt to make quick work of the puddle that had gathered just inside the door with a deftness that spoke to this not being the first time they'd endured such weather. Still, it made Alfie feel better when a log popped in the grate and he was not the only one who flinched.

He cleared his throat. "Thank you both for your additional assistance with the ladies this morning. Once you're finished here, you should get some rest while you have the chance."

Moira rose and curtseyed. "Thank you, milord. Shall I pass the same on to my mother?"

Alfie thought for a moment, it was hardly fair to keep Mrs. Buie toiling away in an empty kitchen all on her own. "Yes, although I would like hot water ready as soon as the men return, and something warming to eat as well."

Moira nodded, "We can put a pot of water and a pot of stew to warm on either side of the fire."

"As long as you don't get the bathwater and the stew confused!" Alfie's jest was met with only polite smiles. Moira curtseyed again and departed, swallowed quickly into the darkness of the house.

"Oh actually, Janie," he said as the girl collected the damp rags they'd used to clean the floor. She looked up at him with a polite if slightly wary smile that was a far cry from the rapturous joy with which she looked upon Gil.

Her concern at being singled out would be justified amongst many of his peers, but he could hardly explain to the poor girl why she was as safe with him as a mouse in cheese. Her wariness was good though, perhaps it meant the conversation he had to have with her about Gil would be easier. Although he still didn't know how he was going to explain that the ones who seemed kind could be even more dangerous than the ones who seemed cruel.

"Before you retire, could you bring a cup of tea up to the gallery? I thought that reflecting on all that the generations before us endured might make these recent trials seem less terrible."

"I'm sure it will, milord."

As she headed off towards the kitchens, basket cocked against her hip, Alfie couldn't help but mutter, "No, I don't believe it either."

CHAPTER 25

The Wicked Master glared down at him.

Looking up at the painting, Alfie could see how well the artist had captured the rage in Malcolm's eyes, but there was more there. Now that he knew the true story, he could see the defiance, the hope. Alfie looked at the book clutched in one painted hand. Although by the time he'd found it hidden away in the secret passage behind the bookcase its bright red cover had dulled with age, it was undoubtedly the same one. Malcolm's diary.

His heart gave a painful lurch in his chest. According to the diary, he'd posed for this painting in order to have a smaller one made as a gift for Samuel. While the artist mixed his colours, Malcolm would have been thinking of his planned escape, how every brushstroke brought him closer to the day that he could run away with the man he loved. No wonder his eyes held defiance; this portrait was all he planned to leave behind in Balcarres, a farewell to his hateful father. No wonder they held hope; he didn't yet know the terrible tragedy that little red book would record.

"It's awful, isn't it?"

Alfie startled at the unexpected voice. He spun around only to see Janie wide-eyed behind him, a tea tray listing dangerously in her hands. He took it from her and set it on a nearby bench beside his cane, before her profuse apologies caused her to upset it once more.

"It's quite all right, Janie, no harm done. I suppose we're all on edge."

"Aye, milord. Apologies again." She began to back from the room.

"A moment more of your time, please. I have something rather delicate I wish to discuss with you."

If possible, her eyes grew even wider at this statement. Alfie grimaced. There were few positive "delicate matters" an employer could wish to discuss with a servant, and even fewer that a male employer might wish to discuss with a young female one. *Damn.* Why did he agree to this anyway? Dominick was better with words than he was. And what business was it of his to interfere anyway?

It's your business because she is a member of your household and that means something. You may have been born in the gutter but now you're an earl. The title, the land, the money, that all comes with a responsibility, a duty to those under your protection.

Alfie glanced back at the painting behind him, not the one of Malcolm, but the one that hung directly beside it. Malcolm's father Gordon, the eighth Earl of Crawford. An evil man who abused and tormented all those under his power. That was not the kind of earl he wanted to be. Nor did he wish to be a more passive evil, to allow abuses to take place to which he turned a blind eye. He straightened his shoulders.

"I imagine what I have to say, Janie, is rather uncomfortable for the both of us, but I think it needs to be said. While I consider Mr. Charleton a friend, it has not escaped my notice that he... has certain attributes.

Qualities."

He's handsome as the Devil and twice as charming. Good Lord, why is this so difficult?

"That is to say, I have noticed the effect he has on the fairer sex. I just don't want to see you hurt."

Janie was blushing again, her face twisted into a confused frown.

Oh Lord, please don't let me be the one who has to explain how it works between a man and a woman. I have little desire to know myself.

"I see," she said softly. "You don't want what happened to Lily to happen to me."

Alfie heart sunk. "Moira's sister, yes. It *was* him then."

Janie shrugged. "I don't know for certain it was Mr. Charleton, although he was up here often enough, I suppose. All I know is one Sunday she's dressing up extra fine for kirk, saying a good man's asked her to marry him and couldn't she just wait to see the looks on everyone's faces when they heard. But no banns were read that day, were they? So she comes running home crying, and the next day she's gone."

She tucked a flyaway curl back into her cap. "I may not have seen much of the world, but I know how it works, milord. I know the reasons a lass might be desperate for the banns to be read. But I thank you for worrying about me. That's quite kind. Do you really think Mr. Charleton's the type?"

Alfie was still reeling from everything Janie had said. They'd suspected someone had gotten Lily in a family way and that's why she'd gone to Edinburgh, but Lily couldn't have believed Gil—if it was Gil—would actually marry her.

Even the second son of a second son was too close to gentry to marry a kitchen maid. And it would have been cruel to let her believe otherwise. And Gil might be a bit of a cad and a charmer, but cruel?

"I don't know," Alfie said honestly. "I don't think Gil—that is, Mr. Charleton—would do something so awful. Or at least, I don't like to think that he would."

"True. But you men don't always see other men the way us women do," Janie said sadly.

For a moment she didn't look like a flighty girl who giggled at jokes and believed in ghosts, but a young woman who had worked all her life and understood things in a way that Alfie never would. Then, like a cloud passing, it was gone and her face lit with her usual smile. "If it makes you feel better, sir, I don't think Mr. Charleton is the type either. A bit of a chancer for certain, but a real gentleman at heart. Unlike *him*."

She pointed at the portrait of Malcolm. "Aye, I hate getting any closer to that one than I have to, for all that he's just paint and canvas. And aren't I always the one sent to dust in here too!"

Alfie smiled, content to let the topic change. Janie seemed versed enough in matters of the heart—and other things—for his conscience to be assuaged, and he would rather discuss quite literally anything else, even poor maligned Malcolm.

"Really? What is it about him that's so awful?"

"Well, he's the Wicked Master of course, that's enough to send a shiver down your spine all on its own. And then there's the way his eyes seem to follow you about the room. Unnatural it is."

Alfie opened his mouth to explain how the common painting technique worked, a process that had seemed like magic when his tutor first explained it to him.

"But that's not the worst of it," Janie continued.

"No?"

"No," Janie shook her head. "You see, my ma is a one for needlework. She did the kirk altar cloth herself, and most any bit of decoration you see in the village. And she tells me that if you're making an embroidery for a wedding gift or such, you don't just sew the names, but add pictures of roses for love. Or holly if it's a fruitful union they're seeking."

She winked, and Alfie regretted ever presuming he needed to explain anything to her.

"But *that* flower," she continued, pointing at the field of yellow blooms painted around Malcolm. "That's not one you'd ever stitch. It's said to be bad luck, for both the one that gets it and the one that gifts it both."

"Really?" Alfie was intrigued. "Why is that? Is there some folk story or legend about it?"

"Nothing so flash as that. Look."

She walked over to the painting and leaned in, her nose mere inches from the canvas. Clearly whatever detail she wanted to show was so small you had to be looking for it, or close enough to brush the dust from it. Alfie peered closer. In the hand not holding the book, Malcolm had been painted clutching a bundle of the plants he was walking through, the ones that were peppered with bright yellow flowers. Alfie gasped.

He hadn't noticed before, but the bundle was tied with a long blue ribbon with red trim. He'd seen that ribbon before, it was the one that Malcolm had been given by Samuel and had wrapped around his diary. But even that wasn't what caught his breath.

This close, he could see the long thorns that stuck out from green stalks. The painter had done an admirable job. Now that he knew to look for it, Alfie could see where Malcolm's clothes appeared to be pulled back, caught on the thorns, the sleeve of his coat slightly torn. And the hand that held the bundle... There, half hidden in painted shadow, blood ran down the inside of Malcolm's hand, and yet still he gripped the flowers so tightly that his knuckles were white.

Why had Malcolm asked to be painted this way? The flowers pulled at him, pierced him, but still he would not let them go.

"I did say it was awful," said Janie. "Makes me shudder every time. They grow all around Balcarres, you know, and across the moors? You wouldn't recognise them this time of year, not so many flowers on them now. Big thick bushes with spines that could take out your eye?"

"Yes, I've seen them. Gorse, I believe it's called?"

"Aye sir, I've heard that name for them. Furze, too, is another name for it up north. Around here though, it's called whin."

Alfie's blood went cold. *Samuel Whin.* Malcolm's lover. He licked his lips. "Isn't that the name of the farmer the Wicked Master was supposed to have killed?"

"Aye," Janie beamed. "Now you see why I think it's so awful. It's like he's bragging about his wicked deed by having whin all over his portrait. So the reminder of the man he killed would be there forever."

Or the reminder of the man he loved.

Alfie looked up at Malcolm. What a clever man. Too clever for his own good perhaps. He'd found a way to include his lover in his portrait, shown him literally pulling Malcolm away, pricking his heart. The only objects he held in the painting, very literally the only things he held dear, were his lover's namesake flower wrapped in the gift Samuel had given him, and the book that chronicled their love. He wanted to be remembered for these things only in the centuries to follow, long after his death.

Now that he understood, the meaning behind the painting was heartbreakingly clear to Alfie. But was he the only one? Was this what had given away Malcolm's plan to escape and lead to that fateful confrontation with his father? Had the earl seen the painting when it was barely dry and known what it meant? Or had it been something else entirely? In his diary, Malcolm hadn't known for certain what had roused his father's suspicion, only the terrible result. It was likely now that no one ever would.

Alfie looked over at the portrait of Malcolm's father. The eighth earl's portrait was completely unlike his son's. Where Malcolm's portrait was wild and energetic, capturing the man as he was, his father's was staid and composed, portraying the man as he wished to be seen. Unlike the two small reminders of his love that mattered to Malcolm, Gordon Pennington's painting was overflowing with all the things a lord's portrait was expected to have. Musical instruments propped up in chairs, a stack of books on a finely carved table, their spines turned so the viewer could see what fine and improving works they were. One of his hands even rested on a painted globe, its continents

uneven and seas filled with monsters. Behind him was a
bookcase filled with more books, and on one of the shelves,
a vase filled with yellow flowers.

At the sight of the flowers, the entire world went still.
No longer could Alfie hear the rain lashing at the windows
or the creak of the house in the wind.

It might be a coincidence, an artist's attempt to add a
bit of colour to an otherwise dreary background.

He leaned in so close he could smell the oils rising from
the paint even two centuries later. The flowers themselves
were so small as to be but the slightest flicks of the brush,
but there was no mistaking them. Painted behind the earl,
like a trophy on a shelf, was a vase of whin.

Alfie stepped back, his cane knocking loudly to the floor
as he nearly tripped over it. Janie dashed forward to pick it
up, and he took it from her with numb hands.

But why would Gordon have whin, the symbol, the very
name, of his son's lover added to his portrait? Breathing
heavily, Alfie stepped back further, barely noticing the
rustle of skirts as Janie got out of his way. He took in
the painting entirely. The room depicted was unfamiliar to
him. By the stone and scale he assumed it was somewhere
in Balcarres, but it wasn't any place he recognised from the
repeated searches of the house, first for Mr. Gibson, then
for Mr. Bisset. But there was something familiar about it.

Cold dread began to fill him, like seawater rising in a
hulled ship.

The bookcase.

It was of a dark wood, the same as most in Balcarres,
but his eye was caught by the carvings around its painted
edges—scrolls crowned with oak leaves. The bookcase in

the painting was almost identical to the one in his room, the one that opened onto the secret passage. And if this bookcase was built at the same time and by the same artisan...

"Janie, do you know what room that is?"

"Aye, milord, that's the earl's bedchamber. I've only been in once or twice, but the fireplace is the same."

"Thank you!" Alfie called out, tea forgotten as he ran from the gallery as quickly as his injured leg could carry him. He might be too much of an invalid to help solve the mystery of the missing Mr. Bisset, but if he was right, he'd just found the key to solving an even older mystery that haunted the walls of Balcarres.

CHAPTER 26

Alfie hurried down the corridor to the east wing as quickly as he could, the pain in his leg ignored in his excitement. If he was right, there would be another hidden passage behind the bookshelf in the earl's room. Who knew where it might lead or what secrets it held. He wasn't sure, but he had a terrible feeling it might be related to Samuel's disappearance all those centuries ago.

He spun the key ring in his hand. With Mr. Gibson's set still unaccounted for and Mr. Howe's out with him in the rain, he'd had to retrieve the final set from a startled Mrs. Buie in the kitchen. He'd barely taken the time to confirm she'd received the message from Moira about the stew and hot water before tearing off.

His pace slowed as he left the familiar areas of the house and made his way into the forgotten corridors of the east wing. A cold draught coiled around his ankles like a phantom cat. He tucked the keys safely into his pocket and picked up the last source of light before the impenetrable darkness ahead. The lamp was a battered old thing, but its glass chimney was uncracked and its small flame burned brightly. Better still, it had a handle that made it easy to hold one-handed, a fact he appreciated as he ran the fingers of his other hand nervously over the catch that released his cane's hidden blade.

"Stop being ridiculous," he scolded himself in a voice not as strong as he'd like. "What are you going to do, stab a spirit? Gut a ghost?"

He squared his shoulders. It was a good thing Dominick wasn't around. Alfie had—mostly—stopped being afraid of the dark back at the workhouse when he'd learned there were much more tangible things to fear. It wouldn't do for Dominick to see him now and think he'd regressed.

Still, he couldn't quiet the small part of his mind that said he should wait until Dominick returned and they could explore together. But the greater part of him, the part that wanted to prove he was still just as capable as any other man despite his injury, had him stepping forward into the dark.

Besides, he reasoned. *All the suspects are out searching for the minister. Except for me, the only ones left in the house are either phantoms or frightened women. There's nothing in the dark that can hurt me.*

❉ ❉ ❉

By the time he reached the earl's bedchamber, his certainty had waned. Skittering sounds behind closed doors brought to his mind all sorts of frightful, fantastical creatures. The open doors he passed were even worse, the fluttering lamplight warping the shadows of covered furniture into unrecognisable horrors. Nevertheless, he peered into every room, but none of them resembled the one from the painting.

In no time at all he was hopelessly lost. He'd taken so many turns, he was no longer certain which direction he faced. For all he knew, he might have made it right back around to where he started. Peering out one of the dirty windows was no help, the darkness outside returned only his own reflection in the glass.

Perhaps I'll turn the next corner to find a confused Mrs. Buie chopping vegetables for the stew and wondering why I'm back so soon!

Grinning at the thought, unlikely as it was, he pressed on until he could hear nothing but the lashing of the wind against shuttered panes and the uneven step, step, *tap*, step, step, *tap* of his own footsteps and cane.

Finally, he reached a door on its own at the end of a hall. There was nothing on the outside to differentiate it from any of the countless others he'd passed, but somehow he was certain this was the right door. The earl's bedchamber.

He fumbled through the entire key ring twice before one of the keys turned with a soft click and the door groaned open. It was definitely the room from the earl's painting. Despite the decay, the layout and much of the furniture was recognisable, untouched by the generations of earls that had followed. His eyes landed on the cold fireplace. Janie was right, it was clearly the same.

He made his way directly to the bookcase, placing the lamp on a shelf as he explored it with his hands. The raised bumps of carved leaves and the smooth swirls of scrolls slid under his fingertips. As he'd suspected, it was a perfect copy of the one in his room. His fingers brushed along the back of a shelf, coming away with less dust than he'd expected. If he was right, and this bookshelf was built to the same specifications, then the hidden latch to reveal the secret corridor should be right... there!

The bookcase swung out on hidden hinges, causing the lamp to wobble and tilt. Alfie lunged, righting it just before it fell. Images of the terrible fire in his London townhouse flashed behind his eyes. He lifted the lamp carefully off the shelf. If it broke, even if it didn't catch the house ablaze, he'd still be lost in the dark. And he'd just opened a secret passage that might lead to any sort of unknowable horror.

"Unknowable horror?" You read too many novels. It likely leads to a private wine cellar or a peephole into the maid's quarters. And won't it be tricky to explain how you happened across that!

He raised the lamp and peered in. His breath left him in a disappointed huff. The secret passage, such as it was, continued straight back for a few feet before coming to an end. Seeing that vase holding whin flowers in the earl's painting, he'd been certain he had the thread of something. He'd even been right about the bookshelf being a secret door, but for what? A hidden recess? It hardly seemed worth the effort.

His shoulders sagged. He'd been so excited to have something to share when everyone returned. How silly he'd been to think he'd found some clue to a centuries-old story, while all the other men were out doing work to solve a real disappearance.

Glumly, he stepped inside and raised the lamp. Perhaps there was *something* he could share: a clue inscribed on the rock, a map of other hidden passages, a few lewd sixteenth century woodcarvings, anything! He held his breath at what he might see, but the lamp did little but flicker, illuminating only shadows.

He turned, ready to resign in defeat, when something

about the wavering light caught his attention. Why was the flame flickering? His heart beat more quickly and he stood perfectly still.

There, just barely perceivable, a draught brushed his face, smelling of earth and damp.

It was only as he walked to the back of the recess that he saw it. On the left side, hidden from the doorway by the bookcase's shadow, a narrow corridor ran off at a sharp angle. The lamp illuminated a few feet along it before the interior wall jutted into the space and the passage twisted to follow.

He tapped his fingers along his cane in an excited tattoo. "Once more into the breach!"

CHAPTER 27

At first Alfie tried to keep track of where in the house the passage led, but traversing within Balcarres' walls was even more confusing than within its halls. He thought it led him upwards at one point, and he stumbled over shadows only to have them turn out to be several uneven steps.

He stopped a moment to catch his breath as his heart raced, something like panic beginning to crawl at the edges of his mind. If he dropped the lamp, how long would it take him to find his way back? He shuddered at the idea of crawling in the dark, blindly feeling his way along the rough stone of the passage that seemed narrower and narrower with every step, a rodent's tunnel carved into the walls of the house.

If he couldn't find his way out, would anyone hear his calls for help? Or would he vanish like Mr. Bisset? His hand shook, causing the flame to dip and quiver. He imagined turning a corner and running into the minister, half-mad with cold and fear, eyes blinded by the sudden light, his mouth opening and closing with horrific clicks, voice gone from screaming.

"Stop it, stop it, stop it!" Alfie's voice echoed off the stone. "There's *nothing* here. You are *not* afraid. There's no possible reason the minister would have gone all the way through the house, into a locked room, discovered a secret passage, and gotten lost. In the dark. On his own. There's no one else here."

He checked the level of oil in the lamp, blinking blue spots from his eyes.

"You have plenty of oil, and even *if* the lamp does go out, you just turn right around and go back the way you came. It's a labyrinth, not a maze. One way in, one way out."

Feeling slightly better, he took a moment to get his bearings. It felt like he'd been walking forever, but Balcarres was only so big, he couldn't have actually gone that far. The dips and turns had probably been to avoid where the walls narrowed enough for windows, but the passage had been deliberately built, meaning that it had to lead somewhere. And since it started from the earl's room, it probably went somewhere important. Perhaps a secret escape in the event of attack, or if Alfie was lucky, a room filled with treasure.

He then remembered the painted vase of yellow flowers and felt uneasy. The earl had those painted deliberately. Whatever secrets lay at the end of the passage might be better left undiscovered.

He put a hand on the wall to steady himself. There was a hollow there, like one of the rocks that made up the wall had fallen out, but there was no trace of it on the floor. He'd noticed several such hollows along the passage, becoming more frequent as he went on. He raised the lamp, and saw something even more worrying. Long white lines marred the walls on either side of the tunnel. Something had scratched and scraped its way through the passage, and it had done so more than once.

From ghoulies and ghosties and long-legged beasties and things that go bump in the night...

He shivered and placed a hand against one of the scratches. Surely the marks were too uneven to be the claws of some great beast?

He frowned and touched the wall again. Was it a trick of the mind, or did the wall feel warmer there? He closed his eyes and tried to envision the layout of Balcarres. He had to be in the inhabited part of the house by now, and he'd been going upwards... He opened his eyes with a surprised blink. He must be by Dominick's and his rooms.

He took a few more steps, and his suspicion was confirmed; the corridor dipped down, then rose back up before turning a right angle, just as it would to avoid the window in Dominick's room, then veering to follow the adjacent wall. He accidentally kicked a small stone, sending it skittering forward. It clicked and clattered as it went, the noise echoing in the confined space before it dropped into the dark, bouncing rhythmically down another steep stairwell.

Alfie thought of Dominick's ghost, heard only in his room but never in Alfie's. Had this been the source? No ghostly entity at all but merely mice or rats running through the hidden passage behind his bed? If Alfie's room lay past where the stairs descended, it would explain why they hadn't heard the sounds there. The rats would have been scurrying around Dominick's room on two sides but been forced to follow the stairs down before they reached Alfie's.

Unless it was something bigger than rats.

He shook the thought from his head. He'd already set aside childish ideas about monsters. He wouldn't return to them now.

Not monsters, not ghosts. Someone living, walking the same corridor. A watcher in the walls.

Alfie adjusted his grip so his thumb rested right over the latch on his cane. If someone walking through the walls could be heard from Dominick's room, was the reverse true? Could they hear what happened in Dominick's room as well?

Well, if they had, then so be it. Alfie had been blackmailed before, and he would not allow himself to be blackmailed again. If anyone had been sneaking around and heard something they shouldn't, he'd deal with it if they tried to come after him. And if they tried to come after Dominick instead, God help them.

The heat of his anger propelled him down the staircase. He swiftly descended one floor, then another, then further still. The walls began to glisten with damp in the lamplight, and the air took on the musty odor of wet earth with something foul around the edges, mold perhaps. Or rot.

When the stairs ended, he raised the lamp high, expecting more of the same narrow passage, but it seemed he'd reached his destination. The steps opened onto a large storeroom or perhaps some sort of underground stable. The main body of the room was empty, but there were six arched alcoves, three along either side of the length of the room.

He took a cautious step forward. Unlike the relatively even footing thus far, here the floor was jagged and deeply pitted. It looked as if many of the stones had been pulled out like rotten teeth, leaving only deep cavities behind.

And it was easy to see where they had gone.

Of the six alcoves, the three along the right-hand wall were empty, their hollow depths going back only a few feet, bare of anything except for a few broken stones where they too had been pried apart. The one furthest along on the left was the same.

But the two closest alcoves were walled up.

The one in the middle was only partially done, the stones stacked to the level of his waist but no higher. Beside the opening was a small pile of rocks, some still damp with clinging dirt, that sat ready to complete the task. As if whoever was building the wall had pulled up what stones they could, and even ventured back to remove more from the passage itself to ensure they had enough ready to complete their work when the time came.

From the look of the pile however, there still weren't enough rocks to finish the wall. Yet enough had already been put in place that from where he stood, he couldn't see what—if anything—lay behind it.

The alcove closest to him was different. The wall there reached to the ceiling, but rather than just being stacked, its stones appeared to have been mortared together. It must have been solid when it was built, but at the base of it was a line of light powder where the mortar had flaked off with time and fallen.

Even more noticeable was the hole that gaped in the middle. It yawned, an open mouth drawing Alfie in. Had the person building the second wall cannibalised the first one for parts, giving up after finding the stones too well-mortared? Or had they simply wanted to know what lay behind it?

The same curiosity ran through Alfie, pounding in his veins with every beat of his heart. He stepped closer, compelled by the beckoning mystery. He leaned his cane against the wall so he could brace himself with his free hand. The remaining mortar stuck to his palm in a grey grit. The foul smell was thicker here, clinging as if it had been absorbed into the very stones themselves. He raised the lamp and maneuvered it into the hole so its light would illuminate the walled-in space. He had an image of the wall suddenly biting down, his arm trapped in its stony teeth as it claimed its prey.

He shook his head to clear the terror that spiked through him, and in defiance of his own fear, thrust his head through the opening to see what lay inside. It took his eyes a moment to adjust, but when they did he gasped at the terrible sight.

The soft yellow glow filled the small room, shifting as his hand shook in horror and dancing in the empty eye sockets of the skeleton within.

Alfie reeled back, nearly losing his footing on the uneven stones. He took several deep breaths as the room spun. His first thought was that he had found Mr. Bisset and discovered his terrible fate. But that was impossible. The minister had been missing less than a day. Even if he was dead, his body wouldn't have decayed so much in so short a time. No, that body must have been lying there for years. Long enough to have withered to nothing more than bones, and for the mortar in the wall to crack and crumble.

Oh no. A terrible suspicion tugged at Alfie's heart.

Taking a deep breath, he peered back into the opening.

The body was curled up facing him, its knees tucked into its chest like a child and its skeletal hands curled against its mouth. Its clothes were in tatters, mouldered away to rags in the damp and dark.

He shifted the lamp, trying to see if there was anything hidden in the corners of the room that gave a hint as to the body's identity. There was nothing he could see, but the walls themselves were covered in long straight lines. His stomach roiled when he realised what they were.

Fingernail marks.

Whoever this man was, he hadn't just been killed and had his body hidden, he'd been entombed alive.

Alfie imagined his terrible final days. He must have screamed. This far down, had no one heard his cries for help, or had they simply been ignored? Aware of his fate, he'd clawed and scratched at the stone with his bare hands for any way out. In his desperation, he must have worn his fingers to the bone to leave such visible gouges not just in one place, but all over the room, anywhere he could reach. The marks closer to the floor were lighter, shallower. How long had it taken him to lose his strength, to succumb to suffocation or starvation?

Alfie's heart ached for the man, dying in such a terrible way in such a forgotten place. He shuddered. As he was about to pull away from the awful scene, the lamplight caught on something glinting between the skeleton's fingers.

"Sorry, I'll try to be gentle," Alfie murmured as he grabbed his cane.

He aimed it as carefully as he could, but it was hard

to hold both the cane and lamp in the small space. He murmured further apologies as more than one of the skeleton's fingers broke under his prodding, falling to the side. The way the body was curled around it, it was almost as if the man had died with the object to his lips, kissing it. Alfie hoped it had brought him some measure of comfort.

"I'm so sorry," he said again as he was finally able to free the object and, with a few careful taps of his cane, maneuver it into the lamplight.

It was a small painting, its colours shockingly bright in the darkness. No bigger than a man's palm, its oval frame glinted gold in the light, perfectly matching the beauty of the man whose portrait it held. His painted hair shone the same rich gold and his mouth was set in a soft smile beneath sparkling eyes. Alfie had only ever seen that mouth set in a sneer before, but he would know those piercing blue eyes anywhere. They belonged to the Wicked Master, Malcolm Pennington. And if the painting was of him, that meant this was the portrait he had given to his lover. His lover who had mysteriously gone missing, presumed murdered.

"Hello, Samuel," Alfie whispered.

"I didn't kill that one," said a voice behind him.

Then everything went dark.

CHAPTER 28

Dominick scrabbled at his boot one more time before giving up with a curse. His reddened hands were too numb to get any purchase on the muddy leather, sliding right off no matter how he tugged. Trying to toe the boots off did nothing more than scuff the leather.

From his perch on the edge of his bed, he leaned back on his hands in defeat. He wanted nothing more than to fall back onto the mattress and wrap himself in the quilt, but his clothing was in as bad a shape as his boots and he hadn't been able to manage so much as the buttons on his overcoat. The idea of giving in now only to have to face sodden bedsheets again in a few hours time held no appeal.

He groaned in defeat. He'd lost track of the hours they spent searching in the freezing storm, but he'd rather go a round in the ring with Bill "The Bodysnatcher" Nunn than spend another minute out there. Christ, it was miserable.

"Gone soft already," he huffed.

Thinking of the old, bad days, he took a moment to count his blessings, and thank God for his main one, who had come back into his life and filled it with warmth.

Speaking of the little sod, where was Alfie anyway? He'd promised to be awaiting Dominick's return with a hot bath and had so far failed on both fronts. Every muscle protested as he shook the frost from his limbs and jerkily shambled to his feet. He made his way creakingly over the passage between their rooms and entered without so much as a knock.

"Alfie, I need your help undressing. I'd threaten to ring for Jarrett but he looked even more frozen than myself. A good man would've offered to let him keep the first round of hot water, but you know I'm not…"

He trailed off. The fire was lit in the hearth, but neither Alfie nor the washtub was anywhere to be seen. He cursed under his breath. First he'd spent all day with Charleton of all people, turning over every rock in Scotland looking for that blasted minister with nothing to show for it, and now when he'd been promised a warm bath and a hero's welcome, neither tub nor welcoming committee was anywhere to be found.

Honestly, he should've known better. He'd spent most of his childhood telling Alfie to stay put, then hunting him down when he inevitably didn't and got himself into trouble. Why should it be any different now? All that changed when Alfie had grown was that his trouble had grown with him.

A flicker of unease tensed Dominick's spine. A missing minister and a murdered butler? That was just the sort of overgrown trouble that Alfie would get himself mixed up in when left unattended.

But how? They'd searched the house thoroughly last night. If there was any trouble to be found within its walls, surely it would've been discovered then. And besides, ignoring Carnbee's ridiculous ideas about a band of roving murderer-thieves, all of the suspects had been outside today. It would've taken a person of considerable strength to strangle Mr. Gibson barehanded, and if the minister hadn't wandered off on his own accord but been snatched, his attacker would've had to overpower him as well. But everyone capable of that had been outside and under the watchful eye of their search partner. Alfie had been alone all day with just the women. He couldn't have been safer.

Unless... They'd been assuming a single culprit was responsible. If it was a team, then one of the searching pairs could have come back to the house while the rest of the men were out. A single man sneaking away would've been noticed by his partner, but if they were both in on it?

Dominick caught himself against a bed post as sudden worry turned his knees to jelly.

It was possible. But which two? He'd been paired with Charleton and hadn't taken his eyes off him. At least, not until the third time he'd slid on wet stone from not paying enough attention to his surroundings. The damned man had actually grabbed Dominick's arm to keep him from cracking his skull open. He'd relaxed his scrutiny somewhat after that, but had still been barely a dozen paces from him all day.

It had to be one of the other two groups then, Carnbee and Mr. Howe, or Jarrett and Graham. Neither pair seemed particularly likely.

Though Mr. Howe *had* advanced in his position after Mr. Gibson's murder, Dominick couldn't see Carnbee being able to bluff at whist, never mind conceal his involvement in a murder or kidnapping. That left Jarrett and Graham, but if Dominick had a thousand years he couldn't imagine a more unlikely murderous duo than the flirtatious footman and the dour stablemaster. He supposed anything was possible, and Jarrett's motives could be the same as Mr. Howe's—advancement. But if the lusty idiot was capable of thinking with anything other than his cock, Dominick hadn't seen any sign of it. Graham was more of an unknown, but the man seemed to want nothing more than to be left alone with his horses. Besides, there was no way a man of his goliath proportions could have snuck through the halls of Balcarres unnoticed.

Still, his conscience couldn't let him completely rule out either group.

Christ. He was missing something.

It nagged at him, a loose tooth that he just couldn't get out no matter how much he worried at it. If only Alfie was around... But if Alfie was around, Dominick wouldn't be concerned in the first place.

He checked the room once more for any sign of his whereabouts. There was nothing. His cane was gone, so wherever he was, it wasn't just a quick trip. But Dominick had no way of telling if Alfie had even been back to his room since their farewell that morning. Another search of his own room provided no further clues either. Knocking items off his dresser in hopes of finding some note of explanation, he tried to tamp down his growing anxiety. Perhaps Alfie was just in the library, so lost in a book he hadn't noticed the rest of the men return.

Dominick had a hand on the door, intent on hunting down his wayward earl, when there was a knock on the other side. He wrenched it open and nearly crashed into Janie, who was leaning against the door jamb, some sort of *contraption* over her shoulders. He'd seen similar things before in Spitalfields, but usually carried by men larger than he was, not girls half his size.

"Oh Mr. Trent! You gave me a start! Mrs. Finley said you'd be waiting, but I didn't expect you to be right at the door!"

Over her shoulders was spread a large wooden beam, carved into a heavy bow, like the sort of yoke used to tether horses to a particularly heavy cart, or oxen to plough. This yoke didn't appear to be much smaller, despite the fact she was hardly bigger than a mayfly. But rather than dragging a plough down the hall behind her, she had a large bucket tied to either end of the yoke. As Dominick watched in astonishment, she executed a brief curtsey, a single drop of water spilling from one of the buckets to dampen the floor.

He stood still, struck dumb in surprise. After a moment, she shifted her weight nervously, the whole contraption swaying with her.

"If you'll beg my pardon, sir. The water won't stay warm for too much longer, and His Lordship was most insistent earlier that you have a hot bath ready and waiting when you got back."

"O-of course," Dominick stepped back to let her into the room. She turned sideways so the yoke would clear the door and scuttled through like a crab. She reminded him of some of the overly fashionable ladies he'd seen, whose bonnets were too large to allow them to enter or exit a carriage without assistance.

He reached out to offer a belated hand, but she was already halfway across the room, setting the buckets down by the fireplace with more grace than he would have suspected.

"Ach," she clicked her tongue. "I suppose it was too

much to ask that Moira had already brought up the tub. Give me just a minute, sir, to fetch it. Or I can send Jarrett if you need assistance?"

"No! I mean, no thank you, Janie." Dominick thought about the tub, an enormous thing like a barrel, made of oak and banded with iron. He looked at the buckets brimming with steaming water. Each had to weigh forty pounds on its own, without even considering the yoke.

That nagging worry wiggled a little more. "You didn't carry that all the way up from the kitchens on your own, did you?"

"Oh aye, sir. Of course. It's a bit of a struggle on the stairs not to tip, but better balanced than you'd think. And saves half the number of trips that carrying them up one at a time would take."

"But it must be incredibly heavy."

She shrugged, her slight shoulders barely the width of Dominick's spread hand. "I suppose. Been carrying water for this or that since I was a bairn. I guess it's no harder than bringing up wood for the fire, or some of those big trays for supper."

Cold washed over Dominick as certainly as if he'd still been out in the storm.

Oh Christ! Oh Christ! They'd been idiots.

He had only himself to blame. He'd been so concerned with never fitting into Alfie's world of fancy toffs that he hadn't realised he'd already started thinking like them. He'd seen the strength it took to kill Mr. Gibson and hadn't considered for a moment that a woman could have done it. He'd thought only of the society ladies who did nothing but pay calls all day, and mistaken the servant women's quiet for meekness.

How quickly he'd forgotten Mrs. Hirkins, who ruled Alfie's townhouse with an iron fist. Or Jimmy's wife, Maeve, who faced down any drunk who caused commotion in her pub with a sharp word and a sharper right hook. Or the lifetime of women he'd known in Spitalfields—flower sellers, costers, other prostitutes. Each and every one of them working all the hours of the day just to get by. And even the society women, didn't they dance all night then get up at dawn to start beautifying themselves for another day, long before the men in their lives stirred from slumber? What kind of fortitude must that take, year in and year out?

And Dominick had dismissed all of this. He'd left Alfie behind, thinking he would be safe with the "weaker" sex, but in truth he'd been in absolute peril. And now he was missing.

His heart tripped in his chest as he looked down at Janie. Could she be the killer? It didn't seem possible, but he no longer trusted his own judgment. He licked his dry lips.

"Janie, do you know where Lord Crawford is?"

"Not for certain, sir. I haven't seen him since this morning. He asked me to bring him a cup of tea to the gallery and we had a bit of a chat." She pushed a stray curl back into her cap nervously.

Ah, *that* conversation.

"I told him a bit about a painting, and he came over all queer and rushed off. And that's the last I seen him."

Dominick frowned. "What painting?"

"Well, it was the one of the Wicked Master as I was talking about, but he gets excited about the one next to it and asks if I ken the room it's painted in. The father's picture I think that is. So I tell him and off he goes."

"And what room *is* it?"

Janie blinked up at him. "Why, the earl's room, of course."

Dominick tore down the halls, his boots echoing thunderously against the stone. Alfie must have seen something in the painting they missed before and gone exploring without waiting for Dominick to return.

That little fool. If he's gotten himself murdered, I'm going to kill him.

The thought sent Dominick stumbling. Surely not. Alfie was fine, he had to be. Janie said he'd gone to the earl's chambers. There was nothing in that part of the house but dust and cobwebs.

Unless he discovered something only the murderer knows about. Perhaps Alfie stumbled across hi-her at her work. Had he uncovered the murderer's lair? Or had he gone running into a trap?

That was a thought. Why should Dominick believe Janie's story? If she was the one behind it all, he could be headed straight for the same trap she'd set for Alfie.

He shook his head. He couldn't think straight. He'd never been able to when Alfie was in danger—always rushing in, fists raised, hoping for the best. But that wouldn't help him now. He didn't know what he should do. The world was topsy turvy, and with Alfie missing he didn't have anyone he could trust to help him sort it out.

Well.

There was one person. The only person he knew for certain couldn't be involved. *Trust* was too strong a word, but at this point Dominick would take what he could get.

Moments later he found himself pounding frantically on a different bedroom door. Gil Charleton emerged, still in his sodden clothes, smiling and wiping his spectacles on a bit of dry silk.

He didn't school his face quickly enough to hide his disappointment at seeing Dominick at his door, but Dominick didn't have time to figure out who he'd been expecting instead.

"Mr. Trent. To what do I-"

"Alfie's missing. I need your help."

Charleton nodded once, the smile dropping from his face as he straightened his shoulders. He righted his spectacles on his nose with the precise movements of a knight stepping upon the field of battle, or a fighter at the first bell.

"Lead on."

CHAPTER 29

Alfie awoke in darkness.

He blinked his eyes to clear them, but the darkness remained absolute. The last thing he remembered was being knocked on the head from behind. Had the blow damaged his vision? Frantic, he tried to sit up, only to collapse back down when the movement sent his head aching and the world tilting out from underneath him.

His groan of pain was muffled by a gag tied around his head. He worked his jaw, attempting to dislodge it, but no luck. Behind the cloth his breaths came faster, thick dust scratching his throat and choking him. He twisted, trying to reach up and tear the gag away, but his hands were bound behind his back. Terror set in and he kicked out, only to find his feet tied as well. His heart beat in his ears as he lashed and flailed like a landed fish, mindless in his panic.

Stay calm! A voice in his head that sounded like Dominick yelled. *You can still breathe. Deep breaths, in and out. Slowly. There you go.*

Through a great force of will Alfie made himself lie still and focus on his breathing, inhaling through his nose then letting it out slowly through his mouth. The dust still stung his nostrils and the material of the gag turned damp with every breath, but slowly he calmed enough that his terrified confusion subsided and he was able to take in his surroundings.

His thrashing had not been entirely in vain. Now rolled onto his back, his tied hands pressed painfully between his spine and the stone floor, but he was able to see that his darkness was not absolute. The wall to his left didn't quite reach the ceiling, and over the top of it came the weak yellow glow of lamplight. He blinked again and lay still, letting his eyes adjust. The gap above the wall looked vaulted.

Oh God. I'm in one of the alcoves!

The horror of his situation froze him, stopping even his noisy breaths, and that was when he heard it, a low scraping noise in the distance. He strained to listen, helpless to do otherwise as all sorts of spectres flashed through his mind; giant rats with steel claws, highwaymen hiding in the walls, Samuel's ghost with a skeletal grin, Doctor Barlowe surrounded in flame and laughing.

The scraping grew louder. It was coming closer.

His terror returned in full force. He jerked and twisted in his bonds, feeling blood well up at his wrists as he tore the skin trying to break free. The scraping sound grew ever louder, ever closer.

His eyes locked on the narrow opening above the wall. Somewhere on the other side, something was coming for him. The light coming through the gap flickered as a shadow passed in front of it. He wriggled backwards, trying to get as far away from the *thing* as he could, until he hit something solid. He stretched his fingers back, expecting cold stone, but instead met with something soft. He frowned and moved his hand. Definitely fabric, but something else as well, something soft and cool.

He rolled over and came face-to-face with Mr. Bisset. His open eyes stared blankly back.

Behind the gag, Alfie cried out in shock.

He scrambled away from the body, pulling himself upright with the strength of pure fear, until his back pressed against the stacked wall. Whatever imagined horror was on the other side of it could be no worse than the terror that lay before him.

Even in the dim light, it was clear the minister was dead. His eyes bulged out of their sockets and his tongue protruded from his mouth, swollen and black. Alfie shuddered as he realised the cool surface he'd felt had been the corpse's skin. The minister's head was arched back and beneath his beard—the red of it garish against his waxy flesh—Alfie could see the ring of dark bruises around his neck.

Behind him, the scraping noises stopped.

"Milord?" a soft voice floated over the wall, barely carrying through the darkness.

Alfie shook his head, setting off another round of nausea. It took him a minute to place the voice.

"Moira! Run, fetch help!" he tried to shout, but the gag reduced it all to unintelligible moaning.

"Oh sir, forgive me! I didn't think you'd wake up."

The scraping came again, and Alfie looked up in time to see another stone slotted into the gap in the wall. The light above him dimmed.

He struggled frantically, clawing at the bindings around his wrists with fingers numb from cold and slick with his own blood. He kicked out with his bound feet, the wild motion doing nothing but causing him to topple over. His shoulder hit the floor and he let out another cry, desperately trying to keep from rolling into the minister's body in his struggles.

Moira's repeated apologies were muffled now, coming through only the small hole that remained in the wall. The scraping noise was back as well. It was the sound, he realised with horror, of Moira pulling the blocks of stone from the very walls and floor of the tunnel with her bare hands and dragging them into place, leaning the loosened rocks against the walls as she walked to help bear the heavy load, leaving long scratches in her wake.

Between his own harsh panting and the stone swallowing up her voice, he could hear little of what she said, but with each word his dread increased.

"...am sorry. You don't seem like *them* but it's too late... I hoped you'd just stay asleep..."

Alfie tried to shout around the gag, to tell her she didn't have to do this, then another stone slotted into place.

Only the smallest hole still remained, barely a trickle of light coming through. Moira's voice faded as she moved away, then came the chilling scraping of her working another rock from the tunnel walls.

One last block to seal his fate.

He begged, but his words were trapped in the cloth. Hot tears blurred his eyes and dripped down onto the stone beneath his cheek.

Please, not like this. Not trapped in the dark with only a corpse to keep him company.

Two corpses, he thought, remembering the skeleton in the alcove next to the one he would share forever with

Mr. Bisset. *Poor Samuel.* This is what had happened to him then. Walled up alive by the evil earl, left to starve or suffocate in the blackness. How much he had suffered? How much Alfie would suffer, sharing his fate?

Samuel, Mr. Bisset, and now him. All the missing men of Balcarres House tucked away in the same hiding spot. At least Moira had been kind enough to strangle the minister first. He and Samuel hadn't been so lucky. Would Dominick search as Malcolm once did, looking for some sign of what had happened to his love, but finding only the unbearable silence of being alone?

He sniffled, his vision blurring with dust and tears, but unwilling to close his eyes against the last light he would ever see. He drew up memories of Dominick's face. His smile lit with a warmth that Alfie would never feel again, never hear his laugh in the unending quiet of this tomb. Even in death, Samuel's body was curled around Malcolm's portrait. His final thoughts must have been the same, the hope of one last farewell with the man he loved.

For a moment, the air seemed to warm, and Alfie thought he caught the smell of fresh hay and summer flowers. An image of Malcolm's diary came into his mind, the words so vivid it was as if the book was before him.

As I hovered near death, I could have sworn I heard my Samuel crying and calling out to me. It was for his voice alone that I returned to the land of the living.

Oh God. Malcolm had heard him. He'd been feverish, too weak to help or even know the voice was real, but Samuel had called out, and Malcolm had *heard* him.

He felt a fresh wave of sympathy for the doomed lovers, torn apart by another man's cruelty. Did Malcolm find out the truth when he confronted his father or had the earl kept it from him? Doubtless the earl picked the option he thought would cause the most misery. If Alfie died down here before Dominick found him, he hoped his love never knew how close he'd been the whole time.

The warm air came again, fresh as a summer's breeze, and cleared the haze of fear and sorrow.

Wait. If Malcolm had heard Samuel while recovering in his room, then Dominick might be able to hear him! Dominick's room was directly atop the accursed tunnel, if Alfie could only get this damned gag out of his mouth, surely *someone* would hear him. Although whether they arrived in time...

The scraping of the final stone echoed loudly. Moira must have returned to the chamber.

He gave one last pull on his bonds, but there was no breaking them. Frantic, he rubbed his face against the floor, hoping for friction, a rough patch, anything that would help. He cried out as the edge of one of the rocks cut into his cheek.

There. Again, do that again.

He wriggled and this time when he moved his head, the fabric of the gag caught, not enough to tear, but enough to feel a little looser. Hot blood welled up as he scraped his face against the floor, but the fabric gave more with every pass. His jaw banged against the stone as he tried to work the gag free.

The scraping sound stopped. He envisioned Moira lifting the rock in her arms, raising it above her head. He gave his head a rough shake, and the gag went limp. He spit it out.

"I really am sorry, milord."

Alfie turned as Moira slotted the last stone into place. As he sunk into darkness, he screamed.

CHAPTER 30

Seeing the bookshelf in the earl's room flung open, Dominick barely waited for Charleton to return with a pair of lanterns before diving into the darkness.

He wasn't sure how much of his story Charleton even believed, but it didn't matter. The man was here now, following him into the bowels of the damned house to find Alfie. If they came out of this, Dominick might have to rethink his opinion of him.

"For God's sake, Trent. Slow down!"

A hand grabbed at Dominick's sleeve, pulling him back. He barely contained a snarl.

Charleton let go of his arm and raised both hands, one open, the other carrying the lantern. Its light lit up the mollifying look on his face.

"Easy," he continued. "I just wanted to say you won't do Alfie any good if you lose your footing in the dark and break your neck. Who knows when these passages were built or what kind of condition they're in. If he's gotten lost or hurt, he may need our help getting back, and by God, there's no way I could drag you both out!"

Dominick bristled at his tone, but what Charleton said made sense. What mattered was getting Alfie out, and getting him out safely. If that meant a little more time spent on caution, then so be it.

He took a deep breath, and turned around, picking his steps slowly through the worn and broken stones. Just then, a piercing scream rushed up out of the blackness of the tunnel. It echoed off the walls, an awful, ghostly wail of fear and torment. Even through the animalistic terror the cry awoke in him, Dominick knew that voice.

Alfie.

The scream stopped suddenly. No, not stopped. Dominick could still hear it, reverberating through the stones in a horrible wail, as if Balcarres itself was weeping. But now he couldn't tell exactly where it was coming from. Sometimes in front of him, sometimes behind, for a moment it seemed to come from the very wall beneath his hand.

No. The scream—*Alfie*—had been in front of him, somewhere in the pitch blackness of the tunnel. Dominick took off again, barely hearing Charleton's curse behind him. He sprinted down the passage, clattering up and down stairs, rebounding off the walls when a turn was too sharp for him to stop, the light from his lantern illuminating only seconds ahead of his mad flight. The cries seemed softer already, more irregular.

Up ahead, he swore he could see the faintest glow peeking around a turn in the passage. He put on another burst of speed and rounded the corner, colliding with the person on either side. Before he could see who it was, both their lights went flying, crashing onto the stones and shattering, plunging them both into darkness. The figure let out a cry and scrabbled back, but the voice wasn't Alfie's.

If it's not Alfie, then it's the person who made him scream.

That thought was all it took for Dominick to stumble

to his feet, blindly staggering ahead with one hand on the wall, the other reaching forward to grasp his prey. Several times his fingertips brushed fabric, but his quarry knew these passages far better, and pulled out of reach each time.

The wall under his hand abruptly vanished and he faltered, taking one last leap forward as he lost his footing. Whether it was skill or sheer luck he didn't care, but he hit someone as he went down and dragged them down with him.

The figure cried out again and struck him. The blow came from an object, perhaps a stick or a poker, but Dominick's attacker was just as blind as he was, and the blows were glancing at best. He finally managed to grab the object and pull it from their grasp. The moment he felt its weight in his hand he knew what it was. Alfie's sword cane, its blade still sheathed.

The realisation only froze him for a moment, but that was all the time his assailant needed. Cold hands gripped his throat, crushing down and cutting off his air.

He fell back, dropping the cane as he tried to pry the hands off, but it was no use. They wrapped tighter and tighter around his neck. He kicked and clawed for air, bubbles of light bursting at the edges of his sight.

Then the light was real. Charleton rushed into the room, lantern in hand. Dominick had just enough time to see Moira's eyes widen in shock as Charleton yanked her off him.

Dominick collapsed onto his side, gasping.

Moira?

He'd known there was a chance it could be a woman, but he'd expected the wiry strength of Mrs. Buie, built from a lifetime of toiling in the kitchen, not her mousey slip of a daughter.

Coughing, he looked over. Charleton held her from behind, one arm wrapped around her throat while the other, still holding the lantern, clamped onto her waist. She struggled weakly in his grasp, shaking and crying too much to put up a fight. The lantern light reflected off Charleton's spectacles, making his eyes glow like the pits of hell, and Dominick remembered the terrible things that had been done to her sister. Dominick was hunting more than one monster tonight.

"Let her go," he said hoarsely, picking up Alfie's cane and using it to push himself to his feet.

"You can't be serious! She just tried to strangle you!"

Dominick flicked the hidden switch on the side of the cane and drew out the blade. Charleton and Moira let out matching gasps.

"I said, 'Let her go.' "

Charleton did, and Moira dropped to the ground at his feet, sobbing. She might have tried to kill him, but Dominick wouldn't let the rogue harm her. Still, he kept the sword pointed at them both. He had questions for her that needed answering too. He hoped they couldn't see how he swayed slightly as he tried to blink the greying edges from his eyes.

He made his voice as soft as he could, "Moira, is he the man who hurt your sister? I swear, if Charleton abused her, or you, or anyone else in the past, I'll make sure he faces justice. Just tell me where Alfie is."

"I would never!" Charleton cried out indignantly. The rest of his protest was cut off when Dominick raised the sword higher.

"It wasn't him," Moira sniffed, wiping her face with her tattered apron. The entire bottom half seemed to have been torn completely off. In her flight from Dominick perhaps? But he didn't see the scrap of fabric anywhere.

"Mr. Charleton never hurt a soul. And the ones that need justice already faced it. I saw to that." There was pride in her voice.

Slowly, the pieces began to fall into place, but Dominick couldn't believe it, *wouldn't* believe it, until he heard it from Moira herself.

"The butler, Mr. Gibson. He was the one who..."

"Who raped Lily, aye. All charming he came over, at first. He was a handsome man when he smiled. Promised her he'd get her better pay and a better job when His Lordship arrived, perhaps even a cottage of their own. But once she let him have his way, he turned mean, cruel. Even tried to use me as..."

She buried her face in her apron again. Dominick let the sword dip slightly. He'd had clients like that, especially when he was young. Men who had intentionally hurt him. Who had gotten enjoyment from it and from making threats of worse to come. But even in the worst times, he'd known there was a way out. If he just held on a little longer, he could collect his pennies and escape, and never see the man again. To be in Lily's position, or Moira's, trapped in the same house as the man, forced to see him every day, work with him, defer to his orders? Dominick couldn't even begin to imagine how terrible that had been.

"Then Lily found out she was with child and things got better for a bit," Moira continued. "He stopped looking at anyone else, and was sweet to her, saying he'd marry her, have the banns read just that week so they could be wed before the baby came.

"The Sunday service came and she was so excited, but nothing happened. She stayed after to speak with the minister. That night, crying fit to burst, she told me what he said. Mr. Bisset had called her all sorts of names— whore, jezebel, and worse. He said she was a sinner and a temptress and it was all her fault. He said there'd never be any banns read in his kirk for a woman who defiled herself in such a way, and if she was still corrupting the village with her filth by next Sunday, he would tell everyone just what she was."

Moira spat on the floor. " *'Her filth,'* he said. When he was just as bad as Mr. Gibson. Worse. Look in the village. How many bairns are there with hollow-eyed mothers and red hair that don't match their father's? Even put up one of his by-blows in the house here, as an 'orphan'. Poor thing. I doubt she even knows."

"She doesn't," said Charleton softly. "Janie believes her father was a sailor. There's quite a lot of red-haired sailors' children in the parish."

He glanced at Dominick and shrugged. "It's an open secret, but what can we do?"

"We can punish them." Moira's voice, usually so timid, was fierce with rage.

"Moira," Dominick licked his lips, afraid to ask. "Where's Alfie?"

Moira continued on as if he hadn't spoken, lost in her own story. "My sister ran. She couldn't bear the things Mr. Bisset said about her. She begged Mr. Gibson to go with her, but he laughed, said she needed to solve her own problems. My ma and I gave her all the coin we had. She made it to Edinburgh, but she was so lonely there. She thought, if she didn't have the child, she could come home. She wrote us she'd found someone who could make it go away.

"That was her last letter. She was found bled to death in one of the mews. No one cared. No one was punished. So I decided, if no one else would do it, I would."

"You strangled Mr. Gibson."

"Aye. I meant to do it before you arrived, but never had the chance. Then when I tried to lure him up closer to the earl's quarters, the old goat grabbed me and pulled me into a room off the library. I didn't think I could do it, but then I thought of Lily…"

She looked down at her hands. The lantern light twisted their shadows into grotesque shapes, but nothing could match the real horrors that had been committed in Balcarres House.

"His Lordship nearly caught me," she whispered. "I went to fetch rope to drag the body away, but he saw me in the halls. I ran back, and locked myself in, afraid of what would happen if he found the body. When I snuck out later and saw him asleep in the library with the door open, I knew I wouldn't be able to hide what I'd done. And after all my planning! All the nights spent piling up stones! I took Mr. Gibson's keys to use later, and left him there to be found."

"And what about Mr. Bisset?" Charleton asked.

Moira shrugged. "He was easier. Followed me right where I wanted him to go. Tongue lolling and panting like a dog."

She sighed, and set her apron back upon her lap. Pressing it down with her hands, her attempts to smooth it back into respectability were in vain.

"I wanted to make it look like they just disappeared. The way everyone said Lily did. The way they said that farmer did, generations ago. But Buies know the truth. It's his ghost, not the Wicked Master's, who haunts Balcarres. My grandfather's grandfather's grandfather heard the screams in the walls when they sealed him in. Seemed a fair fate for a minister and a butler too, to be walled up and forgotten. Only you found the butler too quickly."

Dominick's arm holding the sword began to shake. He hadn't heard any more of the cries since he'd caught Moira.

"*Where's Alfie?*"

Eyes downcast, she raised a hand and pointed at a rough-hewn wall.

"He's with the minister."

CHAPTER 31

Dominick didn't remember dropping the sword. He didn't remember running his hands over the stacked stones or calling out Alfie's name. He remembered only the terrible silence when he got no response. He began scrabbling at the stacked rock, pulling at anything he could grab. Not caring when his palms were cut or his fingernails tore.

"Stop. Stop!"

For the second time, Charleton pulled at his sleeve. This time Dominick didn't even acknowledge him with a snarl, just shook him off and continued his work.

"For God's sake, stop! Do you want to bring this whole thing down on his head?"

Dominick paused. Charleton squeezed his arm once, then dropped it to adjust his spectacles. He peered at the wall, head darting back and forth. Then he pointed.

"That one. Then the two below it. I'll get the big one to the left."

They worked quickly, Dominick removing the stones in the order Charleton pointed out, the two of them lifting each one carefully to prevent the wall from toppling like a house of cards, before tossing them aside and moving on to the next.

When the wall was no more than chest high, Dominick

could wait no longer. He grabbed the lantern and against Charleton's protests, scrambled over, careful to land gently on the other side, lest he step on something precious.

Two bodies lay on the other side of the wall. From the bright red beard, Dominick could clearly make out that the one in the back of the alcove was Mr. Bisset. For a moment he thought the minister was alive, but the flicker in his eyes was only a reflection from the lantern.

The second body lay only inches from Dominick's feet. Eyes closed and hair matted with blood, but Dominick knew that face better than his own.

He dropped to his knees. The air this side of the wall was thick with dust and Alfie was coated in it, a fine powder settled on his clothes and coating his skin.

That's why he looks so pale and grey, Dominick told himself. *No other reason. And he's lying still so he can save his strength. That's why.*

He lay a trembling hand on Alfie's cheek, eyes closing when he felt the coldness of his skin.

"Please, no."

"N-nick?"

It was barely more than a croak, but Dominick's eyes flew open. Alfie's cheek moved beneath his palm as cracked lips tried to form more words. Alfie gasped, then immediately started to cough.

"Hush, don't try to speak. I've got you." Dominick gathered Alfie up in his arms. His face was a mess, the side that had been lying on the floor bloody from hairline to chin. There were flecks of stone and dirt ground in, and a few places still bled sluggishly, but when his lashes fluttered open and those blue eyes looked into his,

Dominick swore he'd never seen a more beautiful sight.

He couldn't help but press a quick kiss against those chapped lips. "You can't scare me like that, love."

"Hurts, Nick. Hands."

Dominick looked down. In his rush to get to Alfie's side, he hadn't noticed the cloth binding his hands. It was tied so tightly his fingers were turning blue and Alfie's cuffs were dark with blood. A quick glance showed his feet tied the same way, the long strips of white fabric that bound him revealing what had happened to the rest of Moira's apron.

Rage rose in him like bile, hot and bitter, but he bit it down. There would be time for that later. Now he had to focus on Alfie.

"All right, let me set you down. Just for a moment, I promise. I'm not going anywhere." He sealed his words with another kiss, cradling Alfie's head gently in his palm as he lowered him back to the floor. He tried to pretend the pained noise Alfie made didn't break his heart.

He approached the bindings at Alfie's feet first, too scared to look at his hands. The knot took a moment to pick apart, having pulled tight in Alfie's struggles. Alfie let out a hiss when it finally fell free, but his boots seemed to have protected him from the worst damage. Dominick moved to examine the ties around his hands, turning Alfie carefully onto his stomach to do so, keeping up a litany of soothing words and endearments. His hands hovered, uncertain. Even if it hadn't been someone he loved, the sight before him would have turned his stomach. The fabric had embedded into the skin, cut deep into his wrists as Alfie tried to free himself, and what flesh wasn't worn raw and bleeding was bruised nearly black.

"Here."

He looked up. Charleton held out Alfie's sword, hilt first. He'd taken down several more layers of stones, lowering the wall to almost hip height. Charleton. If he'd been standing there when Dominick kissed Alfie, had he seen? Had he heard him call Alfie "love"?

Dominick shook his head. Another thing to worry about later, after Alfie was safe.

"Thank you." He took the blade and cut through the bindings. It was difficult to use a large blade on such fine work when the slightest twitch in the wrong direction could cause Alfie even more harm.

Alfie cried out when the ties were finally cut through, then again when Dominick slowly unwrapped them. He gathered Alfie back into his arms, rubbing feeling back into his hands, chapping them between his palms until they finally lost their stiffness and curled around his. Alfie's wrists would need to be seen by a doctor—and quickly—or else infection would set in.

He couldn't help but press a kiss to Alfie's knuckles. Whatever Charleton saw, he saw. What mattered was letting Alfie know he was cared for and safe.

"Knew you'd come for me, Nick," Alfie whispered.

" 'Course I did. Don't I always pull you out of trouble? Mind, I'd prefer you stop finding it so often, and in such damned inconvenient places."

"I have to keep you interested somehow," Alfie smiled, then winced when it pulled at his dry lips.

Dominick let out a laugh that could have been a sob. Any tears that fell on Alfie's shirt were caught in the dust and flaked away. He knew they'd have to move soon, to get Alfie proper care and deal with Moira and Charleton, but Dominick needed just one more minute to hold his Alfie in his arms and convince himself he was safe. From how tightly Alfie's hands gripped his, he needed it too.

It was not to be, however. Charleton jumped over the now much-reduced wall, and put a hand on Dominick's shoulder.

"How can I help? I assume you don't want to let him go?"

Dominick raised an eyebrow. He knew he should wait to confront him until they were somewhere where there wasn't only one lantern and one way out, but he couldn't help himself. "Problem?"

"Ah no, not at all." Charleton dropped his voice to a whisper. "There's more than one way to keep a secret. Some men introduce their male companion as a cousin from Cornwall. Other men find that a man who flirts with all lasses is so easily tarred as a rake that no one notices when he beds none."

He winked and picked up the lantern, rising to his feet. "Let me get on the other side of the wall, and I can support him while you get back over."

The awkward maneuver completed and, after a near-disaster proved Alfie couldn't support himself on his own feet, Dominick hoisted him back into his arms to only mild grumbling. Alfie was heavy, but his weight was a reassurance that he was real, he was safe.

Charleton leaned back over the wall and grabbed Alfie's sword, sheathing it neatly and tucking it under his arm.

"What should we do about that one?" He pointed at

the minister's body. "There's another one in the hidey-hole next to it. Mr. Samuel Whin, I presume."

"We'll come back for them later. Not like they're going anywhere."

Charleton nodded. "And her?"

Moira still sat in the same spot, crumpled in on herself and crying softly.

Dominick was at a loss. The rage was still there, boiling away, but he didn't know how they'd handle getting Alfie to safety while escorting a prisoner with only a single light between the two of them. All she had to do was knock the lantern out of Charleton's hand and run. She knew the passage well and would be long gone by the time they fumbled their way out. And what about Alfie's injuries? A delay like that might kill him.

"Let her go," Alfie croaked.

"No. Absolutely not! She tried to kill you!"

"She didn't. She was scared and trapped and reacted badly."

"She tied you up and left you-"

"But you found me," Alfie breathed, his voice clicking with the strain. "I'm fine."

"She killed two other men!"

"Because they hurt someone she loved," said Charleton. He looked at Dominick significantly, glancing down at Alfie, then back up. "While her anger is understandable, continuing the cycle seems... painful, and I think this house has seen enough pain."

Dominick looked down at Moira, and tried to imagine what she'd felt. Balcarres was gloomy enough already, but to be trapped in it with a predator, to see someone you loved destroyed and feel completely helpless must have been a living nightmare. He'd had similar fears all those years ago in the workhouse, clutching a sleeping Alfie tight and knowing that every night might be the one when something terrible happened. He'd been lucky, she had not.

He thought too about the other miseries the house held. The awful dread in Malcolm's diary. The fears he recorded, the dashed dreams of escape.

The monsters remembered as good men.

Charleton was right. It was long past time to break the cycle. Let Balcarres be a place of mercy for once. Of hope.

"Too many secrets in the walls," Alfie murmured. Dominick couldn't help but agree.

"Go," he said to Moira. She looked up at him with wide eyes red from crying. "You can find your way back without a light, I take it? Then go. It'll be full night by now. The entire household is exhausted and the stables will be unguarded. We'll wait until morning to tell everyone what happened. I won't help you if you're caught, but by the time the hue and cry is raised, you'll have a good head start."

She got unsteadily to her feet. "Thank you."

"I'm not doing it for you."

She nodded, and without another look, dashed off down the corridor into the darkness. Dominick waited for the patter of her footsteps to fade away, then adjusted his grip under Alfie's shoulders and knees.

"I'd best follow you," he nodded at Charleton. "I'll even listen to your advice and go slower this time."

Charleton smiled. Then he picked up the lantern and led them out of the dark.

EPILOGUE

One Month Later

Dominick scowled at his reflection and ripped the cravat from his neck. The damned knot seemed so simple when Mr. Howe tied it the other day, but now Dominick looked less like an elegant gentleman and more like he'd been trying to bandage a neck wound. Sighing at the limp fabric in his hand, he went to fetch another. He was on his third cravat already.

The chiming of the hall clock confirmed what he already knew, he was somewhere between fashionably and unforgivably late and still had his coat and outerwear to deal with. He'd just wanted to be especially presentable for the occasion and impress Alfie with his memory of some of their etiquette lessons that related to fashion.

"Can I help you, sir?"

Oh wonderful. Just what he needed to make his frustration complete. He tossed the fresh cravat at Jarrett with a grimace.

"You might as well try. I doubt you can make more of a mess of it than I did. I was attempting a barrel knot, but a mathematical would also do."

Jarrett fumbled, nearly dropping the cravat entirely, a look of surprise on his face.

That's fair enough, Dominick mused. *I did accuse him of*

trying to slit my throat before. I suppose he didn't expect me to let him make a second attempt.

Jarrett hesitated a moment, clearly thinking the same. "A jest about strangulation would be in poor taste."

"It would," Dominick said, as sternly as possible.

"Apologies, sir."

"It would also be very funny."

Jarrett quirked a small smile, then focused on his work. When he stepped away a few minutes later, Dominick examined his results in the mirror.

"Jarrett?"

"Aye, sir?"

"Not to be unkind, but do you have hands or hooves?"

The wad of laundry somehow affixed to his throat sagged under Jarrett's and his reflected stares. As they watched, it unraveled and fell to the floor. They looked at it in silence.

"Aye, I might," Jarrett admitted. "My mother never actually said my father was a groom, just that he was in the stables. The last house I worked at *was* quite known for its breeding stallions."

Dominick choked. He might not know all the rules of being a gentleman yet, but he was certain that valets, or even footmen for that matter, weren't allowed to make such lewd comments in front of their employer. Of course, they weren't meant to try to get into their employer's trousers either. Just another one of the ways Jarrett didn't act the way a house servant should. Fragments of Jarrett's words and actions over the last weeks came together.

"You weren't a footman before Mr. Gibson hired you, were you?"

Jarrett's eyes went wide, and his shoulders crumpled. "No, sir. Stable lad."

"How on earth did you get the job then?"

"Well, word came up that some new lord was looking to fill a household and needed a footman. I thought he meant the kind that rides on the back of the carriage. Not much chance of advancement where I was, and I thought I might be able to work my way up to driver someday if I took it. So I packed my things and came here. I arrived just a day before you, and Mr. Gibson hired me on the spot. It wasn't until it was too late I realised he meant the other kind of footman. But the pay was twice what I'd been getting, so I kept my mouth shut, didn't I?"

"So, it's just as well I didn't let you shave me."

Jarrett flinched. "Aye, probably. Please don't tell His Lordship, sir. I didn't mean no harm and I'm learning as quick as I can."

Dominick thought about it. His life would certainly be easier if he did. The little bastard might not be a murderer, but he was a liar and a flirt who behaved completely inappropriately and was vastly unsuited for the position in which he now found himself.

And that didn't sound familiar at all.

He sighed. "Fetch another cravat then. Let's see if we can't figure this out together."

❋   ❋   ❋

Dominick rushed out the front door, wildly late now, and crashed into Charleton on the doorstep.

"Sorry, sorry!" he apologised, helping Charleton back to

his feet.

"Quite all right, Mr. Trent. I received the invitation to dinner. I know I'm early..."

"Yes," said Dominick, glancing down the path that led around the side of the house in haste. *Blast.* No Alfie. He must have gone on ahead. "I'm afraid Alfie is busy, but if you want to wait—"

"Oh no, I actually arrived early to speak with you."

Dominick blinked. "Me?"

"Aye, I can see you're in a rush though, is everything all right? Doctor Mills said Alfie would be fine, and when I received the summons I assumed all was well."

"No, no!" Dominick was quick to reassure him. "He's fine. He really is just busy. I'm meant to meet him actually. About a quarter of an hour ago."

"I won't keep you then, we can talk later. I just wanted to let you know I've been thinking about your finances. Alfie mentioned you had no interest in being a landowner —Now don't protest, I mean no insult."

Dominick clicked his teeth shut. The man was right, after all.

"So I was thinking you might be interested in selling the land and reinvesting elsewhere. Lots of interest amongst the beau monde for hunting properties and the like."

"I'm not sure..."

"Of course, of course, don't decide now." Charleton flashed his most charming smile. "I'd have to look more closely at what you have. There's always a market for farmland, especially if you're willing to sell to the families there already. In that case, the price would have to be dropped, of course, but I know a man in Edinburgh who finances a fine goods trade to the Orient. You could fold the profits into that. A bit risky, but it could make very good returns. Think about it, all the wonders of the world brought right to your doorstep!"

Dominick couldn't help but feel overwhelmed. "Thank you, Charleton."

"Gil, please. I think we've been through enough to allow that."

"All right, Gil. Dominick, then. I'd like to hear more about it—in layman's terms—later, but I really am late. We won't be too long. Feel free to wait in the library. Actually…"

Dominick grinned. The idea was too perfect. And really, he did owe Gil for his help and for being such a good friend to Alfie. To them both. Really, it was the least he could do.

"Actually, Gil, do me a favour? I forgot to tell Jarrett that I'll miss my riding lesson this afternoon. Could you tell him? He'll still be in my bedchamber, I think."

Dominick didn't miss the slight flush on Gil's cheeks when he mentioned Jarrett that only deepened when he included the word 'bedchamber'. He added cheekily, "Tell him if he finds someone else to go riding with, Alfie and I are up by the chapel, so he'll have to stargaze elsewhere."

Gil's brow furrowed in confusion. "Stargaze? In the middle of the afternoon?"

✳ ✳ ✳

Alfie heard Dominick chuckling to himself as he made his way into the clearing, his voice quieting as he rounded the back of the chapel. He walked softly over the fallen leaves and stood by Alfie's side.

"You're late," Alfie murmured as he looked down at the fresh mound of dirt behind the chapel. It was marked by a new stone shaped like a broken pillar, a match to the much older monument that stood beside it.

Dominick had told him about Malcolm's grave behind the ruins of the chapel, and after the new minister had finally arrived and said his blessings over Samuel's remains, they could think of no better place for him to rest. They'd made sure the little portrait of Malcolm was buried with him, held in his hands as it had been for so many years. Hopefully the presence of his lover beside him would bring Samuel the peace that the painting never had.

There had been no further vanishing figures or ghostly noises in the night since Moira's disappearance.

"I suppose it was all just her," Dominick said, mirroring Alfie's thoughts.

Alfie shivered as a gust of wind tugged at his scarf. Dominick kept the lantern lit beside his bed now, every night. He blamed it on the December mornings being as black as night, but when Alfie gasped awake in his arms with nightmares of the walls closing in on him, he never awoke in darkness.

"I know it was her you saw in the hall," Dominick continued. "And I suppose so for the rest of it? The noises in the walls, the footsteps, even the wind?" His voice trailed off there, uncertain.

Alfie remembered the diary falling right into his lap, and the smell of hay and summer flowers. He wasn't sure either.

Dominick knelt and pulled a small trowel he'd stolen from the tool shed out of his pocket. He dug a few spadefuls of dirt from Malcolm's grave, the frozen earth ringing against the blade. There wouldn't have been a way to explain doing this at Samuel's burial the day before, but it felt right to do it now, just the two of them.

Alfie pulled the red and blue ribbon from where it was tucked safely inside his glove. The bandages around his wrists had only come off a few days before, but the ribbon was soft as it ran against his raw skin, as comforting as a lover's caress. He passed it carefully to Dominick, making sure the wind didn't carry it away.

Dominick set the ribbon in the hole, weighted it down with a small stone, then folded the earth gently back over the top. Now Samuel lay with Malcolm's gift, and Malcolm lay with his.

By the time they'd emerged from the tunnels, filthy, exhausted, and on the last flickers of lamp oil, Moira was gone. The horse she'd taken was eventually found wandering a few villages over. By the end of the week, the truth about the minister and Mr. Gibson had spread and Mrs. Buie had packed up for parts unknown. Alfie had wanted to slip her a few extra pounds before she left, but Gil convinced him she'd know what the money was for, and there were some things you couldn't buy. She had already lost one daughter. Alfie hoped she knew where to find the other.

He slid his hand into Dominick's as he rose to his feet and dusted off his knees.

"Should we say something?"

Alfie cocked his head to the side. "Religious studies

weren't part of my tutelage. History, politics, literature…"

"I think we've had enough of history. And the dead don't have to worry about politics. What about the last one? There should be something fancy in there."

Alfie cleared his throat.

"But be contented when that fell arrest
Without all bail shall carry me away,
My life hath in this line some interest,
Which for memorial still with thee shall stay.

When thou reviewest this, thou dost review
The very part was consecrate to thee:
The earth can have but earth, which is his due;
My spirit is thine, the better part of me:

So then thou hast but lost the dregs of life,
The prey of worms, my body being dead;
The coward conquest of a wretch's knife,
Too base of thee to be remembered.

The worth of that is that which it contains,
And that is this, and this with thee remains."

The wind rustled through the trees, needles from the pines falling to join their brethren on the ground, while leaves long since fallen from bare branches caught and played around the stone memorials.

"I like that," said Dominick, squeezing Alfie's hand in his. *"And this with thee remains."*

Alfie's heart gave a painful thump in his chest. "We don't have to, you know. Remain here. Not if you don't want to. I know I promised you we'd go on all those adventures. A cold, damp house in Scotland hardly seems like a fair trade."

Dominick laughed, "Alfie love, if you don't consider what this house has already put us through as an adventure, then I worry about your travel plans. Besides, I don't think I'd want to risk crossing the channel in winter. Might as well bunk down here for a bit, until some of us are fully recovered."

"I'll show you fully recovered," Alfie muttered.

"I'll take that as a promise."

Alfie ignored him. "I would like to take the time to learn more about running my estates. I don't want to become like the Wicked Earl, spending my fortune on my own pleasure, while those around me suffer."

"Well, in fairness, you already spent half your fortune on me, and I like to think that I—"

"That you should join me in my lessons with Gil on how to run an estate? What a capital idea, Nick!"

"I suppose you're right, I probably should," Dominick said, a gleam in his eye that Alfie didn't trust. He continued, suspiciously nonchalant. "Do you think he'd make an exchange? I'll let him teach me all about my money and he can have his own riding lessons?"

"I'm sure he can ride quite well already. What makes you think otherwise?"

Dominick shrugged, innocent as sin. "Oh, nothing. Jarrett seems to be quite the clever young man is all. I'm sure there's a thing or two he'd be interested in teaching Gil."

Alfie narrowed his eyes. "You know something."

"I know lots of things," Dominick shrugged again, an enticing little smile tugging at the corner of his mouth.

"For example, I know Janie is attempting to roast a goose for supper, so the sooner you convince Mrs. Hirkins to come up here, the less likely we all are to die of accidental poisoning. I also know that you haven't been exercising your leg nearly as much as Doctor Mills says you should. And... I know there's only enough hot water for one bath before dinner. The last one back to the house will have to use cold."

He let his words hang on the air a moment, then tore off back towards the manor.

Alfie shouted indignantly, then ran after him as quickly as his injured leg would allow. Dominick turned with a laugh. The pale winter light caught on his skin, reflecting like the moon, and Alfie's breath caught. He sent up a prayer in thanks for his bright star, his earthly angel.

"Is that the best you can do?" Dominick taunted.

Alfie grinned and chased his love home.

In the clearing behind them, the sun fell in dappled patches, illuminating two stone markers, side by side at last. The wind came up, scattering yellow blossoms in its wake. It rustled through the forest like soft voices, murmurs of promises kept and whispers of joyful reunions.

The End

AUTHOR'S NOTE

The idea for this book came while researching the first *His Lordship's Mystery* novel and getting hooked on the sensational history of the Crawford earldom. Among other things, the earldom has stories of not only the Wicked Master, but also a bizarre body snatching in the late 1800's, and the tale Gil mentions of an early lord playing cards against the Devil. If you have a free afternoon, I highly recommend reading up on the real stories that inspired this one.

Balcarres House is a real place, and is still owned by the current Earl of Crawford. It isn't open to the public, so I've based the interior layout on what little information I could find and filled in the gaps with images of nearby Charleton House (to which Gil's name is an homage). Please don't drive out to Balcarres expecting a tour, unless you happen to visit during the one day a year when the garden is open for visitors. In which case, send me lots of pictures! The chapel is real, as are the two stones behind it, and the brambles of whin dotting the landscape. There is also a magnificent folly built upon the crag in the 1820's, so I'm absolutely going to have to think of a reason for Alfie to think that a worthwhile investment!

While both the grounds of Balcarres House and the story of the Wicked Master have a basis in fact, I've altered them in this book. On the part of the Balcarres, it was mostly by deciding that a house like that *must* have secret passages, despite not knowing for certain. However, as far as the Wicked Master character, my story as written is a complete work of fiction. While the real history is fascinating, in this book key details including names, crimes, and even the exact time period have been changed and are not intended be taken as fact.

Despite every record I could find calling him all sorts of ghastly things, my favorite being, "He was the irreclaimable enemy of both God and man" I could actually find very little that explained *why* the real Wicked Master was called that, even in court documents of the time. In addition, his father, the earl, was only ever described in the most glowing of terms, which I found suspicious. Two sources I have quoted directly in this book are *The Scottish Journal of Topography, Antiquities, Traditions, Etc, Etc, Etc, Vol I* (Stevenson And Menzies, 1848) and *The Lives of the Lindsays* (Lord Lindsay, 1849). Both give fascinating— although clearly biased—accounts of the story.

It is possible that his father was really just as wonderful as he was described, and the son just as wicked, but the obvious bias in all the documents I found set off alarms for me and led to my retelling of the tale. It is the victors who write the history books after all.

For the rest of the novel, I have tried to be as historically accurate as possible, unless it suited my needs to do otherwise. For example, while most of the book is written in language appropriate to the time period (including some words and phrases that I initially thought far too modern for 1818 but were apparently quite common), I decided that writing Malcolm's diary in actual 1590's vernacular would be too painful for both author and reader. If you compare it to Shakespeare's "Sonnet 74", written about a decade later and quoted at the end of the book, you'll see why!

Finally, I want to close this little history lesson by thanking Margot and Emily, who were again willing to read a rough draft and to Veruska who suggested the tweaks that made this book what it is today.

ABOUT THE AUTHOR

Samantha SoRelle

Sam grew up all over the world and finally settled in Southern California when she soaked up too much sunshine and got too lazy to move.

When she's not writing, she's doing everything possible to keep from writing. This has led to some unusual pastimes including but not limited to: perfecting fake blood recipes, designing her own cross-stitch patterns, and wrapping presents for tigers.

She also enjoys collecting paintings of tall ships and has lost count of the number of succulents she owns.

She can be found online at www.samanthasorelle.com, which has the latest information on upcoming projects, free reads, the mailing list, and all her social media accounts. She can also be contacted by email at samanthasorelle@gmail.com, which she is much better about checking than social media!

Made in United States
North Haven, CT
18 December 2022

29083345R00193